354440
PB GIE
Gibsor
Groom
D0198743

Jac
mar

He'd simply made a statement.

From the shocked look on her face, Eliza hadn't expected the suggestion, either. After several moments of silence, he wondered if Eliza Kelly had been turned speechless.

"Get married? You and me? Why?" She sputtered the words. "What would motivate you to ask me to marry you? Well, you really didn't ask, you suggested. But still, why?"

His lips twitched. So much for speechless. "Yes, get married and yes, you and me."

Again she asked, "Why?"

Jackson sat down on the porch and patted the wood beside him. When she sat, he turned to her. "Look, I know what the ladies are saying. I've put your reputation in danger and I want to make things right."

She offered him a smile. "Look, Jackson. I'm sure your heart is in the right place, but I can't be a good wife to you."

Books by Rhonda Gibson

Love Inspired Historical

The Marshal's Promise
Groom by Arrangement

RHONDA GIBSON

lives in New Mexico with her husband, James. She has two children and two beautiful grandchildren. Reading is something she has enjoyed her whole life, and writing stemmed from that love. When she isn't writing or reading, she enjoys gardening, beading and playing with her dog, Sheba. You can visit her at www.rhondagibson.net, where she enjoys chatting with readers and friends online. Rhonda hopes her writing will entertain, encourage and bring others closer to God.

Groom by Arrangement

RHONDA GIBSON

Thompson-Nicola Regional District
Library System
300 - 465 VICTORIA STREET
KAMLOOPS, B.C. V2C 2A9

HARLEQUIN® LOVE INSPIRED® HISTORICAL

If you purchased this book without a cover you should be aware that this book is stolen property. It was reported as "unsold and destroyed" to the publisher, and neither the author nor the publisher has received any payment for this "stripped book."

™ LOVE INSPIRED BOOKS

Recycling programs for this product may not exist in your area.

ISBN-13: 978-0-373-82954-5

GROOM BY ARRANGEMENT

Copyright © 2013 by Rhonda Gibson

All rights reserved. Except for use in any review, the reproduction or utilization of this work in whole or in part in any form by any electronic, mechanical or other means, now known or hereafter invented, including xerography, photocopying and recording, or in any information storage or retrieval system, is forbidden without the written permission of the editorial office, Love Inspired Books, 233 Broadway, New York, NY 10279 U.S.A.

This is a work of fiction. Names, characters, places and incidents are either the product of the author's imagination or are used fictitiously, and any resemblance to actual persons, living or dead, business establishments, events or locales is entirely coincidental.

This edition published by arrangement with Love Inspired Books.

® and TM are trademarks of Love Inspired Books, used under license. Trademarks indicated with ® are registered in the United States Patent and Trademark Office, the Canadian Trade Marks Office and in other countries.

www.LoveInspiredBooks.com

Printed in U.S.A.

3 5444 00138201 8

Behold, the former things are come to pass,
and new things do I declare.
—*Isaiah* 42:9a

Thank you, Tamela Hancock Murray
for being my friend and my agent. You are a blessing.

Chapter One

Spring 1886
Durango, Colorado

Eliza Kelly's worse fear had just been confirmed.

She couldn't believe she was standing on the train platform waiting for a mail-order groom. One she hadn't ordered!

With shaking fingers, Eliza opened the envelope and pulled out the slip of paper inside. Once more, her eyes scanned the letter that explained how her best friend, Hannah Young, had ordered the expected groom.

My dear friend Eliza,
I know this will come as a shock to you, but I have been writing as you to a Mr. Miles Thatcher. He posted a mail-order bride ad in the same newspaper as my own prospective groom, Mr. Westland. After reading his ad, I answered as you.

Eliza, I think you will like Mr. Thatcher. He will be arriving on the two o'clock train this afternoon.

Before you close your mind to the possibility of being a mail-order bride, know that I've prayed about this and feel I did the right thing in answering Mr. Thatcher's advertisement. Granted I should have told you. For not doing so, I apologize now.

After you read his letters, you can decide if he is a man that you will enjoy spending the rest of your life with. If you decide to send him away, I promise to never do this again.

I'll write once I get to Granite, Texas. I'm looking forward to hearing how you and Mr. Thatcher get along.

Sincerely,
Your friend Hannah

Emotions sliced through her like sharp scissors through cloth. How could Hannah do this to her? Anger at her friend's impulsiveness demanded an answer that wasn't forthcoming. She caught her lower lip between her teeth. What if Mr. Thatcher arrived and refused to return to wherever he came from?

She stuffed the note from Hannah back inside the envelope with Mr. Thatcher's letters. Eliza had read them all so many times she almost had them memorized.

The two o'clock train squealed to a noisy stop. Eliza closed her eyes, said a quick prayer of deliverance and slowly counted to ten.

Jackson Hart lifted his head from the table and held it in his hands for several long seconds, waiting for the sound of grinding breaks to stop pulsating through his brain. He felt as if someone had taken a hatchet to his skull.

Keeping his eyes closed, he did a quick check of his pockets. As expected, they were empty. Whoever had taken advantage of him being alone in the train car and hit him over the head, knocking him out, had also robbed him.

"Sir, we've arrived in Durango."

Jackson looked up at the porter. He rubbed the back of his head and winced. A knot the size of a goose egg pulsated against his skull, but when he pulled his fingers away there wasn't any blood coating them. He was thankful for that and that he'd had the good sense to hide half of his money in his luggage.

He nodded to the young man and stood. "Who do I report a robbery to?"

Ten minutes later, Jackson stepped from the train. He moved off to the side of the platform and tried to ignore the sounds around him as he waited for his bag. It seemed to take forever before the porter lugged his belongings toward him. Taking pity on the young man, Jackson met him halfway and picked up the luggage. It held a few of his favorite tools, clothes and his Bible. Not to mention half the money he'd planned to use to get started in Silverton, Colorado. Again Jackson thanked the Lord that it hadn't been with him at the time of the robbery.

"Sorry for the delay, Mr. Hart. I stopped and reported what happened to you to Special Agent Wilson. He says to assure you he will be looking out for future passengers and if the thief is caught, he'll make sure you are notified."

Jackson nodded. The action cost him as pain sliced

through his skull. The porter hurried away and disappeared from sight. He closed his eyes to narrow slits, trying to shut out the piercing sun and willing the pain to subside. He'd planned to rest a couple of nights in Durango before traveling the fifty miles to Silverton. Now he didn't have enough funds for the train and would have to secure employment of some kind here until he could move on. Jackson sighed. His search for his father would have to wait a little longer.

"Oh, Mr. Thatcher!"

Jackson cracked his eyes and looked to where the high-pitched call came from. He envied Mr. Thatcher as the lovely woman hurried toward him. A wisp of brown hair escaped from her hat; her brown eyes shone but didn't match the smile on her lips. She was waving as if afraid Mr. Thatcher wouldn't notice her. Jackson turned to see who she was frantically waving at.

Seeing no one, Jackson turned back around to find her standing directly in front of him. The silly bluebird on her hat bobbed just below his chin. He tilted his head and looked into her coffee-colored eyes. The woman slipped to the side of him and tucked her arm in his. She began to pull him down the dirt street.

Was the woman insane? What did she think she was doing? Jackson felt like digging his boots into the dirt, but he'd already noticed the attention she was getting from bystanders. His temples throbbed; maybe it would be better to let her get wherever they were going and then tell her she'd made a mistake.

"Come along, Mr. Thatcher. I am Eliza Kelly. I am a little tired and would really like to get back to the boardinghouse and get this situation taken care of, immediately. I know none of this is your fault, but I am exhausted because we were up so early yesterday to make the trip here from Cottonwood Springs, then this morning Hannah had to be at the train station by seven, and that's when she told me about you. My stomach has been in knots all afternoon. At one point I thought I'd be sick. I still can't believe Hannah would do such a thing."

He marveled at the fact that she didn't even take a breath as she continued walking and talking. That the woman had the courage to pull him along also amazed him. Most women took one look at his bulk and turned the other way.

"I hope you don't mind, but I have made arrangements for you to stay at Mrs. Hattie's boardinghouse until we can smooth out this mess. Hannah didn't mean any harm in what she did, but well, I'm afraid she put us both in a very bad situation. You see, I am a widow." She stopped and glanced over at him. A puzzled look crossed her pretty features before she pressed on. "But she probably wrote you that already, at least I hope she did. Anyway, I have asked Mrs. Hattie to make us a nice pot of tea so that we might discuss the situation."

The woman talked faster than anyone he'd ever had the pleasure to meet. Her brown eyes sparkled, or maybe he was still seeing stars from the knock to the head, as she chattered on about Hannah and letters. The scent of vanilla filled his nostrils as he inhaled her fragrance.

When she took a deep breath, he decided now was the time to tell her she was mistaken, that he wasn't Mr. Thatcher. "I…"

"Now, let's not discuss it out here on the street." She lowered her voice to a whisper. "I would hate for the town to find out that you were brought here under false pretenses. Of course, I'm sure Hannah didn't mean for it to happen like that." She paused and her voice returned to normal. "Well, maybe she did. Although, I want you to know that she did apologize to me and promised never to do such a thing again."

Jackson felt as if his brains were swimming in a sea of words. Curiosity caused him to ask, "What did she do?" He noted that they'd arrived at a two-story house with blue shutters. The sign on the front lawn stated they were at Mrs. Hattie's Boardinghouse.

Eliza reached forward and pulled the door open. Once they'd entered and she'd closed the door behind them, Eliza said, "She answered your mail-order bride advertisement. Only you didn't know it was her—you thought it was me."

He allowed himself to be tugged into a sitting room. The furniture was a little worn, but everything looked clean and in its rightful place. Her last words sunk in, and Jackson pulled his arm free of her. He'd not placed any mail-order bride ad and had no intention of marrying Mrs. Kelly or her friend Hannah. Just when he opened his mouth to say so she interrupted again.

"Oh, I'm making a mess of this, aren't I?" Before he could agree or disagree, she continued. "Sit right there." She indicated a rocking chair by the front window. "And I'll go get the tea." Her skirts made a soft swishing sound as she hurried away.

Did the woman ever stop talking? Jackson watched her disappear down a short hallway before he eased into the chair and took a deep breath. The smells of baking bread filled the air and his stomach growled in response.

What had he gotten himself into? He was in a strange town, without enough money to make it to Silverton, with a fast-talking woman who didn't make sense. He rested his aching head in his hands and sighed.

"It's not that bad," Eliza said as she reentered the room. "I know you were expecting to get married today but—"

"What?" Jackson raised his head and looked at the woman. The sudden action sent new pain through his temples, and he groaned aloud. She'd taken off the silly bird hat, and dark brown hair curled about her face. A very pretty face. He still had no intention of getting married. As soon as she settled down, Jackson planned on telling her so in the nicest way he knew how.

He'd not be ruled by another woman.

"I am sorry, Mr. Thatcher." She continued forward with a tea serving tray extended before her. "Since I didn't write the letters, I would think you'd understand that I can't marry you. I know this has to be a disappointment to you."

Jackson held up his hand to silence her incisive chatter and tell her he was far from disappointed. He was surprised when the action worked. She placed the tea set and sandwiches on the table in front of him and waited.

The calluses on his hands scratched his cheeks as he ran them over his face. He shut his eyes for a brief moment to gather his thoughts and figure out a way to break the news to her. If only his head would stop hurting.

Jackson sighed and looked her in the eyes. "You have the wrong man."

She picked up the teakettle and opened her mouth to speak.

He quickly raised his hand again to stop the flood of words that he was sure would be forthcoming. "My name is Jackson Hart, and I'm a blacksmith headed to Silverton, Colorado. I'm not your Mr. Thatcher."

The metal teakettle slipped from her fingers and clattered to the floor. Hot tea splashed his legs and boots.

Chapter Two

Eliza placed a finger against the throbbing pulse in her neck and felt the color drain from her face. Her stomach did a flopping thing, and her hands shook. For the second time today, she felt as if she were going to be sick. Her mind frantically worked to make sense of his words. If he wasn't Mr. Miles Thatcher, then who was he?

It abruptly dawned on her that she'd dragged a complete stranger into Mrs. Hattie's boardinghouse.

Her gaze moved to his boots and pant legs. A dark stain ran down his limbs, and liquid pooled at his feet. "I am so sorry. You must think me a complete fool." She picked up the teapot and saw a crack across the bottom. "Oh, I've ruined Mrs. Hattie's teapot, your boots and pants. What more can I ruin today?"

Hattie hurried from the kitchen, carrying a dishcloth. "Are you all right?" she asked Eliza. Her eyes swept the room and landed on Jackson and the pool of tea he now stood in.

Tears sprung to Eliza's eyes. "I'm fine, but I've made quite a mess of things." A sob tore from her lips as she covered her face to hide her shame.

His clear deep voice echoed the statement she'd said to him earlier. "It's not that bad, Mrs. Kelly." When she uncovered her face, he continued. "I can take the pot to the nearest blacksmith and he'll fix it up. Boots can be wiped off and pants washed, so see? No harm done."

Hattie patted her shoulder. "He's right. I have another teakettle and we can clean up this spill in no time."

No harm done? Who was he kidding? She'd dragged him from the train station and rambled on about being a mail-order bride. And to make matters worse, she had no idea where the real Mr. Thatcher was or what he looked like.

She studied the man before her. How could she have mistaken him for a scholar? He was big, taller than her by at least a foot. Large sinewy hands and brawny arms marked him as a man who was used to physical labor. Guarded cobalt-blue eyes stared back at her. Fresh flames of heat licked up her neck and into her cheeks.

Eliza jumped to her feet. "I have to find the real Mr. Thatcher. I'm so sorry to have caused this inconvenience, Mr. Hart. If you will excuse me." Hoping she hadn't sounded as breathless as he made her feel, she hurried from the room and scooped her hat from the kitchen table. She took a couple of deep breaths before returning to the main room.

Eliza didn't want to face Jackson Hart again but knew she'd have to go back through the main sitting room to exit the house. She exhaled and slowly walked back the way she'd come.

Hattie was wiping up the mess, and Jackson Hart still stood where he'd been a few moments ago. A bewildered expression rested on his handsome face. He held his hat in his hands and stared down at the mess she'd made.

She hurried across the room and yanked the door open to escape. Her shoes pounded the wooden sidewalk. It wasn't until she was halfway to the train station that Eliza and her heartbeat slowed down.

Eliza stopped and tried to picture the train station as it had appeared when she'd dragged Mr. Hart away. She closed her eyes and focused, recreating the memory in her mind. Jackson Hart had been standing beside the platform with a pained expression on his face. She'd thought he looked lost. Her gaze had scanned the train yard. Seeing no other passengers emerge from the train, she'd assumed he was Miles Thatcher.

She sighed and opened her eyes. Maybe Mr. Thatcher had changed his mind and hadn't come. Or maybe she hadn't waited long enough for him to have exited from the train. What if he was lost and searching for her? He could be anywhere, she thought.

"He's probably long gone by now."

Eliza jumped at the sound of Jackson's voice so close to her elbow. How long had he been standing behind her? Taking a deep breath to calm her nerves, she turned to face him.

"You're probably right." The cracked teakettle dangled from his hand, and she reached for it. "I'll take that to the blacksmith. I'm the one who broke it. I should be the one to get it fixed."

He shook his head. "I'll take it—I have business there, anyway."

Nerves prickled up her arms and into her hairline. She felt as nervous as a fly trapped in a spider's web. Only she'd created this web. No, on second thought,

Hannah had. The first chance she got, Eliza intended to write her friend and tell her what a mess she'd gotten her into.

Eliza nodded and turned away from him. She decided to return to the boardinghouse. "I can't believe the day I've had," she grumbled under her breath.

"Me, either," Jackson agreed as he turned to walk toward Main Street.

Eliza watched him leave and for a brief moment wondered what it would have been like to get to know Jackson. His wide shoulders swayed as he walked away. He was a handsome man, but handsome or not, Eliza knew he wasn't for her. No man was. She shook the sad thought off and hurried back to the boardinghouse, praying tomorrow would be a better day.

The next morning, Eliza smoothed the quilt over her legs. She wasn't ready to get up and face the world this morning. She'd not seen Mr. Hart any more the day before, and she felt grateful.

How could Hannah have done such a thing as to order her a mail-order groom? It dawned on Eliza that she'd never shared her deepest secret with her friend. Hannah had no idea that Eliza was barren and could never marry a man who wanted children. Mr. Thatcher's letter had been clear that he wanted not one, but a houseful.

Eliza sighed and got up. As she dressed, she thought of Jackson Hart and wondered what had happened to him. Had he returned and collected his bag or was he staying on at the boardinghouse? She hadn't dared ask Mrs. Hattie the night before.

Heat filled her face once more as she reviewed the

events of the previous day. She'd hurried back to the boardinghouse, pleaded a headache and gone to her room early. Her stomach growled, reminding her that she'd skipped dinner.

The grandfather clock ticked off the hour downstairs. She counted along with it and when the chiming stopped Eliza grabbed her bag and began stuffing clothes inside. She was late. Seth Billings, her friend Rebecca's husband, would be waiting for her, and he'd said he wanted an early start back to Cottonwood Springs.

She looked around the room to make sure she wasn't leaving anything behind and then hurried to the kitchen. U.S. Marshal Seth Billings, Jackson Hart and Mrs. Hattie sat at the table drinking coffee.

Aware of their gazes upon her, Eliza focused on Seth. "I am so sorry, Seth, I overslept." Eliza held her bag with both hands and waited for him to stand.

Seth motioned for her to take the fourth chair at the table. "Please sit down, Eliza. I need to talk to you."

What did the U.S. Marshal want to talk about? She knew he was in a hurry to get back to Rebecca and his girls. Eliza looked to Jackson Hart; his focus seemed to be on something in the bottom of his cup.

Had he filed a complaint against her for dragging him from the train station? Why else would Seth be acting so formal? Heat filled her face. Eliza wasn't sure if it was from the anger she felt toward Jackson Hart or if it was because of her embarrassment at having Seth learn what she'd done the day before.

Mrs. Hattie smiled and nodded to the chair. "Can I get you a cup of coffee or tea, dear?"

Eliza slid into the chair and lowered her bag to the floor. "No thanks. I'm sure that Seth is about ready to head home." She turned her attention to Seth. Her stomach took that moment to grumble noisily.

Mrs. Hattie's laughed softly. "I'll go fix you some breakfast and a strong pot of tea." She pushed away from the table and walked to the kitchen.

Seth took a deep breath. "Eliza, I can't leave Durango just yet. The trial I'm here for is being held over, there's nothing I can do but stay."

Her mind worked frantically. She needed to get back to her dress shop. Millie Hamilton was seventeen years old and had only agreed to watch the store for a week. They were expected home today. Would the girl be able to watch her shop for a few more days?

She caught Jackson sneaking a peak at her over his mug. Eliza felt as if she'd made a fool of herself enough for one visit to Durango. All she wanted right now was to go home and try to forget Jackson Hart and Miles Thatcher ever existed.

His blue eyes drilled into hers. She took a deep breath and dismissed him. Eliza returned her focus to the marshal. "I understand, Seth. I'll rent a wagon and horse from the livery."

Seth's gaze bore into hers. "No, you won't."

She knew that stubborn look and opened her mouth to protest. "I need to get back to Cottonwood Springs, Seth. I have a store to run."

He nodded. "I'm aware of that, Eliza. I've made arrangements to have you escorted home today."

Eliza felt she knew the answer before she asked. "Who shall be escorting me?"

Seth took a drink and his eyes moved to Jackson Hart. He lowered the cup once more. "Mr. Hart has agreed to accompany you."

Just as she feared.

Seth held up his hand to stop her from protesting. "I know he's a stranger to you, Eliza, but I met and worked with Jackson a couple of years ago and trust me when I tell you, he's a good man. You'll be perfectly safe with Jackson as your escort."

Eliza swallowed hard. A full day with Jackson Hart. Hadn't she suffered enough embarrassment in the presence of this man? "Seth, I'm sure Mr. Hart has his own business to attend to."

Seth placed his mug on the table. "Mr. Hart and I have already established a fee, and he's agreed to take you. The matter is settled, Eliza." He paused and gave her a grave look. "Unless you want to spend another week, maybe two, here in Durango."

Eliza wanted to stomp her foot and demand to be allowed to return home alone. She was an adult. What was to stop her from leaving on her own?

A plan began to form in her mind. She could agree to stay and then simply change her mind and head home later in the morning. The thought of traveling alone both excited and scared her.

She felt Seth studying her. Eliza raised her head and tried not to look guilty. Her gaze met his.

"Don't even think about it, Eliza Kelly. If I have to track you down and find you halfway home…" He let the threat hang in the air between them.

What would he do? Throw her in jail? Eliza saw his jaw harden. Possibly. Her heart sank, and she realized she couldn't have lied to him, anyway. That wouldn't have been the right thing for her to do. Instead, Eliza had a choice to make, spend her day with Jackson or stay in Durango for who knew how long.

She glanced across the table at the blacksmith and caught Jackson's grin just before he hid it behind his cup of coffee. Today he wore a blue shirt that brought the rich blue color out of his eyes. Eyes that seemed to twinkle at her predicament. His short brown hair looked wet, as if he'd just taken a bath. Strong hands held the cup.

Seth cleared his throat. Eliza swung her gaze back to him. "Well, seeing as I really don't have a choice, I suppose Mr. Hart can escort me today."

Mrs. Hattie set a small plate before her with a piece of toast and egg upon it. "Here, eat this while you wait for Mr. Hart to get the wagon ready," she instructed. "I'll bring you a hot cup of tea to go with it, too. You have a long day of travel ahead of you, so eat up."

Jackson pushed his chair back. "It shouldn't take more than five minutes. As soon as the wagon is ready, I'll return to collect you and your things, Mrs. Kelly." He left the room.

"Seth, I'm not sure about this. What do we know about Jackson Hart?" Eliza spread strawberry jam onto the slice of toast.

He leaned toward her. "Are you afraid of Jackson, Eliza? Because if you are, just say the word and I'll fire him now." His brown eyes searched hers.

She trusted Seth with her life. If he thought Jackson was reliable, then that was good enough for her. Eliza didn't really know why she was protesting so much, other than the fact that she'd completely embarrassed herself with the man the day before. "No, I'm not afraid of him. I just don't know him."

Mrs. Hattie snorted and set a teacup beside Eliza's

plate. "And yet yesterday you dragged him back here as husband material."

"I did not! I brought him here to tell him there had been a mistake," Eliza protested, dropping the toast back on its plate and crossing her arms over her chest. If Mrs. Hattie thought she'd intended to marry Mr. Hart, what must he think? She tried to remember if she'd told him differently.

She had. Eliza replayed the conversation in her mind and was sure of it.

Hattie slipped back into her chair. "I'm sorry, child. I didn't mean any harm in my teasing."

"Hannah really put you in an awkward position, didn't she?" Seth said.

Eliza turned to look at him. How did he know what Hannah had done? Had Jackson told him?

Seth continued. "Rebecca tried to talk her out of it, but that woman can be stubborn." He finished drinking the coffee from his cup.

Her hands fell to her side. "Rebecca knew?" Disbelief and hurt filled her voice. Rebecca Billings was supposed to be her best friend, too.

He looked up and understanding crossed his face. "I..." Seth sighed. "Yes, she did. Hannah's been talking about it for weeks. I'm surprised they were able to keep the secret from you."

Eliza felt betrayed. She looked down at the toast and egg, no longer hungry. How could they have done this to her? And why did they think she needed a new husband?

Both of them knew of her love for her deceased husband, Charlie. Her inner voice defended them. *But he died five years ago and you never shared with your friends his unhappiness at never having fathered a child.*

"Anyway, I think you will be safe with Mr. Hart." Seth pushed away from the table and headed for the door. "I'll see you outside, ladies." And with that he left the room.

Hattie cleared her throat. She reached out and took one of Eliza's cold hands. "I heard Mr. Hart promise Seth he'd take care of you and make sure you got home safe. So I believe you will be secure and protected with him around."

"I'm sure I will be." Eliza picked up the toast and took a bite. The sweet strawberry jam would have tasted wonderful if she hadn't been so upset with her friends. Plus, it didn't help that the butterflies in her stomach were determined to make her day miserable.

If only Hannah hadn't sent for Miles Thatcher, she would never have met Jackson Hart. Was God at work here?

Chapter Three

Jackson finished hitching up the wagon and took a deep breath. He'd agreed to take Eliza Kelly to Cottonwood Springs for two reasons: one, he needed the money and two, the marshal had said the blacksmith there was leaving town and required a journeyman to run his business.

Seth had told him that Eliza's husband was dead and that he'd been watching out for her ever since they'd met. Why he'd promise to protect Eliza on the trip home and to watch out for her until Seth Billings's return to Cottonwood Springs was another matter. One Jackson didn't want to study too hard.

He pulled the wagon in front of the house and waited beside the horses as Mrs. Hattie handed Eliza a picnic basket. Jackson listened as they said their goodbyes and hugged. He saw Seth push away from the side of the house and wondered again why the marshal had taken such a liking to him.

"Now try to rest on the trip home. And keep your hat on since that sun can be brutal," Mrs. Hattie said as she patted Eliza's back.

"I will. Thanks for everything."

Jackson took the basket from her and set it behind the seat. Seth handed him Eliza's bag, and he put it beside the basket. Then he turned to help Eliza up.

Seth beat him to her, and Jackson watched as the marshal assisted the petite woman up onto the wagon. He dropped his hands from her tiny waist and said, "Tell Rebecca I'll be home as soon as this trial is over."

"I will, Seth," Eliza promised. She smoothed down her pretty brown dress and straightened her back.

Today she wore a floppy straw hat with an orange-and-yellow scarf tied in a bow that wrapped around the crown. Jackson smiled as he realized that oversize hats seemed to be an obsession for Eliza Kelly.

"Ready?" he asked as he swung into the wagon and took the reins.

Eliza nodded and waved to her friends.

Jackson turned the team to head out of town. He wondered if she realized her emotions flickered across her face much like a hummingbird flutters from flower to flower. The thought startled him. He flicked the reins across the horses' backs. The sooner he got Eliza Kelly home, the better he'd feel.

She grabbed his arm. "Wait! We have to go by Sally's Dress Shop. I have cloth, ribbons and other sewing things to pick up."

The warmth of her fingers seeped into the sleeve of his shirt. Jackson eased back on the reins and pulled the animals to a stop. He nodded and turned the horses around.

"Sally's is over one street and up one block," Eliza instructed in a soft voice.

Jackson enjoyed the soft singsong way she spoke this

morning. The day before she'd sounded breathless and overexcited. He found himself grinning as he guided the horses to Sally's. Maybe getting to know Eliza Kelly wouldn't be so bad.

Earlier she'd noticed that Jackson had worn a dark brown coat, but he'd taken it off while loading the wagon. Her gaze moved to his shirtsleeves, which were rolled up to the elbows. Eliza had admired the muscles that worked in his arms as he loaded her supplies into the wagon.

She smiled her thanks as Jackson finished arranging the last of her purchases in the wagon bed and climbed aboard the wagon ready to go. The air smelled of the light rain they'd received earlier in the morning. She prayed they wouldn't get caught in another spring rainstorm. The water could ruin several of her fabrics.

Once they were out of town, Eliza turned to him with what she hoped was an encouraging smile in place. "Seth tells me you are a journeyman. Have you been one long?" She picked up her sewing project, a small cloth doll, and began stitching on its little dress.

He gently slapped the reins over the horses' backs. "A few years now."

"Uh-huh." Eliza admired the tall trees they passed under. Jackson Hart didn't seem as if he was in a talkative mood. But she wanted to know more about him. She asked, "How does one become a journeyman? Didn't you say you were a blacksmith? Is a blacksmith the same as a journeyman?" She pulled the little dress over the rag doll's head and tied the string around its neck.

"Journeymen travel from place to place helping other

blacksmiths. So, yes, they are blacksmiths. And most blacksmiths start out as apprentices."

Eliza placed the doll back on the bench. When it became obvious that he wasn't going to say anything else, she looked at him. Large muscles bulged in his arms as he held the reins. "So, you've been traveling around? Were you very young when you became an apprentice?" she asked.

"I was ten." He kept his gaze trained straight ahead.

"I see." She wanted to ask more questions. Like how long had he apprenticed. And had he ever trained anyone else to be a blacksmith? But from the set of his jaw, Eliza decided she might be annoying him.

Since he wasn't in a talkative mood and was looking straight ahead, she took the opportunity to study him. He was a big man with wide shoulders. As she thought about it, Eliza realized that Jackson Hart was probably the biggest man she'd ever met. The blacksmith in Cottonwood Springs, Dan Tucker, wasn't as big as Jackson. He had muscles but not like Jackson.

Jackson had sandy-brown hair, cobalt-blue eyes and a cleft in his chin that she couldn't seem to pull her gaze away from. His face seemed chiseled and strong. She decided she liked that in a man. Her eyes traveled up to his, and she found him staring back at her.

Eliza ignored the heated sensation that took over her face and said, "I was just thinking. If you are going to live in Cottonwood Springs, I should tell you a little about the people who live there."

When he didn't answer or say he wasn't planning on living in Cottonwood Springs, Eliza took that as her cue that he was interested. She talked nonstop for the next few hours. Oh, she didn't gossip about the townspeople;

she simply told him that Mr. and Mrs. Miller owned one general store and Mrs. Walker and her husband owned another. Mrs. Velarde owned the diner; Mr. Browning ran the livery. And the list of businesses continued.

She told him that Dr. Clark had been the town doctor ever since she'd moved to Cottonwood Springs over five years ago. Then she'd continued by telling him about the circuit preacher, Reverend Griffin, who came through town once or twice a month unless the weather was bad. If the reverend wasn't in town, then the local men took turns leading service.

Jackson nodded in all the right places. She decided he must have been interested in what she was saying. As soon as she finished with who lived in town, Eliza filled him in on who owned the local farms and ranches.

After a while, Eliza noted that rain seemed to be falling in the distance. Once more she worried about her fabrics and sent a swift prayer heavenward to keep the rain at bay at least until they got home.

Eliza picked up the doll. Jackson's gaze fluttered to the toy, and she thought his eyes had been curious. Without him asking, Eliza began to tell him about the doll and the Parker family. "Little Bessie Parker is having her fourth birthday next week. Her pa died last spring and her ma has been having a hard time of it so I'm giving her ma, Georgia, this doll to give to Bessie." She smoothed out the little dolls dress and then sat it back on the bench beside her. "I think she'll like it."

He grinned at her. "I believe you are right."

Something in the grin tickled her tummy. In just a short amount of time she'd gotten used to looking into his stormy-blue eyes. She shook her head at such foolish thoughts. Eliza looked up into the sky, pretending his smile hadn't affected her in any way.

Two colorful arches filled the heavens. "Look! Mr. Hart! A double rainbow." She turned from the spectacular view and looked over at him. "You know what it means?" Eliza didn't give him time to answer. "I love rainbows and believe they are promises. Promises from God that He will never destroy the entire world again by flooding. And I believe they are also a sign that no matter what we go through, He will be there for us. Those are the promises I hold fast to."

Her awe-filled voice touched his heart. She was a widow who still believed in promises from God. He'd met a few widows in his life and the ones he'd met were bitter about the loss of their husbands. But Eliza Kelly didn't strike him as a bitter woman. That was one of the things he liked about her. At that thought, Jackson turned from the rainbows and the pretty woman beside him.

Silence hung between them. The birds chirping in the trees and the sound of the horses' hooves clomping through the mud were the only sounds filling the air.

Jackson felt her studying his profile and fought the urge to squirm. He lowered his hat to shade his eyes. Her brown gaze moved over his face and down his shoulder and continued until she came to his boots. Then he watched from the corner of his eye as she examined herself.

Eliza removed her sun hat. Her hands went to her hair. She released it from the knot she'd piled on top of her head. Next her fingers combed the locks until they hung shiny and soft about her shoulders. Then she began braiding it. He surreptitiously watched as she twisted the braid into a crown on the top of her head.

Realizing she must be preparing to enter town, he returned his focus to the road ahead. After a few minutes, the strong scent of smoke touched his nostrils.

Jackson's gaze searched the tree line and surrounding area for the source of the smell. He searched the sky for signs of it in the air. Nothing.

"Smells like something is on fire," Eliza said, raising her nose into the air.

It amazed him that she'd just seemed to notice. Had her mind been focused elsewhere or was Eliza Kelly one of those women who were unaware of their surroundings? He realized she was staring at him and decided to answer. "Yes, but I don't detect the smoke. Do you see it?"

She'd replaced her hat. Eliza shook her head. "No, could be it's an old fire. We're getting closer to town. Maybe someone is burning his trash."

Jackson saw the homestead Seth had said was standing just outside Cottonwood Springs. He could hear the river gurgling on each side of him and smiled, enjoying the soothing sound. "Maybe so."

The wagon began the slow climb up the hill. "We'll be home in just a few minutes," Eliza told him. Excitement filled her voice at the prospect.

Home. The word sounded promising. Would he find a home in Cottonwood Springs? Or would it just be another town that he'd pass through? For years he'd been searching for his father who had abandoned him and his mother when he was a child. But the hope of finding his father and a home was simply that, a hope. Jackson only wanted to know why his father had left. Was that too much to ask?

Jackson took a deep breath to clear his mind. The acrid smell of smoke seemed stronger. His gaze moved to Eliza once more. He wondered if he and Eliza would become friends once they arrived in Cottonwood Springs or if she would go on with her life and forget all about him.

He found himself hoping she wouldn't forget about him. Eliza Kelly had made him feel liked today. She'd shared about her hometown and friends as if she thought they'd be friends, too.

Eliza chose that moment to look over at him and give him a dazzling smile. Her smile disarmed him for a moment. It seemed as if all her wholesomeness was in that grin. He found his lips spreading and returning the smile. For a brief moment he wished he was Miles Thatcher and that they were two people in love, returning to their home in Cottonwood Springs. She faced forward once more and the spell was broken.

Jackson shook his head to clear it. It was only a dream. He had faced the truth a long time ago; no woman would ever love him.

His own mother despised him, mainly because he was a reminder that his father had deserted them. If his own mother didn't love him, then Jackson felt sure no woman could.

They topped the hill, and he found himself looking down on the town below. Eliza gasped beside him. He turned to see shock on her face. His gaze followed hers.

A recent fire had claimed one of the businesses in the valley below. Smoke still drifted up into the air from the ruins. He turned to look at Eliza again. Tears rolled down her pale cheeks, and he knew without being told that the burned building was her dress shop.

Jackson stopped the team and tied the reins down. He reached across and pulled Eliza into his arms. Her tears wet his shoulder as they fell like rain. He looked at the town below and wondered what she would do now.

As if to confirm his thoughts, she cried, "Oh, Mr. Hart, what am I going to do?" She sniffled and then pulled a frilly white handkerchief from her sleeve. In defeat Eliza rested her head on his chest once more. A huge sigh lifted her shoulders, and then her body went still.

He knew with the words he was about to utter that he'd open a part of himself that he'd managed to protect for a long time. "I don't know what you'll do, but if you need me, I'm here. You are not alone." Jackson had felt that sense of hopelessness all his life and could not stand to let Eliza endure it alone.

She straightened away from him and looked deeply into his eyes. Eliza took a deep breath and slowly let it out. She nodded and tried to offer him a wobbly smile. He studied every expression that crossed her features. Right now insecurity and fear fought with determination and acceptance.

"Thank you. I guess we should go down and see what happened." She scooted over and twisted forward on the seat.

Jackson knew at that moment he would keep his promise to Seth. He would protect and care for Eliza for as long as she'd allow him to. By his own vow, he'd be there for her for as long as she needed him.

* * *

Eliza's emotions were all over the place. She felt shocked that her home and business had burned to the ground, scared because she had no idea what she'd do now and confused as to why God would allow this to happen.

"Where do you want to go first? Home or to the store?"

Jackson asked as he guided the wagon down the hill.

She tried to control the shake in her voice. "The store was my home." The pungent scent of burnt wood filled her nostrils and coated her tongue.

He nodded as if she'd told him where to go. The strong jaw she'd admired moments before was clenched, and his hands gripped the reins so tight that his knuckles were turning white.

What must he be thinking? Surely he didn't think she'd want him to take her in. Jackson had said he'd be there for her, but surely he didn't expect her to take him up on the kind offer.

Eliza would have laughed at the thought if her situation weren't so bleak. When the wagon came to a stop in front of her store, she rose to get down.

For a big man, Jackson was fast. Before she could climb from the wagon, he stood beside it, waiting to help her down. He placed both big hands around her waist and lowered her to the ground.

He held her for just a moment longer than necessary and looked deeply into her eyes. Did he see the fear? The helplessness she felt?

"This too shall pass," Jackson reminded her before releasing her and stepping away. A fresh tear slid unbidden down her cheek.

"Oh, Eliza! I am so sorry."

Eliza turned to see Rebecca Billings hurrying to her. Her friend grabbed her and hugged her close. "We tried to save it, but, well, it was late last night and..." Her words drifted away on the afternoon breeze much like Eliza's hope for ever having another shop.

"I'm sorry," Rebecca offered again. She released her hold on Eliza and stepped back.

Others began gathering about them and presented their condolences, as well. Her gaze searched the crowd for Millie Hamilton. The girl was nowhere in sight. Fear and sorrow warred within her as Eliza continued to search the girl out.

"Rebecca, is Millie all right? Did she get out in time?" Eliza heard the panic in her voice begin to rise. She sent up a silent prayer. *Lord, please don't let her be hurt or worse.* It would all be her fault.

Rebecca rubbed Eliza's shoulder in a gesture of comfort. "Calm yourself, Eliza. Millie is fine. She wasn't here when the fire started."

Eliza exhaled and silently thanked the Lord. She would never have forgiven herself if something had happened to the seventeen-year-old girl.

Dan Tucker, the blacksmith, and his wife, Sally, stepped forward. Sally gathered Eliza's hands in her own. The woman's warm palms felt comforting. "Eliza, Dan and I talked about it last night and we have decided that you should use our house while yours is being replaced. We're leaving in a couple of days to visit my parents until the baby comes. I don't like the thought of our house standing empty. So, if that would be all right with you, we sure would be grateful." She squeezed

Eliza's hands before releasing them and moving back to her husband's side.

Eliza felt a sob begin to choke her at the Tuckers' kindness. She swallowed the lump. "Thank you. I appreciate the offer." Tears clouded her vision.

From the corner of her eye, Eliza watched as a short man in a brown suit stepped away from the growing crowd of people steadily pouring from storefronts and homes. She was surprised when he called her name. "Eliza Kelly?"

She nodded, wondering who he could be and how he knew her. Eliza rubbed the tears from her eyes so she could see him more clearly.

He walked up to her with a big grin that didn't quite reach his eyes. "I'm Miles Thatcher." He swept a dark brown derby-type hat with short red feathers sticking out of the band on the side off his head, revealing light brown, thinning hair.

Inwardly Eliza groaned. Her mail-order groom was the last complication she needed right now. She didn't know what to say, and even if she did, Eliza knew she didn't want to say anything in front of her friends and neighbors.

"I realize you've had quite a shock, but I've been waiting for you and I don't plan on waiting any longer." He stepped even closer. "Since we are to be wed, I would like to discuss a few matters with you."

What he planned to do Eliza had no idea, but she felt Jackson move up to stand next to her. She welcomed his presence much like a freezing man welcomed a fur-lined coat.

His baritone voice stopped Miles Thatcher. "I'm afraid your business with Mrs. Kelly will have to wait,

Mr. Thatcher." Jackson crossed his arms over his wide chest as if daring the other man to press the issue.

She wanted to hug Jackson. Thankfully, he seemed to understand that Mr. Thatcher was the last person she wanted to deal with at this moment. Eliza dismissed the little man by turning her gaze back to Rebecca.

With the loss of her home and shop, Eliza felt as if the weight of the world had been placed on her shoulders. The look in Rebecca's eyes said she understood.

Rebecca took her hand and pulled slightly. "You've had quite a shock. Let's go to my house for a hot cup of tea."

The nasal voice of Miles Thatcher caused Eliza to pause. "It's nice to meet you, Mr. Billings. Your wife has been most gracious in your absence."

She turned around to see who he was speaking to. Eliza found him extending his hand out to Jackson and waiting for the other man to respond. Poor Mr. Hart, this was the second time in two days that he'd been mistaken for another man.

Jackson took the extended hand and gave it a firm shake. His voice carried a sharp edge to it. "I'm Jackson Hart. The marshal is still in Durango." He released Miles's hand.

A hard glint entered the scholar's eyes. "It was my understanding that Mr. Billings would be escorting my future bride home. Isn't that correct, Mrs. Billings?"

Eliza felt the change in Rebecca's composure as the scholar turned his attention on her. Dislike seemed to radiate from her friend.

With her back straight and her shoulders squared, Rebecca's voice hardened to match her accuser's. "I can assure you, Mr. Thatcher, that is the truth as I knew it at the time. My husband's plans must have changed."

"I can see that," he snarled back at her. His beady green eyes riveted back onto Jackson, reminding her of a snake about to strike out again. "What is going on here?"

Eliza sighed. She'd have to deal with Miles Thatcher now, but she didn't want a public viewing of their situation. "Mr. Thatcher, if you would be so kind as to come with us to the Billingses' home, we'll explain everything."

He stomped his foot and crossed his arms over his narrow chest much like Jackson had done a few moments earlier, only instead of looking like a force to be reckoned with, Miles Thatcher resembled an angry child. "I will not have this postponed, madam. I want to know who this man is and what he is to you." His voice dripped poison.

The crowd around them gasped at the underlining implication. Eliza couldn't believe her ears. Her gaze searched out Jackson's. His blue eyes locked with hers. Then, without taking his gaze from Eliza, he stepped so close to Miles that their noses were almost touching. His jaw clenched as he answered the man. "I told you, my name is Jackson Hart. What I am or am not to this woman is none of your business."

Eliza felt flames of embarrassment lick up her neck and into her face. She wanted to crawl into a hole and never return. Now the whole town was curious as to who he was and what his business was with her. She saw several of the older ladies standing off to one side. Their heads were together, and the whispering had commenced.

Miles's thin face paled as if he'd just realized the danger he'd put himself in by confronting her in public. His shoulders squared and he lifted his head. In a steady voice he announced, "Mrs. Kelly, under the circumstances, I cannot marry a fallen woman."

Chapter Four

If he lived to be a hundred, Jackson would never forget the gasps of surprise arising from the gathered group of people. He advanced on the little man once more. How dare he defile Eliza's reputation in such a manner!

"Mr. Hart, wait." Eliza's cool voice stopped him in midstep. He looked at her face and saw rage in her molten-brown eyes.

He stepped away from the man when all he wanted to do was give him a good shake. Jackson watched in amazement as Eliza's shoulders straightened, her chin came even farther up and she took a step toward Miles Thatcher.

"I'll have you know, I have not now or ever planned on marrying you. I didn't write those letters, and I am not obligated to stand behind any promises that might or might not have been made in them. Mr. Thatcher, I think your business here is done. I suggest you leave town the same way you arrived." With that Eliza scooped up her skirt and walked away. Rebecca Billings trotted along after her.

Jackson glared at the little man with the beady eyes.

"I suggest you do as the lady says," he growled low in his throat.

Miles jumped back and lifted his head before turning around and walking away in the opposite direction.

He was thankful Eliza had mistaken him for the little man. Jackson had to wonder, if the circumstances had been different, would she have married Miles Thatcher? No, he didn't believe she would have. He'd been proud of the way she'd stood up to her mail-order groom.

"Mr. Hart, please bring the wagon to the Billingses'." Eliza called over her shoulder. Jackson nodded; he tried to ignore the soft quiver in her voice.

The rest of the crowd began to return to their shops and homes. He noticed an older group of women whispering to one another and heard the word *shameful* hissed by one of them as they left.

"Better do as Eliza says—she's in a mood now." Jackson recognized the man who spoke as the one who'd just offered his home to Eliza. He wore a leather apron, and his shirtsleeves were rolled up.

"I suppose you're right." Jackson grabbed the horses' halter and proceeded to pull them in the same direction the women were headed. He knew without introductions that the man was Dan Tucker, the blacksmith. His leather apron and bulging biceps gave away his occupation.

When Dan fell into step beside him, Jackson silently prayed this was God's way of bringing them together.

"Name is Dan Tucker," the big man offered.

"Jackson Hart." He stopped the horses and extended his hand. "And you are just the man I wanted to see."

"Looking for a blacksmith, are ya?" Dan cocked a blond eyebrow at Jackson.

"Not just any blacksmith—you." Jackson continued pulling the horses in the direction Eliza and Rebecca were headed. He watched the marshal's wife lead Eliza into the house; she turned and pointed toward the barn.

Jackson waved and nodded that he understood. She smiled and entered the house. He felt sure Rebecca Billings would have lots of questions for Eliza regarding him.

Dan walked along beside him. He rubbed his chin and asked, "What do ya need me for?"

"The marshal suggested you are in need of a journeyman to watch over the shop while you and the missus travel back east." Jackson entered the barn. The sweet fragrance of hay greeted him. He began to unharness the team, allowing Dan time to mull over his words. He took one mare and led her to a stall while Dan did the same with the other.

Dan handed him a brush. "So, Seth sent you my way." He began grooming the horse he'd taken charge over.

"Yes, sir. He did."

A warm chuckle erupted from the blacksmith. "Now, don't start calling me sir. Just call me Dan. You'll find if you stick around that most folks here go by first names. We're more laid-back than city folks."

"All right." Jackson worked the sides of the mare with the brush. "Dan, the truth of the matter is, I need a job and Seth thought you could use me."

Dan placed his brush on a bale of hay and turned to face Jackson. "Seeing how Seth is the one making the recommendation, I think you'd be perfect for the job." He leaned against the stall door. "Would you be able to stay on a year?"

Jackson thought about Eliza Kelly. If he stayed on for that long he'd be able to help her get her shop rebuilt and save enough money to go to Silverton. He hoped his father would stay there long enough for him to catch up. Jackson nodded. "I figure I could."

"I can only offer you two dollars a day and the use of a room off the smithy while we're gone." Dan leaned on the side of the horse. His blond eyebrow was cocked once more as he waited for Jackson's answer.

Jackson saw a sack of oats sitting against the barn wall. He walked over and filled two buckets. Two dollars a day was fair pay, especially since Dan was willing to let him use the room, too. He gave the horses the oats and dusted off his hands. "I think it's only fair to tell you that Seth and I are not close friends."

Dan laughed. "Seth Billings is a good judge of character. He trusted you to escort Eliza Kelly home, and you did just that. I also saw the way you defended the little lady, and that made me like you even more. Plus, it didn't hurt that you just confessed you weren't a close friend of our marshal. So if you want the job, it's yours." Dan pushed away from the stall and stepped closer to Jackson.

Jackson extended his hand. "I'll work hard."

"I believe you will," Dan answered as they shook hands.

He started to walk out of the barn but stopped halfway through the door. "Come on over once you get Eliza settled. I reckon the poor woman is going to have a rough time of it for a while." He shook his head and walked out.

Jackson thought about Eliza as he secured the wagon. What was she going to do? Would she take the Tuckers up on their offer of a home? His gaze moved over the fabric and boxes of supplies she'd bought for her store. He thought about driving them over to the Tuckers' home, but she hadn't agreed to stay at their place. The supplies might be all right overnight in the barn, but he didn't think they should be left out in the barn much longer than that. Tomorrow he'd ask if she wanted them moved someplace else.

Jackson pulled his bag and Eliza's from behind the seat. He saw the little doll she'd worked on earlier in the day and gently placed it inside Eliza's bag. The woman was precious; her consideration for others touched his heart. He wondered if her community realized what a jewel they had.

He took his time walking toward Rebecca and Seth's house. His gaze moved about what he could see of the town. It seemed as if everyone had returned to their businesses and homes.

Thankfully, he didn't see Miles Thatcher anywhere about. He'd already decided that if he did see the little man again, he'd make sure Miles left town. Even if he had to tie him to the saddle. He pushed the thought away and prayed the little man hadn't damaged Eliza's standing in town.

Jackson sighed. Cottonwood Springs was to be his home for a full year. He prayed he'd fit in here better than he had in other small towns. It seemed odd that Miles Thatcher was the man who was supposed to have moved here and now he found himself taking the little man's place.

As he reached the side of the house, Eliza's voice came through the open window. Jackson stopped and leaned against the building. He tilted his head to the side to hear her better. She sounded both sad and desperate. He rubbed the stubble on his chin as he listened.

"What am I going to do? I can't stay here. Now don't interrupt, you know it's true. You have the baby, Janie, Seth and Ruthann plus yourself living here in a three-bedroom house. There is no room for me. Not that I'm blaming you, I just can't ask you to add another person to the mix." She didn't give Rebecca time to answer. "I am so glad Millie had already gone home when it happened, but I'd love to know how the fire started. Did Millie say?"

Rebecca's soothing voice floated to him. "You can stay here until the Tuckers leave town and then take them up on their offer of using their house until yours is rebuilt."

Eliza's miserable sigh drifted to him. "What about Seth?"

Loneliness filled Rebecca's voice as she answered, "What about him? He's in Durango for who knows how long. You and I both know those trials can last weeks."

Eliza's voice lost all sounds of desperation as she reassured her, "I'm sorry, Rebecca. I know you miss him."

She'd seemed to have put her own concerns to the side to comfort her friend. Jackson wondered if Eliza was always this giving to others.

"Oh, you stop that!" Rebecca giggled. "I'm supposed to be comforting you, not the other way around."

Sadness reentered Eliza's voice. "What am I going to do about the business? I don't have enough funds in the bank to rebuild. I bought a few supplies in Durango but didn't buy buttons. I should have bought buttons."

Rebecca chuckled. "Only you would think about buttons at a time like this, Eliza."

Eliza's soft twinkling laugh joined her friend's. "I do tend to have a liking for them, don't I?" Her voice sobered and she said, "It doesn't matter now, does it? What am I going to do, Rebecca?"

Jackson wanted to help but didn't know what he could do. The thought that the Bible spoke of helping widows troubled him. It was his duty to help Eliza Kelly. He frowned as he tried to figure out how. If only Miles Thatcher had been a decent man, he could have married Eliza and she'd have a home again.

He frowned, not liking that thought at all.

Why had her friend Hannah ventured outside the community to find them husbands? Earlier in the day, Eliza had explained that Cottonwood Springs had a new schoolteacher because Hannah had been accused of being fresh with one of her students. Hannah had been mortified that the residents of the town would believe such a lie and had decided to become a mail-order bride. But why had she searched for a husband for Eliza, too? Weren't there any eligible men in the area to marry?

Rebecca's voice reached his ears again. "We'll figure out something. Now as soon as your Mr. Hart brings us your bag, we'll get you into a hot bath and tonight you can sleep in my room with me."

"All right but you didn't answer my question."

One of the ladies blew her nose. Jackson suspected it was Eliza.

Rebecca laughed. "Which question? You ask them and then speed along until I forget what you asked."

Jackson almost chuckled. He was glad he wasn't the only one who had problems keeping up with Eliza's train of thought.

A huff filled the air before Eliza repeated her question. "Did Millie know what started the fire?"

"No, but since both the sheriff and Seth are out of town, Reverend Griffin did a little snooping around and found a half-smoked cigar behind your house. The men are speculating that some of the local boys might have snuck back there for a smoke. And Mr. Walker confirmed that several of the nasty things were missing from a new shipment he'd gotten in his last order."

Eliza asked the question Jackson was thinking. "If there was only one cigar behind my house, why do they think a group of boys were smoking back there? I mean, that doesn't make sense, does it? No, I would think they would have found more cigars. Maybe it was just one boy, sneaking a smoke."

Rebecca added, "Maybe the other boys took theirs with them. Anyway, Seth will figure it out when he gets home." Rebecca's voice took on a motherly tone as she soothed. "Come on now, drink your tea and I'll go out to the barn and check on your Mr. Hart."

"He's not mine."

Rebecca giggled. "If you say so."

Jackson pushed away from the wall and headed toward the front of the house. He didn't want the women to know he was eavesdropping on their conversation. Now that he thought about it, it really wasn't a nice thing to do.

After delivering Eliza's bag and assuring Rebecca that the animals were settled in, Jackson walked to the smithy. Rebecca Billings had called him Eliza's Mr. Hart. He shook his head. Women said the strangest things, but he couldn't help but wonder what it would be like to be married to Eliza and be her Mr. Hart.

He pushed the thought away. She seemed like a sweet woman, but he didn't delude himself into thinking she'd ever care about him. And why should she? He wasn't loveable and didn't deserve her care. He didn't enjoy his feelings of protection where Eliza was concerned. Would he become too attached to her if he stayed here?

Jackson pushed the worrisome thought away and focused on the small town as he walked. New trees had been planted along Main Street in front of the newspaper office and the doctor's office. Several of the stores had flowerpots sitting in front of them with fresh green shoots coming up. Soon there would be colorful flowers in them.

The wind blew from the opposite end of town, bringing with it the scent of sawdust from the sawmill and the burnt odor of Eliza's shop. How was Eliza going to refinance her store?

He didn't have far to go to find the smithy. Dan's home was right behind the druggist. The livery sat beside that, and the smithy was across the street from the livery. He took a deep breath and entered the smithy. The smell of heated metal filled his nostrils. Comfort eased over his taunt shoulders. His eyes began adjusting to the dimmer light. This felt like home.

Home. Jackson's thoughts returned to Eliza and the fact that she didn't have a home or the money to restart her business or build a new house. Upon reflection, he realized that he'd come into town and gotten a job and roof over his head in a matter of hours. She'd come into town and realized within minutes that she was homeless and without a job. It didn't seem quite fair.

He released the air in his lungs and silently prayed. *Lord, please rebuild Eliza's life. And, Father, if I am to be part of her restoration, help me to do and say the right things. Amen.*

The thought entered his mind: What if God asked him to do more for Eliza than he wanted?

Chapter Five

Eliza looked about the spacious sitting room. She held her bag tightly in her hands, aware that all her belongings were in the bag.

"Please sit, Eliza. I made a pot of tea. I remember how much you enjoy tea." Sally Tucker indicated a rocking chair across from where she sat on the sofa.

After sitting, Eliza placed her bag beside the chair at her feet. "Thank you," she muttered, wishing she could be anywhere else.

Rebecca had promised this would be easy—that Sally was a friend—but it wasn't easy. Taking charity from others was never easy. Now Eliza understood why some women shunned her help when she offered them new dresses to replace their worn-out ones. It had been shame at needing such things.

She looked up to find Sally's pale blue eyes full of compassion. Sally wore a yellow day dress with black ribbons around the top and skirt. A row of black buttons lined the front of her blouse; her rounded tummy caused the buttons to gather slightly. Eliza had the urge to tell her that she could let the ribbon out slightly to give her baby more room to grow.

Sally handed her a cup of tea. "Help yourself to cream and sugar," she offered.

"It's fine, thank you." Eliza took a sip of the tea. She felt awkward and little beads of perspiration formed on the back of her neck.

Sally added both sugar and cream to her cup. "Dan and I appreciate you taking care of the house for us, Eliza. I was so unhappy to leave it, but now, knowing you are here puts my fears to rest."

Did Sally really think she was helping them and not the other way around? Or was she just being kind? Eliza swallowed. "It is I who should be thanking you."

"Nonsense." She smiled at Eliza. "It's nice to have friends who can help each other out. You've been there for us several times. Remember when Dan burned his leg? You made him a brace to help keep his pant legs from touching the raw flesh. And then there was the time I needed to bake a cake for the church social and I was short on cash that week, you stepped right in and gave me a cake to take."

Eliza opened her mouth to speak, but Sally held up a hand to silence her. "There were other times, too, but I think I've made my point. You are a good friend, Eliza. We all feel lucky to have you. So please don't feel uncomfortable about using our home while we are gone."

"You really feel that way?" Eliza wanted to believe that she was being a help and not a charity case.

Sally nodded. "Of course."

Eliza felt a smile pull at her lips. "I'm glad."

"Didn't you arrive with a wagonload of supplies?" Sally asked, setting her cup back down on the table.

Reminded of the material, threads and other notations, Eliza nodded. “Yes, but I’m not sure what I’m going to do with them now,” she confessed.

Sally scooted forward on the sofa, and her eyes sparkled. “I have an idea.”

Eliza tilted her head sideways and studied the other woman. “Oh?”

“This room is the main sitting room. There is a smaller one in the back of the house that Dan and I use when not entertaining. I was thinking that you might be able to turn this one into a small shop. It wouldn’t be as fine as the one you had, but I think it would make a nice storefront, if you wanted to use it as such.” She looked down at her stomach and spread the material over it.

Eliza looked about the room. It would be nice. A large window faced the road, and she could have a sign made to hang in it, announcing she had hats and dresses for sale. She began to envision how to display her goods. Her gaze moved back to Sally. “Are you sure you and Dan wouldn’t mind?”

The young woman’s face broke out into a wide grin. “We’d love it. Last night I thought of it, and he said if you agreed, he’d have Mr. Hart help him move the furniture from this room to one of the back bedrooms. We’ve already moved the stuff that was in there against one wall, so now there is plenty of room for this furniture.”

Tears filled Eliza’s eyes at her friends’ kindness. She’d have wanted to do just what they proposed but wouldn’t have done so without their permission. “Oh, thank you. If I can open my shop here, I’ll be able to save the money to rebuild.” Eliza jumped to her feet. “We can put my supplies in that corner until I can start making dresses. Oh, but I don’t have a sewing machine." She felt as if the wind had been knocked out of her. Once more she was reminded of just how much she'd lost in the fire. Everything.

"You can use mine," Sally offered.

Eliza dropped back down into her chair. "I didn't know you had a sewing machine."

Pink colored Sally's cheeks as she confessed, "Dan bought it for me as a wedding present, but I have no idea how to use it."

Once more Eliza felt her face break into a smile. "I'll teach you when you come home."

Sally clapped her hands. "That would be wonderful. We'll start with baby clothes. I still can't believe I'm going to have a baby." Her eyes sparkled with joy.

Eliza felt a moment of remorse. She'd never have a baby and wondered what it would feel like. Charlie had wanted children, but after three years of marriage, they'd not had any. He had said it didn't matter but she'd seen him watching children playing and knew that she'd disappointed him. She never wanted to see such deep disappointment in a man's eyes again. Thankfully, she hadn't been obliged to tell Miles Thatcher that she could never have children; she'd been saved from him turning away from her. Deep in her heart, Eliza believed no man could love a barren woman.

Jackson carried the small table toward the back of the house to the spare bedroom where they'd carried all the other heavy furniture. His back was tired, but the joy on Eliza's face would be worth it. He still marveled that the Tuckers were so free with their home and business.

"Why don't you stay and have dinner with us, Jackson?" Dan offered, slapping him on the back.

"Sounds good." Jackson followed Dan into the dining room. The Tucker home was bigger on the inside than it looked from the road. So far he'd seen the main sitting room, three bedrooms and a dining room, and he knew there was a kitchen somewhere because the warm smells of pot roast filled the house.

"Smells good, too," Dan said, taking a seat at the square table. "Sally's the best cook in town."

Jackson smiled. "I'm sure she is." He sat down at the other end of the table.

Sally entered the dining room, carrying a large platter of meat. "Have you men washed up?" She eyed Dan.

He wiped his hands on his pants and nodded.

"With soap and water?" she asked, placing the meat on the table.

Jackson hid the grin that twitched at his lips. Dan reminded him of a boy with his hand caught in the cookie jar.

"Come on, Jackson. She won't believe us until she can smell the soap." Dan's chair scraped against the hardwood floor.

"Dinner will be ready when you get back," Sally called after them.

Jackson couldn't help but envy the warmth between the couple. Dan Tucker loved his wife, and she returned that love. It was in their eyes and voices every time they were together. He wondered if his parents had ever felt that way toward each other. If so, he'd never witnessed it.

His father had left long before he could even walk. For years Jackson questioned why his pa had left them. Was it because he was so unlovable, as his mother had said? This was one of the questions he planned on asking John Hart, if he ever caught up to him.

Where had those thoughts crept up from? Jackson finished washing his hands and they returned to the dining room. He was sure Dan had been talking the whole time, but for the life of him he couldn't recall a word the other man had said.

The table was set, and steaming bowls of potatoes, green beans and fresh rolls blended with the aroma of pot roast. How long had it been since he'd sat at such a fine dinner table? Too long.

"What's on your mind this evening, Jackson?" Dan asked.

Jackson looked up. "Not much." He hoped he hadn't insulted his host with his quiet nature.

Dan nodded. "I've been trying to think if there is anything else I need to tell you before we leave tomorrow."

"Did you mention Peter?" Sally took a seat next to Dan.

Dan looked surprised. "I'd plumb forgotten about the boy. Let's say grace and then I'll fill you in, Jackson."

Jackson listened as Dan offered thanks. Not only did he bless the food, but he asked for travel mercies, as well. Sally added her amen at the end of the prayer. Jackson joined in. "Amen."

A soft knock sounded on the front door. "Excuse me." Sally stood. "That will be Eliza Kelly. I invited her to dinner, as well."

"Give me a couple of minutes with Jackson, honey." Dan reached for the green beans and began filling his plate.

Sally nodded. "You better talk fast. I don't want my

dinner to get cold." Her smile took the sting out of the words.

Dan grinned back at his wife and watched her sashay toward the front of the house. Then he turned his attention back to Jackson. "This afternoon, Peter arrived at the smithy asking if I needed an apprentice. I told him no, and he started to cry."

"He started to cry?" Jackson almost dropped his fork.

Dan nodded. "Yep. Boy is six years old and has no place else to go."

"So where is he now?" Jackson asked, wondering how anyone could turn out a six-year-old child.

"In the front sitting room with Sally and Eliza. I sent him to Eliza this afternoon, until I could ask you if you will apprentice the boy." Dan served himself a hunk of meat.

Jackson frowned. "Where's the boy's family?"

"Don't know. He won't say. He's not a local. I figured if you'd agree to apprentice him, when Seth gets back into town he can find the boy's parents. Until then, I can't just turn him out." Dan plopped a big spoonful of potatoes onto his plate. "So what do you say? Will you take him on?"

Take on a small boy? Was he kidding? From the serious expression and the hiked-up eyebrow, Jackson assumed not. "There isn't enough room for me and the boy in the small room off the smithy."

"Oh, I didn't mean keep him with you in the room. I meant will you train him? At least until his parents can be found. He'll be living here with Eliza and working with you during the day. She's agreed to feed him and make sure he's taken care of." Dan added a couple of hot rolls to his plate.

Jackson took a deep breath. "I suppose I can do that."

"Good." Dan pushed away from the table. "I'll go tell the women to come in now."

Every moment in Cottonwood Springs brought on new responsibilities. Jackson groaned. What had he gotten himself into?

Chapter Six

Eliza was in love.

Peter, with his big green eyes, blond hair and dimples, had melted her heart the moment she'd met him. He didn't talk much, but an easy smile covered his face as he explored everything around him.

She held his hand as they entered the Tuckers' dining room. Jackson sat at the table looking as if he'd eaten persimmons. His pinched face and stiff jaw said he wasn't happy about the arrangement he'd made with Dan.

Both Dan and Sally ignored his sour face and sat down at the table. Eliza placed Peter beside her and smiled at Jackson. His frown dissolved for a moment and he offered her a lopsided grin.

She hadn't seen him all day and felt her heart do a little flutter. What was it about the man that made her feel like a silly schoolgirl?

Turning away from the handsome man, Eliza focused on her plate. "This looks and smells wonderful, Sally," she complimented her friend as she took her place at the table.

"It's my ma's recipe. I can't wait to see her again and tell her about the baby." She picked up the potatoes and passed them to Eliza.

Eliza noticed Jackson focused on his meal and didn't say much. "You haven't told them you are coming?" she asked, taking a sip of iced tea.

Dan answered for his wife. "They know we are coming, just not about the baby."

"Oh, I see. Do you have room in your bags for a couple of baby blankets I've made up for you?" Eliza dished food onto Peter's plate.

Surprise filled Sally's face. She smiled and replied, "I do. Thank you, Eliza. How did you know I'd need them?"

"Every mother needs blankets. I make them all the time to give to the young mothers in the area. And they don't take long to whip up. Last night I borrowed Rebecca's sewing machine and made up a couple for you to take."

Sally continued to smile at her. "You have the kindest heart, Eliza. Thank you."

Embarrassed at the compliment, Eliza turned to Peter. The little boy's big eyes stared at Jackson. He titled his head sideways and tried to see into Jackson's face.

Dan must have noticed, too, because he said, "Peter, I'd like you to meet Mr. Hart. He's going to teach you how to be a blacksmith."

"Really?" Peter's small voice asked in awe.

Dan laughed. "Really."

"Nice to meet you, sir." Peter held out his hand.

For a moment, Eliza wasn't sure how Jackson would react. She almost sighed when he reached across the table and took the small hand into his own. "Nice to meet you, too, Peter. Just call me Jackson."

"All right, Jackson."

The little boy continued to stare at Jackson for the remainder of the meal. Eliza noticed he seemed to ignore the rest of the adults as the conversation flowed around him. Jackson paid no attention to the little boy's stares. He answered questions when asked and every once in a while would ask a question of Dan regarding the smithy.

She leaned over and whispered in Peter's ear, "Peter, it's not nice to stare."

Peter turned his attention to his food and occasionally peeked up at Jackson. He muttered the word *sorry* before shoving a spoonful of meat into his mouth.

Eliza could imagine the boy was in awe of Jackson's size. She'd noticed that he towered over Dan, and his arms were twice as large. His chest and his shoulders were wide, yet he had a flat stomach. Muscles seemed to ripple when he moved. Yes, Jackson Hart was a big man and a handsome man and, from her experiences, a kind man.

"Miss Eliza, I thought you said it wasn't nice to stare." Peter's young voice pulled her from her observation.

Everyone looked at her. She felt heat ignite in her face. Eliza jerked her eyes to her food and whispered, "It's not, Peter. Now eat your food." Eliza wished the floor would open up and swallow her. No lady stared at a man like she'd been doing.

Later that night, Jackson smiled up at the ceiling. The pretty pink in Eliza's cheeks had blessed his heart. Peter didn't really understand what he'd done to embarrass his new friend, but he knew to leave well enough alone.

After supper he'd helped Dan load their wagon and then said good-night. He'd watched Eliza and Peter say their goodbyes to the Tuckers and then head toward Rebecca Billings's home.

To ensure they made it there safely, Jackson had followed them. He'd stayed well enough behind that they'd been unaware of his presence. Once they were inside the house, he returned to his room and climbed between the cool sheets on his bed.

When Dan had said they had a small room off the smithy, he'd expected just that, a small room similar to a woodshed. It turned out his room was twelve-by-twelve and had a small potbelly stove in one corner. His bed, a side table and washbasin sat beside the stove.

On the opposite wall, Sally had arranged a writing desk and a large chair with a fluffy cushion for him. She'd managed to place a small bookshelf beside the chair and had filled it with several books.

A window allowed light to flow in during the day. Yes, his room was as good as any hotel room. Only it was cheery and clean.

He hadn't realized how close the smithy and the Tucker home were. If they were much closer, his room would be part of the house. Jackson wondered how Eliza felt about him living so close. He realized she'd said very few words to him tonight.

Jackson missed her constant chatter. Was she trying to be a good example for Peter? Or did she just feel as if she no longer had to talk to him? Then he remembered that the boy had embarrassed her; perhaps that was the cause of her silence.

He turned over on his side and thumped his pillow. Jackson reminded himself that he needed to get some sleep. A blacksmith worked from sunup to sundown.

The night continued with him getting very little sleep. After several hours, Jackson pushed the covers back and lit a kerosene lantern. He flopped into the big chair and picked up the Bible. He became lost in the story of Joseph and the hardships he'd endured in his young life. Yet God never left him, and everything he put his hand to prospered. A tiny thread of hope wove its way into his heart. He was no Joseph, but if God was no respecter of persons, then God could and would do the same for Jackson Hart. He just needed to get his life in line with God's plans for him.

After a few hours of reading, he walked back to the bed. Jackson did something he'd not done in a long time. He knelt and prayed, first thanking the Lord for not abandoning him, then promising to do his best to follow the Lord's guidance in his life. He climbed into bed and closed his eyes. His last thoughts were of Eliza.

The next morning, Peter ran into the shop. He carried a lunch pail and apple. "I'm here, Jackson."

Jackson had just started working on a new ladle for Mrs. Harper. Seth had told him the woman would be by in the afternoon to pick it up. "I see that."

Peter's blond hair stood on end this morning. His green eyes scanned the blacksmith shop. "Whatcha want me to do first?" he asked.

"You can put your lunch pail over on that bench and then grab that short-handled broom and start sweeping." Jackson watched the door for Eliza. When she didn't arrive, he sighed.

He turned his attention back to the ladle. To make the

ladle's scoop, he heated one end of the rod and formed a lump. Then he held the rod upright with the hot end against the anvil. Jackson took his frustrations out on the metal by pounding the cold end with a hammer to upset the hot end.

"Whatcha doing that for?" Peter asked.

"I'm making a ladle. When I pound the cold end like this it forces the hot end to thicken."

"Oh. I forgot Miss Eliza said to tell you she'll be by later to see how we're doin'." Peter swung the broom. He seemed to be unaware that he was missing the floor as he stared at the heated metal.

"Thanks for telling me. Now move over there and sweep." Jackson pointed to the far side of the room. He didn't want the boy to get curious about the fire. As soon as he finished the ladle, he'd have to show Peter the smithy and tell him what to avoid. He'd also tell him what his jobs were.

Peter moved to the other side of the room. His small shoulders and arms worked as he swept at the floor. Jackson wondered where his family was and why he didn't want to talk about them.

He pounded out the ladle's handle. As he pulverized the rod, he rotated it to make sure the handle would be the same thickness all the way around. His thoughts returned to Eliza's message. She was going to stop in and check on them. Did she think he'd harm the boy?

Jackson had to flatten the upset end of the rod. He pounded the lump with the face of his hammer until it flattened into a round shape. He then forged the round part into a scoop. As he worked, his thoughts continued to focus on Eliza. How was she spending her morning? Would she be setting up her dress shop? Sewing?

Without much thought to what he was doing, Jackson heated the flattened end of the rod again and used the peen end of his hammer to make a curved dent in it. He continued to hit the scoop with the peen until it was totally rounded. When the spoon was fully shaped, he smoothed the ladle's handle with a file.

"Jackson? How much longer do I have to sweep?" Peter called from the other side of the room.

"Until the whole shop is clean," he answered. Jackson grinned as the boy began sweeping again. He knew Peter would be sick of sweeping before the day was over, but that was a big part of what Peter would be doing. Sweeping built arm muscles and taught discipline. The first few years every apprentice learned by cleaning and watching.

He continued to work on the kitchen ladle. Heating the straight end of the rod and then hammering it around the horn of the anvil, Jackson created a finger-size loop. Once it was just the way he wanted it, he began hardening the ladle by plunging it first into the fire and then cold water. He did this several times until the iron was strong and durable.

Once it was cool enough, he held it up for inspection.

"That turned out mighty nice," Peter said.

Jackson turned to study the boy. Peter had moved so silently that he hadn't realized the boy was right behind him until he spoke. "Thank you."

He hung the ladle on a nail by the door and then motioned for Peter to join him. They moved to a quiet corner of the smithy. Jackson picked the little boy up and set him on a barrel. "Peter, you can't be sneaking up behind me like that. You could have been hurt if I had swung around real sudden like."

Peter nodded. His bottom lip came out, and he clamped his top one over it.

"And another thing, big boys don't pout." He eyed the boy.

Peter released his lower lip. "I'm sorry, Jackson. I just wanted to watch."

"You can watch by standing in front of me, not behind. Do we understand one another?" Jackson didn't enjoy scolding the boy, but it was for his own good. The last thing he wanted was for the child to be hurt.

Peter nodded. "Yep, stand in front of you, not behind."

Jackson ruffled his hair. "Very good. Now before we do anything else I want you to look around."

"All right." Peter made a big show of rotating his head and looking about the smithy.

"Do you see the fire pit?"

Peter moved his head to look at the fire pit and nodded.

"That is called a forge. It's very hot and very dangerous. I don't want you getting too close to it." Jackson waited for the little boy to nod again. "Good, now look over there on the big stump."

Peter's gaze followed Jackson's pointing finger. "What's that big thing on top of it?" he asked.

"That is an anvil. See how close it is to the forge?"

"Yep."

Jackson waited until the boy looked up at him again. "Never run or walk between the anvil and the forge. You can trip and fall into the fire. As a rule, you are never to run in the smithy. There are sharp pieces of metal in here, and you have to be very careful not to get cut." As he talked he wondered at the wisdom of having a child so young in the blacksmith shop. From his experience most apprentices were closer to the age of ten, not six.

"I'll be careful, Jackson. My pa taught me to be a good boy. He said I should listen to grown-ups so that I don't get hurt." His eyes moistened and he dropped his head.

Did the boy mean grown-ups would hurt him? Or that they were giving good advice? Jackson continued to study Peter as he swung his feet and avoided looking at him. He cleared his throat. Peter looked up.

Jackson felt his heart open for the boy, and he knew he'd never let anyone or anything hurt the child. Earlier he'd questioned his decision to apprentice the little boy, and now he was thankful that he'd decided to do just that.

"I have only one more thing to say to you, young man, and I expect you to listen." He waited for the child's response.

Big green eyes studied his face, and then Peter nodded and answered, "All right."

Jackson moved to stand directly in front of the little boy. He placed his hands on each side of Peter and leaned down until they were eye level. "I will never hurt you, and if I can prevent it, neither will anyone else. If you get scared or think a grown-up is going to harm you, you come tell me."

Peter stared him in the eyes. His green ones filled with tears and then he flung his arms around Jackson's neck and hugged him tight. In a small voice he asked, "Does that mean you are going to be my new pa?"

Chapter Seven

Eliza stood in the doorway watching and listening. She'd heard the sincerity in Jackson's voice as he'd promised the boy his protection. She held her breath as she waited for him to answer Peter's plea to be his new pa.

Jackson gently pulled the boy back and looked him in the eyes once more. "Where is your pa, Peter?"

She continued to wait with bated breath. Would Peter tell him? Both she and Sally had tried to get the child to tell them where his pa was.

"I don't know." He dropped his head back onto his small chest.

Eliza released the oxygen in her lungs. She'd thought maybe Jackson could get through to the little boy.

Jackson gently raised his chin. "You really don't know?" he asked.

"I really, really don't. Pa left me just outside of town and said to come and ask the blacksmith to teach me, and then he left." Peter's chin quivered.

Jackson pulled the little boy into his strong arms. "When was this, Peter?"

The little boy wrapped his arms around Jackson's neck. "I don't know. A long time ago."

He hugged the small body close to his chest. "Well, then I guess you will just have to stay with me. 'Course, I'll have to get us a house." Jackson pulled out of the little boy's embrace. "It might take a while, though. Do you mind staying with Mrs. Kelly?"

Peter smiled. "Really? I can come live with you when you get a house?"

"Sure can." Jackson ruffled the child's hair.

"Then I reckon I can live with Eliza until then. She's a nice lady."

"Yes, she is." Jackson picked the boy up and placed him on the floor.

Eliza slipped out of the shop. She didn't want Jackson to know she'd been eavesdropping on their conversation. After several long minutes, she reentered.

"Eliza!" Peter called. He started to run to her but then looked to where Jackson stood beside the anvil and slowed to a walk. "Guess what?" he asked, walking as fast as his short legs would carry him.

She smiled at his desire to run and his willingness to obey Jackson. "What?"

He stopped right in front of her. "I'm going to live with Jackson."

"Oh?" Eliza looked at Jackson. This was information she already knew, but she didn't want to spoil the little boy's pleasure in telling her.

"Yep. He said as soon as we can get our own house, I can live with him and he'll be my new pa." Peter smiled up at her. His big green eyes sparkled with joy. "And you can be my ma!"

Eliza didn't know how to answer the boy. She looked

to Jackson, who, with studied interest was beating a piece of iron on the anvil. He seemed to either not have heard them or was deliberately ignoring them. She looked down into Peter's hopeful face. "But what about your parents? Won't they be sad if you call us Ma and Pa?"

"My Pa left me here. He said I was to find a better life. And Ma went to live with Jesus when I was born, so I don't reckon she'd mind. Pa said sometimes he could hear her singing with the angels, but I never heard her. You sing real pretty, though." Peter grinned up at her.

Jackson walked over to them. His gaze met Eliza's. "Maybe we can be Ma and Pa to him, at least until Seth decides what we should do." His blue eyes met and held her own.

A huff behind them caught Eliza's attention. She turned to see Mrs. Walker standing in the doorway. "Playing house now, are we?" She didn't wait for an answer but turned on her heels with the pan she'd brought for Jackson to repair.

Eliza sighed and chose to ignore the woman. Mrs. Walker and her husband owned one of the general stores in town. She and her friends were the local gossips. They'd been horrible to Rebecca when she'd first arrived as a mail-order bride, and even though they were trying to change, it was a long process for them. She could only imagine what the talk of the town would be by afternoon teatime.

"I think that's a good idea," she assured a frowning Jackson and Peter. "I've made lunch if you two would like to come eat." She studied both of the males in front of her. One appeared oblivious to the awkwardness of the situation they found themselves in and the other ready to fight.

Jackson's eyes were glued to the empty doorway. A scowl covered his handsome features. What must he think? She tried to get his attention by clearing her throat.

"I'll have to pass on lunch," he said absently. "I need to get some work done around here."

"I'm hungry, Eliza." Peter grabbed her hand and held on. "Can I call you Ma now?"

Once more Eliza felt at a loss as to how to respond. She didn't know how Seth would feel about the boy being homeless and what liberties she and Jackson would be permitted. Could she simply adopt him? Did Jackson plan on adopting the boy? His earnest eyes looked up at her.

She remembered Jackson's earlier words and decided to humor them both. "Yes. I don't see why not." After all, Seth had allowed Rebecca to adopt Janie after her parents had been murdered last year. As for Jackson adopting Peter, she would have to tell him her plans and then see what his were. But, not until Seth gave his approval.

"Yay! I have a new ma and pa." The little boy hung on to her arm and jumped up and down.

Her gaze moved to Jackson once more. A soft smile touched his eyes and mouth as he looked down at the excited boy. Charlie had had that same look; it meant the man was hungry for a child. Eliza wondered if all men wanted children of their own someday. If so, she knew Jackson could never consider her for a wife. Not that he'd ever acted as if he were interested.

She sighed and told Peter, "Go get your lunch pail,

and I'll put an afternoon treat in it for you and Jackson while you eat lunch." If Jackson wanted the little boy, too, they were going to have a problem because Eliza knew she would never give Peter up.

Over the next couple of days, Jackson fell into a routine with Eliza and Peter. He arrived at the shop early and Peter came in a little later. Eliza picked the boy up each day around noon and returned him midafternoon. Jackson made sure Peter went straight back to Eliza after work.

"Pa, Ma says you should come for supper tonight. She's making chicken potpie. I think that sounds good, don't you?"

Jackson smiled down at the boy. "Sure do."

He and Eliza hadn't spent time together since she'd taken over the Tuckers' house, and he found that he was looking forward to having dinner with her and the boy. Jackson handed Peter a small bucket. "See that box over there?" he asked Peter.

"Yes, Pa."

"Your job this afternoon is to fill it with coal. Do you think you can do that?" He ruffled the boy's hair, something he'd gotten into the habit of doing.

Peter nodded. He didn't look nearly as cheerful as he had when he'd come back from lunch. Jackson suspected that the newness of working in the smithy had worn off for the little boy.

Bart Hamilton came into the shop. He was a small man with a big nose. "Afternoon, Jackson." His wife, Judith, had him doing repairs to their house. He'd already been in once for a bag of nails.

Jackson answered, "Afternoon, Bart."

"Do you have another sack of nails I can buy? Judith's nagging me about putting shutters on her windows. You'd think the woman was rich or something." He chuckled.

Jackson walked over to a shelf and pulled down a sack of nails. He'd made up several bags over the past couple of days and was glad to see these sell. "Sure do. How's the family?"

Bart dug in his pocket to pay for the nails. "Doing good, although Judith seems to think Millie's coming down with something. The girl hasn't had much of an appetite the last few days."

He took the money. "Millie took care of Mrs. Kelly's shop before it burned, didn't she?" Jackson asked, trying to put people and names together. He felt sure Eliza had called the girl Millie.

"Yes, it's a shame about her house. I'm thankful Millie wasn't there when it happened." Bart shook his head. "Judith says if she hadn't changed her mind about letting her spend the night, she might have been."

Jackson had to agree; things might have turned out much worse. "Well, I hope she gets to feeling better soon."

"I think she has allergy problems, so I'm sure she'll be right as rain in no time." Bart took the nails. He stood watching Peter haul coal in. "Have you found out who he belongs to?" Bart asked.

"No, as soon as Seth gets back we'll see what he has to say about the boy." Jackson picked up a couple of pieces of metal to make hinges out of.

Bart nodded. "I guess I should be getting back." He started toward the door, then turned around and came back. "Normally, I wouldn't say anything, but I just want you to know that most folks aren't paying attention to what the gossips are saying about you and Mrs. Kelly."

"And what are they saying?" Jackson asked, not liking the thought of anyone speaking ill of Eliza.

Bart's neck began to turn red. "Oh, you know, about you two coming into town alone, and then Mrs. Walker has voiced her opinion that you and Mrs. Kelly have been playing house and—" he looked pointedly at Peter "—other stuff. Just talk."

Jackson frowned. "There is nothing to talk about."

Bart immediately agreed with him. "Oh, I'm sure there isn't but you know how some women can be."

He didn't, and Jackson was sure he didn't really want to find out. "Are they trying to ruin Mrs. Kelly's reputation? Who are these women?" His voice had hardened and he saw Bart flinch away.

"I've already said too much. Just thought you should know most of us aren't paying them a lick of attention. Thanks for the nails." The man practically ran from the smithy.

What was wrong with those women? Didn't they have enough to do without talking about other people? As he pounded on the hot metal, he wondered if he should tell Eliza what Bart had said. No, that would just be stirring the pot. She'd lived in this town long enough to know how the people were.

Peter smiled over at him every so often. He carried coal in and out of the shop with the small bucket Jackson had made him. The idea had come for the smaller tools when he'd realized Peter was smaller than he'd been when he'd started working in the smithy. He was also four years younger.

The little boy wiped his brow and walked over toward him. "Are you ready for a break?" he asked, sitting down on a small stool.

Jackson grinned at him. "You go ahead and rest. I've got to finish this hinge for Mr. James."

"Oh." Disappointment filled his young voice. Peter stood. His small shoulders slumped as he began walking back toward the coal bin.

Jackson laid the hammer and metal down. "I guess I could use a little break."

Peter hurried back to his stool and sat down. "I'm sure looking forward to Ma's potpie. I think my tummy is touching my backbone." He grinned up at Jackson.

"You sit right there, I'll be back in a moment." Jackson went to his room and found the two cookies Mrs. Velarde had given him at lunch. She ran the diner and always gave him a little extra on his plate or offered a dessert to go. More than once in the past two days he wondered if she felt he needed more food because of his size.

Folks here didn't react to his build like they had in North Carolina. Or maybe he just wasn't as sensitive to their reactions. Most everyone in Cottonwood Springs smiled and nodded when he passed them on the sidewalks. They treated him like everyone else, and he liked that. The folks in North Carolina had ducked their heads and rarely smiled in his direction. He assumed it was because of his size.

He returned to Peter and handed him the cookies. "Think these will fill the space until supper?"

Peter's eyes grew even bigger in his little face. "Sure will, thanks!" He bit into the sugary treat and sighed.

"My aunt made cookies like this," he said around the next bite.

"Where does she live?" Jackson asked, settling down on a barrel.

Peter swallowed. "In heaven." His voice sounded sad. "She died a few weeks ago."

"I'm sorry to hear that." And Jackson was. He felt the boy had lost all his family in such a short time.

"That's all right—I have a new ma and pa now." Peter shoved the rest of the cookie in his mouth and chewed happily.

A new ma and pa.

Jackson still couldn't believe he'd agreed to be the boy's father. But he'd done so for the same reason he'd not wanted to take the boy on as his apprentice. Peter was too young to be an apprentice and too young to be without a pa. He planned on traveling to Silverton when his year was up here in Cottonwood Springs. Would the boy be devastated? Or would he want to come with him and leave Eliza behind? And hadn't he promised the boy a house? He'd not even looked for one.

If they did leave, what about Eliza? Every day she grew closer and closer to the boy. Could he hurt Eliza by taking Peter away?

Chapter Eight

Jackson scraped the mud off his boots and then Peter's before entering Eliza's home. When he stepped into the doorway Jackson stopped.

Peter ran past him, yelling, "Ma! We're home!" He ran through the sitting room toward the kitchen.

When did she have time to do all this and take care of a little boy? His gaze moved about the room in wonder. Last time he'd seen this space, it had been bare. Today, it housed clotheslines along the walls with dresses, hats, scarves and other items hanging from them. In the center of the room were tables. Two held bolts of fabric in different colors. One held baskets with what looked like thread, needles and notations in them. A display of ribbons and basic hats filled two other tables.

Lastly, he noticed that she'd set up a sewing machine and he could see a half-sewn garment on it.

"What do you think? Too much?" Eliza stood in the entryway, studying his face. "Rebecca and I set it up, and I think it will work for a temporary shop. Of course, in my other store, I only sold ready-made dresses and hats, but now I don't have time to make them all myself. Rebecca thought I should open up a sewing shop instead. You know, just sell the sewing goods to the ladies so they can make their own dresses, and I can make up special orders. What do you think?"

Jackson smiled. She'd asked the same question twice without much of a breather in between. "I like it."

He heard her exhale of breath. Had she been holding it in anticipation of his approval? If so, that was something new for Jackson to experience. Most women didn't care what he thought.

Peter ran up behind her. "Ma, I washed my hands and set the table."

"Thank you, Peter." She placed her hand on Peter's thin shoulder, and they turned to walk back to the dining area.

Jackson followed and was surprised to see she'd changed that room, as well. The dining table now sat beside the window. She'd placed a sideboard next to the table and hot dishes of food waited to be served. A pretty bouquet of flowers decorated the center, giving it a homey look that he appreciated.

Eliza pointed to the head of the table. "Jackson, you sit over there. Peter here. And I'll sit here." She walked over to the sideboard as they took their seats. "How was your day, Peter?"

Peter snuck a look at him and flushed red. "It was good."

She placed a plate of steaming food in front of him. "What did you do?"

The boy rolled his eyes. "Man stuff."

Jackson looked out the window to keep from laughing. This side of the house faced an apple orchard that was just starting to bloom. He listened to Eliza continue her line of questioning and Peter's short answers. The woman could sure hound a guy when she wanted answers. He smiled.

No sooner had the thought crossed his mind that he was glad it was Peter and not him that was the focus of her questioning when she asked, "And how was your day, Jackson?"

He liked the way his name rolled off her tongue. It sounded warm and almost loving. Jackson sputtered at the thought. "Good."

She placed a plate of food in front of him that smelled wonderful. He couldn't wait to try her crust. It looked buttery and flaky.

"And what did you do today?" Eliza returned to the sideboard for her own plate.

Jackson shared a grin with Peter and said, "Man stuff."

She took her place at the table and smiled sweetly at both of them. "I see. Well, I did woman stuff today. I went over to Rebecca's shortly after you men left and had tea. That's when she and I put our heads together and came up with the idea to make my shop into a sewing store. Jackson, will you say grace, please?"

Jackson nodded and said a quick prayer. Since that first night when he couldn't sleep and had read his Bible and prayed, he'd been more consistent in his devotion time with the Lord. It had gotten easier to voice the requests on his heart, and just now his prayer must not have sounded too awkward because as soon as he finished Eliza continued as if nothing was amiss.

"We went to the general stores first. Mrs. Miller had lots of fabric and notations. Thankfully I have a running line of credit with her and was able to get all her stock. Now, Mrs. Walker, that's another story. She told me that she had a business to run, too, so I could just forget buying all her goods. She said something about not selling to the likes of me. I wonder what has gotten into her?" Eliza took a bite of potpie and stared out the window as if contemplating Mrs. Walker's behavior.

So Mrs. Walker had taken a personal jab at Eliza. Surely she had understood what the woman meant by her unkind words. He thought about going over there first thing in the morning and setting the woman straight. But what would that accomplish?

"Some folks are just mean, Ma." Peter took a drink of milk.

The old saying "out of the mouths of babes" came to mind. How many times had he been misjudged in the past because of his size? Or rumors that others had spread? All because of meanness. "He's right, you know."

She swallowed. "Yes, well, I'm happy with what I bought from Mrs. Miller and with the things we brought back from Durango. I have a nice start. After Rebecca and I unloaded the wagon and set up the room, I sold enough fabric and thread to make any gal happy, and tomorrow I know I'll do much better. Mr. Sayer, over at the sawmill, is bringing over a sign he's been working on for me. Which reminds me, Jackson, do you think you can burn the words 'Miz Eliza's Sewing Goods and More' into the sign? Or should I just stick with 'Sewing Goods and More' as the name of my business?"

He looked up. Was she going to stop and let him answer? Jackson waited.

Six-year-old Peter looked at Jackson, smiled and said, "I think it's your turn, Pa."

Jackson wiped his mouth to cover the grin he couldn't seem to control. "Sure, I'll put whichever one you want on it."

The little boy seemed amused at the way he'd answered her. "Pa, you forgot to answer her question." He turned his attention to Eliza. "I think 'Sewing Goods and More' sounds good, Ma."

She smiled at him. "It does, doesn't it?"

"Yes, ma'am. You are gonna have the bestest shop in this whole town." Peter shoveled more potpie into his mouth. Jackson watched her face as she turned her attention back to the orchard just past the blue-and-white curtains. For a few moments he witnessed hurt and anxiety cross her delicate features. Was she thinking about Mrs. Walker? She turned and caught him staring.

"Dinner tastes great. Thank you."

"You're welcome." Eliza stood, picked up her barely touched plate and carried it to the scrap bowl.

Peter pushed his chair back, as well, and took his plate to her. When she took it, he asked, "Can I go look at the picture book now?"

She smiled down at him. "You may."

Peter scampered off down the hall.

Jackson finished his meal and then carried his plate to the scrap bowl. Eliza filled a washbasin full of hot water and soap. He scraped out the crumbs and handed the plate to her.

Their eyes met as she took it. With a sigh she said, "Peter really is a good boy but I'm not sure he should be staying with me." Her voice cracked and tears filled her eyes.

He should walk away, Jackson told himself even as he asked, "Why not?"

* * *

A sob tore from her dry throat. Eliza tried to control the tears that she knew were coming. She wasn't Jackson's problem. He didn't need to know that in just the past couple of days she'd been christened the town harlot. Eliza wiped her hands off on a towel. Who was she kidding? He probably already knew.

"Some of the ladies believe that, well, that…" She couldn't bring herself to say that they thought she and he had spent the night together. How did you say such a thing to a man? "Never mind, it's not important." She turned away from him, wiped the moisture from her eyes and pulled her shoulders back.

His sigh tickled the back of her neck, sending goose bumps down her arms. She moved farther away from him. He wasn't the man she needed to talk to about Peter—Seth Billings was. Eliza dunked the dirty dishes into the hot water and began to scrub.

"I'm sorry, Eliza. I've heard some of what the ladies are saying." She heard him pull out a chair from the table and sit.

It was her time to sigh. "I'm not blaming you, Jackson. People gossip." She stacked the dishes on a dish towel.

"So what are we going to do about it?"

Eliza frowned down at the dirty water. "About what?"

"The gossip."

She swished her hand through the water once more, making sure she hadn't missed any silverware, and then picked up the basin. "Nothing we can do. The gossips will gossip about us no matter what we do."

Eliza walked to the back door and took the wooden steps down to the garden.

His boots clomped as he followed her.

She tossed the water onto the garden and turned back around.

Jackson leaned against the door. His legs were crossed at the ankle and his arms crossed over his broad chest. His sandy-brown hair fluttered in the evening breeze, inviting her fingers to straighten it. He looked relaxed as he offered, "We could get married."

Chapter Nine

Jackson felt anything but relaxed. Sweat beaded on the back of his neck and his hands shook. He'd never asked a woman to marry him before. Come to think of it, he really hadn't asked her. He'd simply made a statement.

From the shocked look on her face, Eliza hadn't expected the suggestion, either. She stared at him as if he'd recommended she go out and kill someone. After several moments of silence, he wondered if Eliza Kelly had been turned speechless.

"Get married? You and me? Why?" she sputtered. "What would motivate you to ask me to marry you? Well, you really didn't ask, you suggested. But still, why?"

His lips twitched. So much for speechless. "Yes, get married, and yes, you and me."

Again she asked, "Why?"

Jackson motioned for her to come to him. He sat down on the porch and patted the wood beside him. When she sat, he turned to her. "Look, I know what the ladies are saying. I've put your reputation in danger and I want to make things right."

She offered him a smile. "Look, Jackson, I'm sure your heart is in the right place, but I can't be a good wife to you." Eliza held up her hand, thinking he might interrupt. "I'm not in love with you. Charlie still holds that part of my heart, he probably always will. I'm sorry if that hurts you, but I have to be honest. A marriage between us would be unfair to you."

Jackson shook his head. "I'm not saying we have to stay married, Eliza. If we marry, it will stop the wagging tongues and help you establish your business. In a year, I plan to go to Silverton and open a new smithy. We can get an annulment then." He focused on the trees. "Besides, I'm not in love with you, either."

She stared at him as if he'd sprouted wings. Her mouth opened and closed. For the second time in the past few minutes, he'd rendered Eliza Kelly speechless. Jackson felt as if ants were crawling up his spine and into his hairline. "Just think about it, Eliza." He stood. "Thanks for dinner." And then he turned and walked away.

Jackson exhaled. Had he messed up by offering Eliza marriage? What if she avoided him like the plague now? What if she accepted? A bead of sweat rolled down his spine.

What was she going to do now? The man had suggested marriage like others suggested having pie for dessert. Eliza heard Peter in the kitchen and stood to join him.

"Are you going to marry Pa?" he asked as soon as she entered the room.

Eliza frowned. "It's not polite to eavesdrop, Peter."

She avoided the question by picking up the dishcloth and wiping down the table.

The little boy sighed. “I’m sorry.”

She realized she’d snapped at him. “I’m sorry, too.” Eliza sat down in one of the wooden chairs and pulled him to her for a quick cuddle. What was she going to do? If the ladies continued to accuse her falsely, Seth might make her give up Peter.

The strong smell of sweaty little boy filled her nose. She tickled him. “You need a bath.”

“I’d rather have a cookie.” He chuckled, squirming out of her arms.

She laughed. “You’ll have both.”

He groaned at the prospect of another bath. “My pa never made me take this many baths.”

“Well, I’d hate to think what he smelled like.” She winked to take the sting out of her words and handed him a fresh sugar cookie.

Peter giggled. “Yeah, my new pa smells much better.”

Eliza had to agree with him on that score. Jackson smelled like leather, iron and the outdoors all rolled up into one manly scent. What would it be like to take Jackson up on his offer of marriage?

That question kept her awake all night. As soon as she got Peter off to the smithy the next morning, Eliza hurried to Rebecca’s for tea. She didn’t take time to look in the mirror before leaving for fear of seeing dark circles under her eyes.

Seth met her at the door. “Good morning, Eliza. I was just on my way to see you.” He held it open for her to enter.

"Good morning, Marshal. When did you get home?" Eliza hurried past him into the sitting room.

Seth closed the door and followed her. "Last night. Rebecca tells me you have a little boy living with you?"

Eliza swallowed. He didn't waste any time getting to the point. She wondered if the local gossips had already made their way to inform him of her suspected unladylike conduct. "I do, and he's the sweetest little thing."

"He's with Jackson Hart now?"

His tone gave her pause. "Yes. Is something wrong, Seth?"

"Yes and no." Seth leaned up against the door frame and studied her. "Rebecca has filled me in on all the events following my absence. She warned me to expect the welcoming committee as soon as they find out I'm home. We suspect they are going to request that Peter be moved to a more respectable home."

"I see."

Rebecca breezed into the room. She had baby Sadie on her hip. One look at them and she scowled at Seth. "Real subtle, were you?"

He stood up taller, and she thrust the baby into his arms and then hurried to Eliza. "Don't fret, Eliza. I told him everything, including what Mrs. Walker and her bunch are saying, so that he can help you keep Peter and find out who burned down your shop."

Eliza felt weariness settle on her shoulders. Seth didn't give the impression that he wanted to help. He acted as though he'd rather be anywhere but in the same room with her. Did he believe the ugly lies?

"Rebecca's probably right, Seth. The ladies heard Miles Thatcher and the way he accused us of spending the night together, and they haven't let it go. I don't think that is cause to take Peter away from me, though. I've done nothing wrong." Eliza looked to Rebecca. "As for my shop burning down, we have no proof that it was done on purpose. And thanks to Rebecca's idea of me opening up a sewing shop, I can rebuild in no time. The sheriff arrived home yesterday and came by to talk to me about it. He thinks that a group of teenage boys were sneaking a smoke, but since he has no proof, he's dropping it. So I don't think you need to concern yourself with that." She took a deep breath.

"What does Jackson have to say about this?" Seth asked as he jiggled the fussing baby.

Should she tell him? Eliza looked to her friend. She'd meant to tell Rebecca, and now Eliza knew that Rebecca would tell him later, anyway. "He suggested we get married."

Seth stopped jiggling the infant and Rebecca gasped. They both stared at her with round eyes.

"What did you say?" Rebecca finally asked.

Eliza sighed. "Nothing. I didn't know what to say."

"Let's sit down." Rebecca led her to the couch.

She sank onto the soft cushion. Seth took the rocking chair and Rebecca sat down beside her. Little Janie climbed down and grabbed the table and began walking circles around it.

Seth cleared his throat. "It's not a bad idea."

"Seth Billings! How can you say that? We don't know the man well enough to suggest Eliza marry up with him."

Janie started at the tone in her mother's voice. She plopped down on her diaper and started to cry.

Eliza wanted to join her. Embarrassed and tired from

the stress of the past few days she fought to hold back her own tears.

Rebecca scooped up the crying baby and soothed her with soft words. She patted the little girl's back and glared at her husband.

Seth waited until Janie calmed down and then said softly, "It's not so far-fetched. Weren't you and Hannah going to marry her off to that Miles Thatcher? What did you know about him? Other than what he told you in a few letters? Letters that he could have lied about himself in."

It was true. Rebecca had schemed with Hannah to marry her off to a man she'd never met.

"That was different," Rebecca said.

"No, he's right, Rebecca. You and Hannah were going to marry me off to a stranger. We haven't talked about it, but you really should have told me before I went to Durango with her."

Eliza heard the hurt in her own voice. "If I had known about him, I might not be in this situation now."

Rebecca turned a shocked face to her. "I'm sorry, Eliza. I didn't realize we would hurt you. The truth of the matter is we didn't want you to be lonely when Hannah left. I truly am sorry."

Seeing the sincerity on her friend's face, Eliza felt like a heel. She patted Rebecca on the shoulder. "It's all right. I'm not angry at you or Hannah anymore. I just wish we could have avoided this whole situation."

Seth stood slowly. "Sadie's asleep. I'm going to go lay her down." He hurried from the room.

Eliza watched him leave. When he was out of earshot she said, "I could leave town. Without my store I have nothing holding me here. Jackson says he's going to Silverton in a year, so as soon as he leaves, the ladies will forget all about us and move on to other things."

"Don't give them the satisfaction, Eliza. I thought after last year they'd changed." She sighed. "You can't leave. I'd miss you something terrible. We're like sisters. And what about Peter?"

Eliza didn't want to leave Cottonwood Springs but didn't know what to do about the gossip. "I'm taking him with me if I go." She didn't want Peter to get hurt and moved into another home. In the short time he'd been with her, the little boy had captured her heart.

"No, you can't leave," Rebecca protested as she rocked side to side holding Janie.

"Then what do you suggest I do?"

When Rebecca stared at her blankly, Eliza realized she would have to choose her own path. Would she marry Jackson? He was a good man. And, if she did, could he raise Peter as an only child? Or would Jackson leave her?

Chapter Ten

Jackson wasn't surprised when Seth came into the smithy. Several of the men had been standing around chatting, and news had it that the marshal had arrived the night before. "Afternoon, Marshal."

"Afternoon, Jackson. I see you've settled in here." Seth's gaze moved to Peter. The little boy was sitting at a barrel, practicing his letters.

"Yep, it's a nice town."

Seth's gaze came back to rest on him. "Is it?"

Jackson looked at the small group of men chatting by the door. "For the most part."

The marshal nodded. "True, but we do have a small group of ladies that like to keep things stirred up."

"Every town does." Jackson returned to shaping the trammel he'd been working on when Seth arrived.

Seth pulled up a crate and sat down not too far from Jackson. "Way I hear it, our little group has been giving you trouble."

Jackson hit the thick metal with his hammer. "Not me."

"No?"

He didn't like the marshal prying into his personal life, but being as Seth was the law, there wasn't much he could do about it. "Nope."

Seth picked up a pair of tongs and examined them. "How's business?"

"Picking up every day." Jackson thrust the metal into a tub of cold water. He turned to face Seth. "Something on your mind, Marshal?"

Seth watched as the men began to depart. "Eliza tells me you proposed to her last night, but that you are going to leave in a year for Silverton."

Jackson laid the hammer down and nodded. "I did and I am."

"Why?" Seth looked up at him. His brown eyes studied Jackson as he waited for the answer.

Jackson glanced at Peter. Could the boy hear their conversation? His face was scrunched up as he copied his letters. Jackson turned his attention back to Seth. "I don't reckon I have to answer you since it really isn't any of your business."

Seth stood. "Well, you are partially right. You see, it isn't any of my business, but Eliza Kelly is."

Jackson felt the old feeling of being measured and didn't like it. He pulled his shoulders back and in a quiet voice that put fear in most men's hearts asked, "How so?"

Seth ignored the stance and tone. His own voice took on an edge as he answered. "I told you in Durango. I decided the day I moved here to keep an eye on her. The Good Book says I am to protect and provide for the widows in my town, and she's my wife's best friend. So I want to know what your intentions are and why you have them."

So that was it. Seth wasn't judging him. He was simply questioning his motives because he cared about his friend. "I suggested we get married. If she says yes, I'm going to marry her. As to why, well, I'll be honest with you. I feel responsible for the hearsay that is going on about her. Her reputation is all she has right now, and I don't want it ruined by the local gossips." Jackson picked up the metal and hammer once more. He didn't feel the need to remind the marshal that he'd promised to protect her.

Seth laid a hand on his shoulder. "I thought it was a good idea at first, too, but my sweet wife gave me reasons to pause and think about it. Have you thought this through? What about the boy? What happens to him when you move to Silverton? Are you going to give him to Eliza and be the second pa to walk out on him in his young life? And what if Eliza falls in love with you during this year of marriage? Are you going to break her heart and leave? I don't mind telling you, Jackson, I don't like the idea of any of that coming to pass. Do me a favor and think about that before you marry Eliza." He walked out the smithy, leaving Jackson feeling confused and foolish.

His gaze moved to Peter. The boy had been abandoned by his father, much like Jackson's had abandoned him. Would he desert the boy, too? Would searching for a man who'd never looked back to his family be worth hurting the boy even further?

And then there was Eliza. If he did leave her in a year, would he be as guilty as his father by turning her into a bitter and spiteful woman like his mother?

Eliza walked back to her shop. After leaving Rebecca and Seth's, she'd delivered a couple of small blankets to the Hudson family. Their girls needed new bedding, and, even though she didn't have the extra material, Eliza made sure they would be a little warmer at night.

Warm spring air lifted her hat. She reached up and grabbed it. Another gust lifted her skirts, and Eliza realized the wind had definitely picked up in the past few minutes.

She turned the corner and sucked in too much air when she saw her likeness sitting on the Tuckers' front porch. It tickled the back of her throat and sent her into a coughing spell. What was her sister, Eve, doing here? The question ran through her mind with such bitterness that Eliza felt taken aback by her own thought.

"Eliza! Is that you?" Eve got to her feet. "It's about time you got home. Where have you been? This wind is trying to rip the hair right off my head, and some woman came by and said to give you this."

Eliza took the piece of paper from her twin's hand. "Why are you here, Eve?" she asked and continued up the steps. Eliza tucked the note into her handbag.

Her sister's skirts swished as she followed her. "Can't a sister come visit you whenever she feels like it?" Eve simpered.

"Not my sister. You want something, so don't play coy."

Eve pouted but didn't say anything. *You get more bees with honey than you do vinegar.* Her mother's voice echoed the words in her mind. How many times had their mother reminded her of that when she and Eve were children?

Eliza sighed. She didn't feel like offering her twin honey. "Eve, just tell me what it is so you can be on your way." Eliza hung her wrap up and tossed her handbag on the nearest table. She turned in time to see Eve push out her bottom lip in what she must have thought was an even more compelling pout.

Her sister flopped down in a chair that Eliza had set beside the door for her waiting customers. "You don't have anything that I want. From what I hear, you have lost everything, your home, your shop and evidently your man."

Shock filled Eliza at the venom in her sister's voice. How long had Eve been in town? Evidently long enough to learn all the local gossip. Eliza wanted nothing more than to toss her uncaring sister out into the street. "Get to the point, Eve."

Eve busied herself by picking at imaginary lint on her skirt. "I just want to stay with you for a while. Is that so bad?"

"It is if you are in trouble. Are you in trouble?" Eliza turned to study Eve. It was almost like looking into a mirror. Eve had the same wavy brown hair and brown eyes. The only difference was that Eve sported a patch of freckles across her pert nose. The green suit she wore at the moment looked a little rough, but that could be expected from traveling.

Eve waved her hand in dismissal. "Of course not. Why would you think such a thing?" She pulled a white handkerchief from her pocketbook and blew her nose.

"Let's see. Why would I think that? For starters, you are here and I haven't seen you in six years. Second, because you would never leave the plantation without a good reason. And third, Daddy wouldn't let you out of his sight." She paused and studied her twitching sister. "Is something wrong with Daddy?"

"So you remember we have a mother and father, do you?"

The sharp and condemning tone set Eliza's teeth on edge.

How could she forget she had parents? Even though they'd disowned her the year before she'd married Charles Kelly, she still loved them and mourned her loss. Bitterness threatened to choke Eliza as she remembered the last time she'd seen her family. She'd been fifteen and had just returned from helping one of their servants deliver a new baby. Instead of being proud of her, they'd accused her of being with a man and then her father had told her to get out.

Their disappointment in her had started early in life. She talked too much for their liking, cared for others too much and didn't value things in the same way her mother and sister did.

Eve, on the other hand, was the perfect daughter. She was everything they wanted in a well-behaved child. She showed signs of being slow to speak, never got dirty, was a quick learner and valued their advice.

Unfortunately, only Eliza knew the truth of her sister's character. She was self-centered, uncaring of others and a petty, spoiled brat. Eve manipulated her parents to get her way, and they thought it was cute. Eliza often wondered what part her sister had played in that dreadful evening when her father had told her to depart from his sight.

It had broken her heart to leave. Alone and unsure where she was going, she'd stumbled onto the Kelly farm. Charles's mother had taken her under her wing, taught her to cook, clean and sew.

A year later, Charles Kelly had proclaimed his love

for her and proposed. The marriage took place a few days after her sixteenth birthday. Eliza had sent her parents an invitation to the wedding, only to have it returned unopened.

"Really, Eliza, if you are just going to stand there and stare out the window, I'm going to go see if you have any food in this place." Eve stood to her feet and looked around. "Which way?"

Eliza pointed down the hall. She just didn't have the strength to argue with her sister. Too much had happened too fast in the past few days. She sighed and followed Eve into the brightly lit kitchen. "You didn't answer my question," she said.

"Mommy and Daddy are well." Eve tossed her pocketbook on the kitchen table and looked about. "This is a cozy kitchen, Eliza. But where are your servants?"

Eliza felt like laughing. "I don't have servants, Eve."

Her sister curled her nose and looked about. "Then how do you function?"

This time Eliza did laugh at her. "I haven't had servants in years, Eve. Believe it or not, I do things for myself."

Eve pulled out a chair at the table. "Oh, well, then do you mind making me some breakfast? I'm starved."

Anger boiled to the surface once more. "As a matter of fact, I do mind. I said I do for myself, not that I am your new servant."

"But, Eliza, I'm hungry."

For a brief moment, Eliza almost felt sorry for her spoiled sister. Eve twirled a curl around her finger and tapped her foot, giving away the fact that her behavior was all an act. Eliza pulled back her shoulders and declared, "Whining isn't going to get you a meal any faster. I'm sure you have money, go to the diner and order something."

Eve looked up at her. The brown in her eyes turned to stone. "Fine. I need to go see the man at the livery, anyway, and tell him to deliver my bags here." She picked up her pocketbook and started for the front door.

Eliza shook her head and hurried after her. "No, you can't have them delivered here. I suggest you go to the Millers' store and ask Mrs. Miller if you can rent a room from her for a few days."

Eve turned around with a gasp. "You aren't going to let me stay here with you?"

"No, I'm not. As you pointed out, this isn't my house and I haven't gotten permission to have a houseguest." Eliza opened the door and motioned for her sister to leave.

Eve's curls bounced down her back as she stomped off the porch. She didn't look back as she headed down the street toward the Miller's store. Eliza held her breath. Why had Eve shown up here? What did she want? And more importantly, why did she have to come now?

Chapter Eleven

That evening, Eliza waited for Peter to get home. She hadn't seen her sister for the rest of the day and for a brief moment worried about what Eve might be up to. "Don't borrow trouble," she muttered as the front door banged open and Peter called out with his familiar, "Ma, I'm home!"

What would Eve think of Peter? Seth had assured her she could keep the sweet little boy as long as his real pa didn't show up for him.

Peter rushed into the kitchen carrying a bouquet of wildflowers. "Look, Ma! Me and Pa picked you some flowers."

Eliza looked over his head and saw Jackson enter the kitchen. His hair looked damp and his face clean shaven. Even white teeth smiled at her from across the room. Her heart did a little skip of happiness.

"They are beautiful, Peter." She turned to the cabinet and pulled out a glass mason jar to put them in. Would Jackson want her answer, about marrying him, tonight? With Eve in town, she didn't know what to do. Her sister was sure to complicate things even further.

Eve couldn't seem to help it; complicating things for Eliza was just what she did. Or at least that's the way it had been when they were children.

The low rumble of Jackson's voice filled the room. "I hope you don't mind my bringing the boy home."

She took a deep breath and turned around with a smile on her face. "Not at all, I'd lost track of time. I should have already come for him. I'm sorry if you felt as if you had to bring him home." Eliza realized she talked more and much faster when Jackson was in the room, but she couldn't quite stop herself. "I guess my mind was on other things."

"Yoo-hoo! Eliza!"

Eliza watched as Jackson and Peter turned to face the front door. She inwardly groaned. *Not now, Eve. Go away.*

Eve could be heard shutting the front door and swishing toward the kitchen. "I managed to get a room at Mrs. Miller's and was wondering if we might have dinner tonight. I'll pay." She came around the corner and stopped short when she saw Jackson and Peter.

"I'm busy tonight, Eve," Eliza answered. She took a big, deep cleansing breath and then made introductions. "Eve, I'd like you to meet Jackson Hart and Peter. Jackson, Peter, this is my sister, Eve."

Jackson extended his large hand. Eliza watched as Eve backed away. What was wrong with her sister? Had she lost all her senses? Or manners? He dropped his hand back to his side.

"It's nice to meet you, Miss Eve."

Eve regained her composure. She extended her small white hand to him. "I'm sorry, Mr. Hart. I was just taken aback at your…presence here."

He cut his eyes at Eliza and then gently took Eve's small hand into his own. "I understand." Jackson released her and moved back a couple of steps.

Peter clung to Eliza's dress and whispered loudly, "She looks just like you, Ma."

Eliza knelt down beside him. "She's my twin sister, Peter." She whispered in his ear, "But if you look closely, she has freckles on her nose and I don't."

"Ma?" The question squeaked from Eve's throat. One hand fluttered to her heart and the other to her stomach. She looked from Jackson to Eliza and then down at Peter once more.

Peter giggled. "She's funny."

Eliza knew Eve was putting on a show. She'd already admitted to hearing the local gossip so more than likely she knew all the circumstances around the three of them. "Yes, she is. Eve, we were about to sit down to supper. Would you like to join us?" Eliza wanted to bite her tongue off. She'd hoped to prepare Peter and Jackson for her sister, but it just wasn't meant to be.

Eve nodded.

"Peter, please set the table. Jackson, you can sit in your regular place. Eve, remember the chair by the door in the store?" Eve nodded. "Go get it." Eliza watched her sister leave the room.

Jackson whispered, "Are you sure you want me to stay?"

She heard the uneasiness in his voice. Eliza nodded and whispered back, "You might as well get to know her."

Jackson took his place at the table. Peter set out plates and silverware while Eliza dished up the chicken casserole and salad. The sound of the chair thumping along the hallway grated on her nerves.

"For goodness' sake, Eve! Pick it up and get in here or we're going to start without you!" Eliza stared at the door.

"But it's heavy," Eve whined back.

Jackson moved as if to push out of his chair. Eliza shook her head at him. "No, she has to do this."

She waited until he was reseated and then called to Eve, "You're not helpless, and we aren't going to do it for you."

More thumping reached their ears.

Eliza filled the plates and sighed as her sister dropped the chair just inside the doorway. Eve puffed as if she'd run for miles. Eliza ignored her while Eve leaned against the door frame dramatically. She poured fresh milk into Peter's glass and coffee in Jackson's mug.

Peter slid out of his chair and hurried to Eve's side. The little boy picked the chair up and carried it the rest of the way to the table. "Here, Miss Eve, you can sit by me."

Eve sashayed to the table. "Thank you, Peter. It's nice to see there is one gentleman in the room. I would be honored." She glared at Eliza and Jackson. "You could have helped me."

Jackson ducked his head and Eliza sighed. "We're not your servants, Eve. You've got to learn to do for yourself or go home." She realized she'd sighed more today then she had in probably a year. Eve had that effect on her. The woman just made her tired.

Her sister tossed her hair over her shoulder and ignored Eliza's statements. "Do you say a blessing over the meal?" Eve asked. She extended her palms face up on the table.

A dark cloud of anger ascended over Eliza. "You know that I do."

"Good." She smiled down at Peter. "When Eliza and I were growing up, we held hands during grace. Doesn't that sound like fun?" Eve wiggled her fingers until both Peter and Jackson placed their hands in hers. "Jackson, please say the prayer."

Eliza wanted to kick her sister under the table, but she was worried she might hit Peter. Who did she think she was? Coming in and taking over her dinner table as if she were some kind of queen? The only reason she wanted to follow the old tradition was so that she could hold Jackson's hand. Anger boiled like overheated water at the thought.

Jackson took her hand in his and gave it a gentle squeeze. Eliza smiled gratefully at him and then bowed her head for the prayer.

"Ma, you're hurting my fingers," Peter protested as soon as Jackson said *amen.*

She jerked her hand loose. "I'm sorry, Peter."

"It's all right. You was focusing mighty hard on the prayer." He grinned at her and then took a big bite of his casserole.

"So tell me, Mr. Hart, what is it that you do?" Eve rested her chin on her hands and batted her eyelashes.

Eliza frowned. Normally Eve's flirting wouldn't bother her but tonight it did. Jackson could very well be her future husband. Her mood soured as she watched Eve's every move.

* * *

Jackson didn't know how much longer he could stand watching Eve blink her eyes like an old owl. She and Eliza looked a lot alike, but their actions were so different. Eve had focused all her energy on him while Eliza had visited with Peter and fussed over the serving of the meal.

As soon as he finished eating he stood to leave. "Thank you for dinner, Eliza." Jackson pushed his chair back and carried his plate to the washbasin.

Eliza followed him to the sink and offered a weak grin. "You're welcome. I hope we didn't talk your ear off this evening."

He would have found that comical coming from her, but the sadness in her eyes touched his heart. After Eve arrived, Eliza hadn't said more than ten words to him throughout the evening. He leaned down and whispered for her ears only, "Actually, I missed your lovely voice tonight." The shock on her face and the smile that slowly spread across her lips warmed his heart.

Jackson straightened and grinned into her eyes. He turned to find Eve and Peter watching them. "Good night, everyone."

"'Night, Pa."

"I'll see you to the door," Eve offered. Her skirt rustled as she stood.

Jackson shook his head. "That won't be necessary."

"I don't mind," Eve insisted.

Jackson shrugged and allowed her to lead the way. He waited while she opened the door.

"It was so nice of you to drop by this evening," Eve said as he walked out onto the porch. She followed, shutting the door behind her.

What was she up to? Why act as if she was the hostess for the evening and they'd just enjoyed a wonderful dinner party? Jackson decided to enlighten her. "Miss Eve, I come by every evening. Most, I simply drop off Peter, but occasionally I stay for supper."

She lightly clapped her hands. "Oh, good. That means I will get to see you again soon."

"I suppose." He turned to leave.

The change in her voice stopped him. "Jackson, what are your intentions toward my sister?" This was a side of Eve he hadn't seen yet. Her words were hard, sharp and demanding.

Jackson turned slowly to face her. Again, he mentally asked himself what she was up to. "My business with your sister is really none of your concern. Good evening." He took the steps down two at a time.

She hurried after him. "I disagree. You see, it would seem that you and Eliza are the talk of the town."

"Again, not your concern." He continued walking.

Eve grabbed his arm to stop him.

Jackson knew he could continue walking and she'd either be forced to release him or be dragged along. He stopped and looked pointedly down at her hand and his arm.

She released him. Once more she spoke in the voice that he guessed turned most men's heads. Concern laced her words. "Look, I'm worried. People are talking in this town. I've only been here one day and I can tell you that my sister went to Durango as a mail-order bride and came back an unmarried woman who spent a full day alone with you. What do you have to say about that?" Eve took a deep breath.

"I've heard that, too." Jackson continued walking. "But, like I said before, it doesn't concern you."

Eve ran along beside him. "It does. She's my sister."

Jackson stopped. "Yes, I've been told that, too. Sister or no sister, I am not answering your questions. Talk to Eliza about it if you must. But I am not airing our business with you or anyone else." He dismissed her by walking away.

After several steps, he released the breath from his lungs. There were no sounds of her following for which he was very grateful. The two sisters did have something in common besides their looks. Both wouldn't let a subject go until they had all the answers they thought they deserved.

He entered his cozy room and plopped down into the chair. Jackson hoped Eliza had better luck answering her sister's questions then he had, because truth be told there was nothing he could do about the rumors and speculations.

Eliza Kelly was the only one who could change the way things were, and Jackson knew that if she accepted his proposal, both their lives would be changed.

Forever.

Chapter Twelve

Eliza watched them from her bedroom window. Her sister's hand rested on Jackson's forearm, and there was just enough sunlight left that she could tell Eve was looking up at him.

Jackson leaned down and said something to her. Eve dropped her hand but her gaze into his face never wavered. Whatever they were saying to each other seemed to aggravate her sister.

"Ma, I'm ready for my story." Peter stood behind her in the doorway.

She dropped the curtain. "All right, what shall we read tonight?" Eliza didn't feel like reading him a Bible story, but it was something that she'd vowed to do as long as Peter lived with her.

He ran down the hall and returned a few moments later with the big family Bible that Charlie had bought shortly after they were married. Peter handed it to her. "How about that fishing story again?"

Eliza smiled at him. "There are lots of fishing stories in the Bible, which one?"

His green eyes grew even bigger in his small face.

"That one where the fish ate that man." Peter climbed into the overstuffed chair by her bed and waited for her to join him.

"Jonah and the big fish?" Eliza asked as she sat down beside him.

He nodded. "Yeah, I still have trouble believing that the fish ate him and then got sick and spit him out. That is so wonderful."

"That is horrible." Disgust filled Eve's voice.

Eliza looked up to find her sister standing in the doorway. "Yes, it is repulsive, but it also shows what Jonah had to endure for not obeying God. Would you like to stay for the story, Eve?"

"No thanks. I just stopped by to say good-night and that I'm heading over to Mrs. Miller's." Eve looked at her and offered a small smile. "We need to sit down and talk tomorrow morning, say, midmorning."

Eliza still didn't know what her sister wanted from her. She guessed she'd find out tomorrow. "All right."

Eve smiled. "If you supply the tea, I'll bring shortbread cookies."

An old-fashioned tea party. Whatever Eve planned on talking to her about must be serious. As little girls, when they wanted to have a serious talk, they'd ask the cook to make tea and shortbread cookies. "I'll put the kettle on at ten."

"Good night, Eliza." Eve started to turn away.

Her heart went out to Eve. Could they go back to being real sisters? Before they became teenagers they'd been close. "'Night."

Peter's young voice reminded them he was in the room. "Good night, Miss Eve."

Eve walked into the room. She knelt in front of Peter

and cupped his face in her hands. "If Eliza is Ma, then I want to be Aunt Eve. Can you call me that?"

His little face lit up. "Yes, ma'am."

She kissed his forehead and then said, "Good night, Peter."

Eliza noticed the tears in Eve's eyes as she stood to leave.

"Good night, Aunt Eve," Peter said as she walked out the door.

Eliza listened as her sister left the house. A glance out the window showed that it was dusky dark. Eve would be fine walking back to the Millers' store.

"Your sister is different, isn't she?" Peter asked. He wiggled next to her and looked down at the Bible in her lap.

"Yes, she is, but I love her." Eliza knew the words were true. No matter what Eve might have done in the past, Eliza could forgive her because she loved her.

Half an hour later, she had Peter tucked into bed and was sipping a hot cup of tea at the kitchen table. Her thoughts were in turmoil. Should she marry Jackson? Would that really stop the wagging tongues? Or would it make it worse?

And then there was her business to consider. She'd been to the bank earlier in the day and been told that because she was single they couldn't give her a small-business loan. But if she were to marry, then they would be happy to extend her the money.

Eve came to mind as a possible source of financing, but Eliza quickly rejected that idea. She still didn't know why Eve was here and she didn't feel she could trust her. Earlier she'd realized she loved her sister, but that didn't mean Eve could be trusted.

She stood and rinsed out her cup. Over the past few days she'd gotten to know Jackson a little better but not much. Eliza knew he felt guilty for the gossip that was circulating about them. Did she want to marry a man because he felt guilty?

But if she did marry him, the bank would give her the money she needed to start work on her store and home. After a year, Jackson would move to Silverton and she'd be free to carry on as before.

That would be a great plan if they didn't have Peter to consider. She wouldn't want the little boy moving to Silverton. Would Jackson be willing to let him stay with her? And if he did, would Peter feel as if he'd been abandoned by another pa?

Thoughts continued to swirl round and round in her tired brain. After a year Jackson planned to leave, would the town gossips start wagging their tongues again? If they had the marriage annulled, she'd be a divorcée. If they stayed married, would the gossips say he'd run out on her and little Peter?

What was she going to do? Time passes quickly. A year would pass fast and then the Tuckers would be back. Without enough money, she could still be homeless. Even so, they wouldn't want her to continue to live here. Opening the shop would supply her with a steady income, but if the wealthier women continued to ignore her business, she would not make enough to rebuild.

Did she really want their business? She could move away. She'd mentioned the idea to Rebecca and Seth and they'd both said they'd rather see her stay. Seth had also pointed out that if she moved away, Peter would have to stay in Cottonwood Springs. Seth still held on to the thought that Peter's father might yet return for him.

Eliza knew she couldn't leave Peter. He'd attached himself to her and Jackson. Jackson wasn't sticking around, so she felt the responsibility of taking care of Peter. Besides, having Peter for a son would fill the void of not being able to have children of her own.

Another sigh escaped her lips. What good would it do to move? She might be able to escape the gossips of this town, but she didn't have enough money in the bank to move and restart her business. Besides, every town had gossips.

Several hours later, Eliza stumbled into the bedroom and fell across the quilted mattress. She was no closer to having any answers than she'd been the night before and now her head hurt.

Marrying Jackson seemed to be the only reasonable answer to her problem. Any woman would be happy to marry him, so why wasn't she?

The next morning, Mr. Sayer stood on the porch. A large piece of wood leaned against the end of the steps. He tipped his hat and smiled. His top two front teeth were missing and he spoke with a lisp. "Mrs. Kelly, I thought I'd deliver your sign myself this morning." His gaze roved over her like he was looking at a new wagon.

Eliza stood a little taller and tried to ignore the queasy feelings that were evoked by his look. "Thank you, Mr. Sayer. If it isn't too much trouble, please take it over to the smithy. Mr. Jackson is going to burn the store name into it."

She turned to enter the house but his voice stopped her.

"We haven't discussed payment."

She frowned. "Of course we did. You agreed that I

could pay you next month." Her gaze ran over the fine scrollwork he'd done around the edges of the sign. He really was a talented man.

"Well, I was thinking we could come to another arrangement." Again he openly ran his gaze over her.

A shiver crept up her spine and into her hair. Was this the way men thought about her now? Eliza shuddered at the thought. She opened her mouth to deliver a stinging put-down, then spied Jackson coming toward them.

The set of his jaw as he approached assured her Jackson was coming to her rescue and she smiled. He was proving to be her personal protector, and Eliza realized she enjoyed the attention.

Jackson marched across the remainder of the front yard. What was wrong with the man? Propositioning a respectable lady like that? His boots stomped across the porch as red flashed before his eyes. With one easy lift, he removed Carl Sayer from the Tucker's porch.

He heard rather than saw Eliza gasp.

He followed Mr. Sayer down the steps and helped the man up by lifting him by his shirtfront. Lowering his voice to a growl, Jackson announced, "From now on, Sayer, all your business arrangements with my fiancée will come through me. Understand?" He lowered Mr. Sayer to the ground but held on to him until he nodded.

"N-next month will be fine, Mrs. Kelly." Mr. Sayer nodded to Jackson and then hurried back toward the sawmill.

Jackson walked back up the stairs. "I'm sorry about that, Eliza. That man just made me so angry, I'm afraid I let my temper get the best of me," he apologized.

She laid a soft hand on his arm. Warmth spread from

her palm into his muscles. "Thank you." Eliza looked up at him with brown eyes that reminded him of molten chocolate. He noticed the dark circles under them before she turned away and opened the front door. "Come on inside. Would you like to stay for breakfast? I'm afraid Peter and I are getting a slow start this morning."

"I'd love some breakfast and I really think you and I need to discuss what happened back there."

She sighed. "I agree."

Peter slid around the corner in his stocking feet. His little body slammed into Jackson's legs. "Mornin', Pa!"

"Whoooa." Jackson steadied the little boy's shoulders. "Are you running in the house?" He held the little boy's shoulders and looked into his eyes.

Peter nodded. "Yes, sir. But Ma never said I couldn't." He raised his chin and looked Jackson square in the face.

Eliza continued into the kitchen. Jackson watched her go and felt a moment of sorrow. She carried so much on her slender shoulders.

He returned his focus to Peter. Jackson leaned forward and whispered, "Fair enough, but if I can talk your ma into marrying me, you'll have to live by my rules and one of them is that we don't run indoors."

A big smile broke out over Peter's face. "You gonna ask Ma to marry you again?" he whispered back in a joyful voice.

"Yep, I sure am. So after breakfast, why don't you head on over to the smithy and start sweeping up?" He released the boy and stood.

Eliza called from the kitchen, "Breakfast is ready."

"I won't let on I know," Peter whispered. He squared

his little shoulders and walked to the kitchen with a bigger-than-life smile planted on his face.

Jackson followed. Peter's smile alone would give him away but he didn't care. The moment he'd called Eliza his fiancée, it had felt right. He didn't know what he was going to do in a year when he'd be leaving town.

But he did know God would have to intervene for him to stay in this small community of gossips.

Chapter Thirteen

Jackson took a deep breath as the front door slammed, announcing Peter's departure for the smithy. He turned his attention to Eliza. She stood at the washbasin, scrubbing their plates. "Eliza, can I talk to you for just a few moments?"

He'd noticed that over breakfast she'd yawned and been fairly silent throughout the meal.

She twisted the water out of her washcloth and laid it on the edge of the dishpan. Eliza turned and looked at him. She kept her hands folded and hanging before her apron. "I know what you are going to say, Jackson, and you are right. We do need to get married."

Jackson didn't know what to make of this statement. He'd thought he would have to convince her that it was a necessity for them to marry. He wanted to ask her a million questions about what had brought her to the same conclusion, but Eliza held her hand up to stop him from speaking.

"Thanks to Mr. Sayer, I now have a good idea of what the men in this town think of me. It's not safe or respectable and it's no wonder the women have been gossiping about me. But if I marry you, Jackson Hart, it has to be a marriage of convenience. I can't be the kind of wife that will keep you warm at night. But I will make sure that no one else knows what our marriage is really like. You will be treated as a true husband, just not in there." Her brown eyes looked down the hall and she pointed a shaking finger in her bedroom's direction.

He opened his mouth to speak, but she silenced him once again with her quick tongue. "You can move in here as soon as we stand before Reverend Griffin and say our vows. But even Peter can't know it's not a real marriage. He's just a little boy and he might give us away. Then I'd be back in that awkward position I found myself in this morning."

A marriage of convenience to a mail-order bride. Jackson had never thought he'd be getting married at all. This woman was a smorgasbord of emotions. One moment she was confident and sure about what she was saying and the next she was shaking like a leaf on a cool autumn morning.

She walked over to the table and sunk into one of the chairs. "I'm sorry. I know this isn't fair to you, but I don't know what else to do." A catch in her voice alerted him that she was close to tears.

Jackson reached out and took one of her hands in his. "Now see here, Eliza Kelly. I'm the one who suggested marriage. Don't you be feeling bad for me. We'll make this work, you'll see."

Tear-filled eyes stared back at him. She cleared her throat before asking, "Are you sure? I mean, if you have changed your mind, I'll understand."

Jackson dropped down on one knee. He gently reached up and brushed the hair from over her eyes.

THOMPSON-NICOLA REGIONAL DISTRICT LIBRARY SYSTEM

Eyes that shone with unshed tears pulled at his soul like no other woman's ever had. In a soft, husky voice he asked, "Eliza Kelly, will you marry me?"

Eliza felt a tear slip down her cheek. She should feel happy. Most women did when a man asked them to marry them, especially a handsome man with big strong shoulders and beautiful blue eyes. Any woman would be thrilled to hear those words cross his lips. But she wasn't. He didn't love her and she didn't love him.

"I will." The words came from her mouth but not her heart.

He leaned forward and gave her a light kiss on the lips. It was a simple touch, but something in her responded. Jackson leaned his forehead against hers. "Thank you."

The sweet scent of coffee and his sincerity washed over her. Eliza hugged him and giggled. "I should be thanking you."

Jackson pulled back just a bit. She saw the teasing in his eyes when he said, "Yes, you should, but I'll settle for a simple wedding. If you can arrange that, it will be enough for me."

"Very simple," Eliza agreed, looking into his blue eyes and wondering if she might lose her heart to this caring man after all. She found the cleft in his chin adorable and thought about reaching out to touch it.

He stood. "Good. Then I better get to the smithy and tell Peter we are getting married." Jackson's boots made a clopping noise as he walked across the hardwood floors.

Eliza missed him immediately. She got up to finish the dishes. A knock on the front door had her changing directions. As she passed the grandfather clock in the hallway she glanced at the time. A little after seven. Maybe this was her first customer of the day.

When she got to the door, Eliza's breath caught in her throat. A man's shadow danced upon the floor of the living room. *Don't be a ninny,* she scolded herself as she reached for the handle. Mr. Sayer wouldn't dare show his face again so soon after Jackson's warning. She opened the door.

"Good morning, Mrs. Kelly." Josiah Miller stood in front of her with a smile on his face. "Ma asked me to come over and see if you got her note yesterday."

Her note? Eliza stared at him for several long moments. For the life of her Eliza didn't remember receiving a note from Mary Miller.

"She said she gave it to Miss Eve to give to you," he explained.

"Oh, that note. I'd completely forgotten about it, Josiah. Tell your mother I'm sorry. Do I need to read it now and give you an answer?"

The boy shrugged and scraped the toe of his boot across the wooden planks. "I don't rightly know, but Ma probably wouldn't have sent me if she didn't want an answer right away." He continued to stare at the porch floor.

"You're right. Let me go get it and I'll see what it says. Would you like to come inside?" She held the door open for him.

"No, thanks. I'll just soak up some of this sunshine while I have the chance." Dimples dotted his cheeks as he grinned at her.

Eliza turned to leave and said, "I'll be right back." She hurried through the house to her bedroom. Josiah worked at the store with his parents. He didn't get out as much as he liked. Eliza decided to take her time and let him enjoy his time outdoors.

Her handbag hung on the oak armoire door. She pulled it down and dug around for the piece of paper. It rested in the bottom. She unfolded it and read the contents.

Dear Eliza, Carl and I are making a quick trip to Durango in a few days. Can we pick up any supplies for you?

A smile touched her lips. Most of the town may be against her but it was nice to know she still had a few good friends she could count on. Eliza found a pencil in Mrs. Tucker's bureau.

For a moment she allowed her mind to dream of the perfect wedding dress. Should she order the materials? She'd want lace, silk, thread and buttons. Maybe even a few pearls would be nice. Yes, nice but expensive. Eliza sighed. No, she'd not have an elaborate dress. She hadn't needed one when she'd married Charlie and she didn't need one now.

Eliza quickly made a list of what she wanted for a simple silk gown, not including the pearls, and added more threads and notations for sewing other things. Peter needed a few new things, as well, so she jotted those down.

Checking twice to make sure the list was complete, Eliza hurried back to Josiah. "Thank you for coming, Josiah, and tell your mother thank you for me, as well."

The boy nodded and took the steps three at a time. He jogged across the lawn and down the street. Eliza leaned against the porch post. She'd need to make another trip to the bank and take out some money to pay the Millers and Mr. Sayer.

Eliza frowned at the thought of Mr. Sayer. She didn't want to owe the man one single coin. The idea that she'd have to go to the mill to give him the money sent a shiver down her spine. Maybe she'd ask Jackson to take care of the actual handing over of payment.

She allowed a small smile to touch her lips. He'd sent Mr. Sayer flying from the porch with one good toss. It seemed wrong to enjoy the man's discomfort, but Mr. Sayer had gotten what was coming to him. Eliza realized that as long as she was married to Jackson Hart, no man would ever be able to hurt her again.

Jackson picked up the horse's leg and began the process of pulling the old nails from her shoe. He could hear Peter whistling some merry tone as the boy cleaned. Of all the people in Cottonwood Springs who'd been told of his upcoming marriage to Eliza, Peter had been the happiest.

He wiped sweat from his forehead and lowered the horse's foot back to the ground. A short man with thinning brown hair entered the smithy.

"Good morning. I see Dan and his wife got away all right." He extended his hand. "I'm Hugh Griffin, the circuit preacher for these parts."

Jackson wiped his palms off and shook the man's hand. "Jackson Hart. What can I do for you, Preacher?"

"Do you think you have time to fix a broken wagon wheel?"

Jackson looked at the horse. "Give me about forty-five minutes and I can start work on it."

The reverend grinned. "Good, don't need it until tomorrow afternoon, so that will be fine."

Jackson went back to the mare and scooped up her hoof. He was aware that the preacher had followed him and wondered if he should mention that he and Eliza were getting married. Or was that something the bride did?

"What do you think of Cottonwood Springs?" the reverend asked.

What did he think of the town? Not much since so far it hadn't been very welcoming and he didn't like the way the folks treated one of their own. 'Course, he did like the marshal, the Millers and Eliza Kelly. His gaze moved to Peter who was busy hauling in fresh coal. He'd also gained a son. "It's has its good points and its bad," he finally answered.

The reverend nodded. "That's true of all towns." He paused and then asked. "Will I be seeing you in church come Sunday?"

"I reckon so."

Hugh Griffin laughed. "You are a man of few words."

Jackson smiled up at him. "That I am."

"Is the boys yours?"

Once more Jackson found himself looking at Peter. "He is now."

"I gather there is a story in that answer." The preacher pulled up a wooden crate and sat down.

Jackson continued shoeing the horse. "He's an orphan, more or less."

Hugh rubbed his chin. "More or less, huh?"

"Yep. His pa dropped him off outside of town and said to go find a new life." He glanced back to see the preacher's reaction.

Sadness filled Hugh Griffin's eyes. "I see. And he found you?"

"He found Dan Tucker." Finished with the front foot, Jackson moved on to the next shoe.

"And Dan found you?"

Around a mouth full of nails, Jackson agreed. "Yep, me and Eliza Kelly."

"Ah, so Mrs. Kelly is involved in this story somehow, is she?"

Inwardly, Jackson groaned. Had the preacher heard the gossip already? And if not, how much should he tell?

Chapter Fourteen

Eliza's back hurt. She looked up at the grandfather clock and sighed. Eve would be arriving any moment. Her gaze moved to the dress that was almost finished. Why hadn't she told her to wait until afternoon tea, instead of agreeing to see her this morning?

The door jingled as Eve came through it.

"Oh, I like the new bell and the open sign." Eve balanced a covered plate in one hand and her handbag in the other. "I brought the shortbread cookies as promised. Did you make the tea?"

Eliza stood and pushed on her lower back. "I always have tea going, you know that." Eliza turned the open sign over to Closed and then followed Eve to the kitchen.

"No, I didn't know that." Eve set the cookies on the table. "There are a lot of things I don't know about you and you about me. That's one of the reasons I stopped by this morning."

Eliza brought the teapot and two teacups with matching saucers to the table. "So is that what this tea party is about?" She smiled at her twin to soften the words.

"In a way." Eve uncovered the cookies and slowly sat down. "I want to know everything that happened after you and Charles left Raleigh."

Eliza laughed. "We only have an hour, Eve, and then I have to reopen the shop." She poured hot tea into their cups and then moved to get the sugar and cream.

"I gather from the talk about town that you are a widow. I wasn't expecting that," Eve said softly.

She placed the bowl and pitcher on the table. "Yes, Charlie was in an avalanche that took his life."

"Why didn't you come home?" Eve asked around a mouthful of cookie.

"How can you ask such a question? Mother and Father made it very clear that I was no longer welcome there. You know that."

Eliza wanted to erase the sound of hurt from her voice.

Eve studied the paisley print on the table cloth. "Mother never wanted you to leave."

"No? Then why didn't she stop Father from casting me out? Or come to my wedding? Or…" There were so many more things she could add but didn't. The pain of losing her family still stabbed deeply into her heart.

"I think Mother always feared Father. She didn't want to end up on the streets like you, and many times she told me she stayed because of me. I'm so sorry, Eliza. I wish I could go back in time and change my part in what happened that night." Eve took a deep breath and gulped at her hot tea.

So her sister *had* done something to cause her father's wrath. Eliza wanted to be angry, but thankfully she'd turned this all over to the Lord the night before and didn't hold any ill feelings toward her sister now.

"It's over and done with, Eve. How are Mother and Father?"

Eve wiped her eyes. "They were good the last time I saw them."

Eliza sipped her tea. "And when was that?"

"Almost a year ago. Shortly after I married Lucas Masters." Eve studied the bottom of her cup.

Who was Lucas Masters? Eliza tried to envision all the people they'd known in Raleigh but couldn't remember him. "I take it Lucas wasn't a local boy?" she asked.

"No, he arrived with a traveling show. Father forbade me to go see it, but you know me. I went, anyway. They were in town for several weeks and I fell in love with Lucas. I knew Father wouldn't allow me to marry him, so we secretly got married. After the deed, I told Father and Mother what I'd done." A sob escaped her lips.

Eliza wondered what kind of traveling show, but it didn't seem important at the moment. She gave Eve a few minutes and then asked, "Then what happened?"

"Well, after what happened to you, Mother refused to let Father cast us out. We moved in with them, but Lucas wasn't happy. So we began traveling." Red filled Eve's cheeks at the memories.

Eliza held her tongue. She wanted to ask more questions but felt this was something Eve had to work out, in her own time.

Her sister blew her nose and then continued. "I hated it but still held on to the belief that I loved Lucas. I knew he drank too much, that he visited the brothels in every town we were in, but it wasn't until I found out he was already married that I…" She covered her face and bawled.

The past few years hadn't been kind to her sister. All

this time, Eliza had thought Eve was the perfect daughter, when all along she'd been traveling the country with a cheating husband. Her heart hurt for her sister and she stood to hug her. "What did you do, Eve?"

Eve hiccupped and sobbed. "I killed him."

Eliza gasped and pulled away enough to look into her sister's red face. "How? Are you sure? Why?" The questions poured from her mouth almost as fast as she thought them. She'd believed that her sister wanted something, but now she knew Eve was simply scared and running.

"I'm sure. There was a lot of blood." Eve's face turned pale at the memory. "He'd been drinking again and told me he was already married and that he was going back to his other wife. I picked up a bottle and smashed him over the head with it. I was just so angry, but I didn't mean to kill him, Eliza. You have to believe me." Her voice had gone up in volume with each word. "I left as fast as I could. What am I going to do now, Eliza? I'm a murderess, wanted by the law!"

Eliza sunk back into her chair. "I don't know, Eve." Her thoughts went to Seth. Was there a wanted poster with her sister's face on it somewhere? "Where did this happen?" She thrust a teacup into Eve's hand. "Here, drink this."

Eve gulped at the remainder of her tea. "Oklahoma territory."

"When?"

"About six months ago. I've been trying to find you."

Eliza looked Eve over. Her sister wore very nice clothes, her hair had an expensive comb in it and the shoes on her feet were made from the finest materials.

How could she afford such luxuries if she wasn't still living with their parents?

"You don't believe me?" Eve's brown eyes grew round.

Eliza picked up her cup and studied Eve over the rim. "I'm trying to, Eve. I thought you grabbed what you could and ran?"

Eve nodded. "I did."

"Then how can you afford such nice things?" She sipped her tea.

Eve sighed. "I never said Lucas was poor. He had lots of money and jewels. He kept a chest of the stuff by the door of the wagon. On my way out the door I took it all." She wiped the tears from her face. "I'm a lot of things, Eliza, but I'm not a liar."

Eliza had to admit her sister had never lied when they were kids. She manipulated the facts to her benefit, but as long as she could remember Eve had never openly lied to her. "How much money?"

"Enough to buy us anything we want."

"Us?" How had she gotten lumped into this mess?

Eve refilled her cup. "Yes, us. I know you aren't doing so well in this town, and with the money I have we can both go anywhere and start over. We can help each other, change our names and make new lives for ourselves. What do you say, Eliza?"

Jackson finished the wheel and wiped the sweat from his brow. "How would you like to go to the diner for lunch?" he called across to Peter.

"Boy, would I! I'm starved." Peter jumped down from the stool he'd been sitting on.

"You about got that arithmetic finished?" Jackson asked as he replaced his tools.

Peter curled his lip. "I don't like doing figures."

Jackson laughed. "So the answer is no."

The little boy hung his head. "No."

"Well, after lunch you'll have to get back on it." Jackson took his apron off and hung it by the door. "Let's go."

Peter skipped ahead of him. "We gonna stop and get Ma?"

"I don't think so. Didn't you mention her sister was going to be there?" Jackson answered.

Peter stopped and looked up at him. "Yes, but how's she gonna know where I am? She might get worried."

Jackson realized that the boy was right. And once they were married, he'd have to check in with her all the time. And he'd have to be around her sister. "I reckon you're right. We'll stop and you can invite her."

A smile brightened Peter's young face. "Good."

He enjoyed watching the boy speed ahead. Peter had more energy than three grown men combined. *If only we could bottle that.* Jackson's thoughts echoed his grandmother's words from the past. The door to the house slammed, and Jackson shook his head as he walked up the steps.

He opened the door and followed Peter inside. Eliza sat at the sewing machine and Eve stood by the window. Eve looked unhappy and Eliza's face was masked in determination. What had he and the boy walked into?

"No Peter, but thank you for inviting me. Eve and I are going to have lunch here and work." Eliza hugged the little boy to her and looked at Eve.

The little boy titled his head. “You aren’t really going to leave, are you, Ma?”

The question shocked Jackson down to his boots. What had the boy overheard? Was Eliza planning on leaving? When was she going to tell him? He had to stop the questions from roaring in his ears and listen to her reply.

“No, sweetheart. Aunt Eve and I were just talking. I’m not moving. I wouldn’t leave you.” She rubbed his back and shook her head at Jackson.

He was surprised at the amount of relief he felt. When had Eliza’s comings and goings started to concern him? Jackson called to Peter, “Come on, Peter. Let’s go grab lunch.”

“I want to stay with Ma.” Peter tried to blend his small body into hers.

Jackson watched as she gently pulled him away. “Why don’t you go have lunch with Jackson? And then instead of working at the smithy this afternoon, maybe you can come here and do your schoolwork.” She wiped tears from the little boy’s face. “I promise. I’m not going anywhere.”

Peter looked at Jackson. “Can I do that?” His face revealed all the fears of losing a parent that a child feels.

“Sure you can.” Jackson wondered if Peter would react that way when he moved to Silverton.

Peter wrapped his small arms around Eliza once more and then returned to Jackson. His small hand clutched Jackson’s. “I’m ready.”

As they walked to the diner, Jackson began to feel trapped. In the past week, he’d adopted a little boy and asked a woman to marry him. He’d managed to acquire in one week what most men spent their lives trying to create.

Like it or not, Jackson was part of a family. The thought came unbidden. *Unless I get out now.*

Chapter Fifteen

Over the next few days, Eliza noticed Jackson was even more quiet and withdrawn than usual. She and Peter attended Sunday morning services. As they got up to leave she saw Jackson rise from the back pew and slip out the door. So he had attended. Something wasn't right. Come to think of it, things hadn't felt right since the day Peter had overheard Eve pleading with her to leave town.

Her thoughts moved from Jackson to her sister. She so wanted to talk to someone about Eve's situation but who? Rebecca was the marshal's wife so she couldn't tell her best friend that her sister had killed a man. She hadn't told Jackson because he hadn't said more than ten words to her.

Julia Harper stepped in front of her. "Excuse me, Eliza." She hefted two-year-old Holly up higher on her hip.

"Hello, Julia. How are you doing?" Eliza felt that if Julia wasn't so busy with her family, they might have become good friends. But her husband, Richard, made sure the young mother was always busy. It was times like these that Eliza realized how much she missed Hannah.

"I'm doing well. I hope you don't find this odd but George was hoping Peter could come to our house this afternoon to play. There are so few boys that are five or six years old." She held on to six-year-old George's hand.

George seemed to be studying Peter with interest.

Peter squeezed her hand. "Please, Ma. I'd like to go play."

Eliza looked into Peter's sweet face. She'd forgotten that little boys needed playtime, too. He had a stuffed puppy that she'd made him, and that he slept with, but other than that, the boy had no toys. She turned her attention back to Julia. "If you are sure he will be no bother."

"Not at all." Julia looked down at Peter with warmth. "We'd love to have him for lunch and then maybe a couple of hours of play. Would it be too much trouble to ask you to pick him up?"

The strong scent of roses passed by them. Eliza looked up in time to see Mrs. Walker leaning toward them. She ignored the woman. "Not at all. I will use this time to plan my wedding."

"You are getting married?" Julia asked with a wide, knowing grin on her face.

Eliza nodded. She felt heat fill her cheeks as Julia made a point of shifting her gaze to Mrs. Walker.

Sincerity filled her voice as she exclaimed, "How wonderful! Congratulations, Eliza." Julia gave her a one-armed hug. "Anytime you want Peter to come play with George, just let me know. I'm so happy for you."

Julia linked her arm in Eliza's and pulled her away

from Mrs. Walker's hearing. "I really am happy for you," she whispered. "Am I to assume you are marrying our new blacksmith?"

"Yes, he asked me a few days ago."

They stepped out into the sunshine. Mr. Harper stood by their wagon. He waved to Julia. "I better go. Thanks for letting Peter come. I'm sure he and George will have a fun time."

"Thank you for inviting him." Eliza knelt down in front of Peter. "You be a good boy for Mr. and Mrs. Harper. I'll come get you in a few hours."

"I will, Ma."

George grabbed Peter's hand and the two boys took off running down the slight hill toward the Harpers' wagon. Peter's laughter floated back to her. Julia followed the boys. Anna Harper and her best friend, Grace Miller, hurried to join the Harper family.

Eliza stood back and watched as they all climbed aboard the wagon. The children were laughing and shoving for what they considered the best spot. Julia and Richard exchanged warm expressions.

What would it feel like to be a part of a real family? She wasn't fooling herself into believing that Jackson was marrying her out of love. No, he was doing it to protect her reputation, and she felt sure he was doing it for Peter also.

As if he sensed her thinking about him, Peter turned around and waved. She waved back. In truth, Peter was part of the reason why she planned to marry Jackson. The boy needed a home. A real home. And, without Jackson's help, neither she nor Peter would have a real home.

"Since the boy isn't going to be with us this afternoon, how would you like to go on a little outing with me?"

Eliza turned around to see Jackson leaning against a big cottonwood tree. His ankles were crossed and he held a basket in his large hand. He grinned at her and tilted his head. It was a look that she couldn't resist. "I'd like that."

"Good, I parked the wagon over there." He pointed toward a buckboard. It looked like the same one they'd arrived in Cottonwood Springs in a week ago today.

How had he known they wouldn't have Peter this afternoon? Normally on Sunday afternoons she visited with Rebecca while the children were napping. This would be the third Sunday in a row that she'd missed spending the afternoon with her friend.

Eliza looked about for Rebecca and her family. She saw Seth escorting them home. Rebecca turned and waved to her. A smile graced her pretty face. "I need to tell Rebecca I won't be coming by for lunch."

Jackson shook his head. "She knows."

She turned her attention to him. "You told her?" A light pink filled his neck and worked its way into his tanned cheeks.

"Yep." He started walking to their wagon.

Eliza followed. Had Rebecca helped him plan this outing? She watched as he put the basket in the bed behind the seat and then turned to face her. Eliza allowed him to help her up.

Once seated, she asked the burning question that was troubling her. "Did Rebecca help you plan this afternoon?"

He nodded, picked up the reins and turned the horses around.

Eliza looked up into the clear sky. "Did she have something to do with Julia Harper taking Peter for the afternoon, too?"

Jackson sighed. "I asked her to help me. We have things to talk about and I didn't think you'd want the boy to hear."

Mixed emotions attacked Eliza at once. She wanted to be happy to be alone with Jackson. After all, they were going to get married. But she also felt angry at her friend for keeping her in the dark about their plans. Hannah had kept the secret of Miles Thatcher from her and look where that had gotten her.

Jackson didn't have a clue what Eliza was thinking. For the first time since he'd met her, she seemed content to keep her thoughts to herself. He hoped she liked the surprises he had in store for her today.

The horses carried them to the spot he'd found a few days before. It opened up into a small meadow beside a sloping hill. Trees and scrubs were scattered about, but it was the green against the hillside that he wanted to spread their blanket beside. His heart beat a little faster at the thought of what she was going to see. He prayed she enjoyed it as much as he'd thought she would; now Jackson was beginning to have doubts. The frown on her face didn't offer much encouragement.

"Have you ever been here?" he asked to break the silence.

Eliza shook her head. "Honestly, I don't get out of town much." She looked about the area and smiled. It seemed she'd made the decision to be happy again. "Is this where we are stopping?"

"We're close. I want to get a little closer to the hill."

He directed the horses forward and searched the slope of the hillside for just the right location. When he saw it, Jackson pulled the horses to a stop and jumped down.

After helping Eliza down, he pulled the basket from the wagon. "I thought this would be a nice spot," he needlessly said as she looked about.

Little brown birds chirped to one another and a light breeze lifted the hair on her forehead. She wore a soft blue dress with tiny yellow flowers. He grinned as she touched the hat upon her head. It was straw with a blue velvet lining and small blue flowers covered its top. Rebecca had told him how Eliza had worked all night to have it ready for attending Sunday services.

"It's beautiful, Jackson."

He returned to the wagon and pulled a small quilt from under the seat. "Can I ask you a question?" Jackson returned to where she stood and spread out the blanket.

"I suppose." She grabbed one corner and helped him smooth it over the grass.

"I noticed you enjoy wearing hats. Do you make them or buy them?" Jackson knew she had made the one she wore now, but his thoughts went to the bird hat she'd been wearing in Durango and he couldn't help but wonder if she'd made it, as well.

"Oh, that's an easy enough question. I make most of them. But every so often I'll go into Sally's in Durango and buy one. Why do you ask?" She knelt on the cover and looked at the basket.

Jackson opened the basket and grinned. "I've never known a woman who wore a hat everywhere she went. You must really enjoy wearing them."

"I do. I think they are fun."

He felt a smile pull at his lips. Her brown eyes drew him in and made him think of coffee. "I have a couple of surprises for you."

"You do? I love surprises." Her eyes took on a sparkle of excitement.

"It's small but here is the first surprise." Jackson looked down into the basket and pulled out a teapot wrapped in a red-and-white-checkered cozy.

Eliza gasped. "You brought tea. Oh, Jackson, how sweet." She took the pot from him and began removing the cozy.

He'd felt silly packing the teapot, but he'd wanted her to feel special. Now he was glad he'd done so. "Here is a cup." He handed her a white teacup that matched the pot.

"You are so sweet to remember I enjoy tea with my meals." She poured a cup of the tea and inhaled its fragrance. "Thank you."

Jackson nodded, then began to unpack the sugar, cream, a dish of finger sandwiches and another of sugar cookies. He added two plates and a mason jar of black coffee for himself. "I'm glad you like it."

Her finger traced the soft blue rose pattern along the side of the pot. "This is very pretty."

He grinned at her. "When I saw it in Mrs. Miller's store, I thought you would like it."

"You bought it for me?" Awe filled her voice.

Jackson grinned. "Call it a prewedding present."

"Oh, thank you, Jackson. I love it. Mine burned up in the house. I'll put Sally's away when we get home." Eliza took over; she placed food on each plate and added sugar and cream to her tea. Once more words poured from her lips much like the tea she served from the pot.

"I'm glad you decided to do this. I need to talk to someone about my sister but can't talk to Rebecca because she's married to Seth. Since he's a lawman, I can't tell her that Eve thinks she killed her husband back in the Oklahoma territory. She also took all his money and valuables when she ran. Eve is rich now. But the fact that the law might think she killed him for the money kind of has her in a pickle. She didn't, of course. She hit him because he was drunk and had confessed he was already married."

He almost choked on the sugar cookie he'd just inserted into his mouth. "I see." Was all he could think of to say.

"I know. This is bad, but what can I do? I can't turn my sister over to the law and I can't run away with her, either. She doesn't know what to do and neither do I. What do you think she should do?" Eliza finally looked at him. Concern laced her pretty features.

Jackson cleared his throat. He stalled for time by saying, "You have had a lot dumped on you this week, haven't you?"

The hat bobbed as she nodded. "I'm scared for her."

He saw the fear in her eyes and knew she was stating the truth, but still, she had to know that they had to tell Seth. Would she hate him when he suggested it? Was fear a big enough motivator to send her into hiding with Eve?

Jackson swallowed hard. This was not turning into the outing he'd planned.

Chapter Sixteen

The surprised look on his face was just what she'd feared. What did he think? Why wasn't he saying something? Anything? She felt hot and decided to remove her hat. Not because it would help, but because it would give her hands something to do.

She placed the hat on the quilt and waited and he still didn't say anything. Eliza started to squirm. It had been a bad idea telling him.

He swallowed the cookie and then cleared his throat. "You aren't going to like what I'm about to say, Eliza. But, I think it's the best thing to do." Jackson stared at her. His jaw worked but no more words came forth.

Eliza felt her throat close but she managed to get out the one word that wanted to be screamed. "What?"

"We have to tell Seth Billings. It's the only answer." He said the words so fast she thought he'd bite his tongue.

"We?" He'd said *we.* Was he going to go with her?

Jackson reached out and took her hand. "Yes, *we.* I'll go with you and maybe I can talk him into not arresting Eve for murder."

"You think he'll listen to you?" Hope filled her at the thought that maybe her sister could be saved from a life in jail or worse, the gallows.

Jackson pulled his hand away from hers. "From what I've learned about Seth, he's a fair man. I don't think he'd condemn her immediately." He unscrewed the top to his mason jar and took a long drink.

Eliza watched his Adam's apple bob with each gulp. Jackson Hart was willing to stand up for her family. She felt warm and fuzzy inside thinking about it. Eliza picked up a finger sandwich and took a small bite. Chicken salad and cheese coated her taste buds.

"I'll suggest that he do some investigating first." He picked up one of the sandwiches and popped it into his mouth.

She grinned as he reached for another. Jackson Hart could take care of himself and those he cared about. She liked that in a man. "Thank you, Jackson. I feel better about Eve's situation now. I'm still scared as to what can happen to her, but knowing you are here to help us both, well, it's just comforting."

"I'm happy I could help." Jackson looked at the hill behind her.

She stared into her teacup. Once more Jackson Hart was stepping in and saving the day. Eliza hoped she wasn't coming to depend on him too much. After all, he hadn't said he'd changed his mind about going to Silverton, so she couldn't put her full trust in him.

Eliza decided to enjoy the day and worry about him leaving when the time came. She finished her sandwich and reached for a sugar cookie. The birds sang around them and the sound of a bee buzzing close by helped her to relax and enjoy a bit of quiet with him. She nibbled on the cookie and leaned back on her elbows.

His blue gaze focused on her once more. "Have you given any more thought about the wedding?"

How could she not have thought more about the wedding? "Yes, Mr. and Mrs. Miller are bringing me material for my dress. I'm hoping to have it made up by the end of next week. That's if I don't get a big order from someone else." She closed her eyes, imagining the dress.

He broke into her daydream. "So we can get married a week from today?"

"Oh!" Eliza sat straight up. "I wasn't insinuating I wanted to get married by next weekend. I was just saying I might be able to get the dress finished by then." A lock of brown hair fell into her eyes and she pushed it back.

Jackson grinned. For the first time she noticed thin white lines within the sea of deep blue in his eyes. "We need to get married as soon as possible, Eliza."

She sighed. Eliza knew what he said was true. The ladies had been coming by and hinting they weren't buying a single dress from her until she was married proper. To her way of thinking they were just being silly. She'd made dresses for all of them in the past and hadn't been married then. "I know."

He reassured her. "I'll not ask you for more in the marriage of convenience than we've already agreed upon."

"I know, and I appreciate that. It just doesn't seem fair that a group of women can control our lives like this." She picked up her hat and began pinning it back into place. Eliza glanced in his direction.

For a brief moment, an alarmed look crossed his features. "It's not your fault."

"No, and it's not yours, either." She began wrapping the teapot back up in the cozy. "Jackson, I've been thinking. If we do get married, I don't want an annulment. If you do, maybe we should just forget the whole thing." Eliza studied the cozy, not wanting to meet his gaze.

"Good, I don't want an annulment, either. I only said that because I thought you might."

Her gaze came up and collided with his. She saw warmth in the depths of his eyes. Eliza's breath caught in her throat. "I still can't be a true wife, Jackson. Not in the biblical sense." She dropped her gaze once more and pulled at a loose string.

"My original offer still stands. I want to marry you and if in time we should fall in love, then we'll discuss the other further. Is that all right?" he asked.

Eliza felt her cheeks burst into flames at the topic of their discussion. She knew they would never truly be man and wife because she wouldn't allow it. Jackson wanted children and she couldn't give them to him. But maybe they could adopt more and he'd never have to know that she wasn't a real woman. Bitterness laced her throat and she looked away from him.

"What will your wedding dress look like?" Jackson asked quickly.

He cared what her dress looked like? She noticed he looked behind her again at the wall and then up at the sun. Eliza looked at the wall behind her. She couldn't see anything out of the ordinary. She answered, "Oh, I'm thinking I want to keep it simple. I asked Mrs. Miller to bring back a light lavender silk material and

I think I might put some tiny beads about the neck and sleeves. Oh, the sleeves will be short cap sleeves. Like I said, nothing too fancy."

Jackson nodded. "Sounds right nice."

"You really think so?"

Again he nodded. She watched as he stretched out on the blanket and folded his hands behind his head. His blue shirt stretched across his chest. She wondered what he'd wear to their wedding.

"I think we should announce that the wedding is next Saturday. Do you think your dress will be ready by then?"

Eliza swallowed. Did she want to get married in less than a week? She did and she didn't. "It will depend on if the Millers come home from Durango today or tomorrow."

He turned to look at her. "One day makes a difference?"

"Dresses don't sew themselves, Jackson. I'll need time to sew it up and then to actually plan the wedding." She smiled at him to take the sting out of her words.

Jackson frowned. "What's to plan?"

She laughed. "People will expect us to have a reception. So I'll need to have a cake made, punch made, entertainment arranged and a place to do all this needs to be found. Putting together a wedding is no simple thing to do."

He grunted. "I thought we'd stand before Reverend Griffin, say I do and go home."

"We can do that, too."

Disappointment must have clung to her words because he sat up and took her hands in his. "If you want a big wedding, we'll have us a big wedding."

"I don't want a big wedding, but I know that there are people in our community who will expect certain things." She sighed. "If it were up to me we'd have a simple wedding, with Peter, Rebecca and Seth in attendance, Mr. and Mrs. Miller and maybe the Harpers."

"Then that's what we'll do. Who says we have to invite the whole town?" He squeezed her hands and then pulled her up.

Eliza looked deeply into his eyes. "What about the gossips?"

"Oh, we'll make sure they know we are getting married and Rebecca and the other two ladies can fill them in on the details." He leaned his forehead against hers.

"All right." She felt as if the air had been sucked out of the world. All she could think about was the big man who held her hands so tight and looked deeply into her eyes.

He raised his head. "Here comes surprise number two." Jackson turned her to look toward the hill.

At that moment, bright rays of color flooded the area. Eliza gasped as rainbows danced about them. She could see that the color came from small holes and cracks in the hillside.

"Oh, Jackson, it's beautiful!" She clasped her hands in front of her and stared in wonder at God's creation.

Jackson watched the surprise and awe that crossed her face. She was beautiful standing in the midst of the rainbows. Her brown eyes danced with joy and excitement just as he'd hoped they would.

"How did you know?" she asked, twirling around in a circle, trying to see all the colors at once.

He clasped his hands behind his back and rocked on

his booted heels. "I stumbled across it the other day. My horse spooked at a rattler and brought me this way. Just when I got the horse stopped, the sun hit the side of the hill just right and I was bathed in the rainbows like we are now."

Eliza ran her hands through the colors. "How is this possible?"

"That mound isn't a hill at all, but a cave of clear stones that reflects the light." Jackson stared at her glowing face. He wanted to create a mental picture of her and the pleasure she was expressing because of his surprise.

Her gaze ran over the hillside. "How can we get in?" Excitement filled her voice.

Jackson laughed. "You can't."

"But I want to see the stones." Eliza turned pleading eyes to him.

He moved to her side and pointed up toward the top. "Eliza, the opening is way up there and it's not safe."

The rainbows were fading as the sun continued on its course. "I'll be careful," she promised. Her eyes begged him to show her the opening and the stones.

"I'm sorry, but I can't risk you getting hurt."

She nodded. "I understand. Thank you for sharing this spot with me. Maybe we can come again. I'd love to see the rainbows again and again."

This was the moment he was waiting for. "What if I told you that you can see the rainbows every day?"

Eliza smiled at him. "I can't come out here every day, Jackson."

He pulled a chain with a large clear stone from his pocket. Jackson cupped the rock within his hand, not quite ready to reveal it to her. "No. But I could give you one of the stones to hang in the window and it will make rainbows for you."

Her squeal pierced the afternoon air. A bird squawked and flew away. "Really?"

Jackson held the chain out to her. He watched as her eyes grew round and she took the chain. Then he slowly opened his hand to reveal the large clear rock.

She gasped and slowly pulled the chain and stone from his hand. He watched as she examined it. No words came from her lips, but her expressive eyes had much to say.

He'd worked many hours on encasing the stone in thin metal wire. It had taken him a long time to craft the chain that held it but the wonder and pleasure in her eyes made it all worthwhile.

"Oh, thank you, Jackson. I shall cherish this always." She held the stone up to the light and rainbows exploded around them.

The joy on her face filled his heart. Jackson prayed she'd get her dress made by next Saturday. He couldn't wait to present her with the wedding ring, made from a smaller version of the stone, and band he'd been working on for the past few days.

Jackson marveled at his own emotions. Bringing her joy felt right.

Chapter Seventeen

Eliza twirled in front of the mirror. The lavender silk of her wedding gown swished about her feet. Tiny cream-colored roses decorated the neck and short sleeves. The V waist made her look tiny. She smiled in spite of herself.

"It's beautiful," Eve gasped from behind her.

"Do you really think so?" Eliza asked as the sensation of warmth filled her cheeks.

Eve nodded. "You are beautiful. Jackson Hart is going to be so proud when you walk down the aisle."

Would he? Since they'd returned from their outing on Sunday, he'd been busy. Always dashing off after bringing Peter home. Eliza fretted that he might regret asking her to marry him.

Eliza realized she missed his easy grin and warm voice. He'd seemed so sure the day they'd gone on the picnic and he'd given her the clear stone. Her gaze moved to the rainbows that reflected throughout her bedroom. She'd hung the stone in the window and awoke each morning with fresh rainbows dancing on the walls and ceiling.

Peter had begged her to let him take it down and play with it but she'd told him no. It was a special gift from Jackson, and she didn't want it accidently broken. Since then, Peter had asked her again and again if they could go find him one.

"Are you going to wear a veil or a hat?" Eve asked, pulling her from her musings.

"Both. A hat with an iridescent veil." She moved to the clothes chest and pulled it out of the hatbox. Eliza held it up for Eve to see. "I created it myself. I made the flowers from the extra fabric from the dress." She ran her hand over the hat. The flowers were large, single lavender petals adorned with a lacy center to create an anemone-like bloom. Lace hung from the brim, creating a delicate veil that would cover half her face. Eliza handed the hat to Eve.

"Oh, Eliza. It is beautiful, too. I wish God had given me half your talent for sewing." Eve ran her fingers over the soft flowers.

Eliza tried to lighten the mood by laughing. "You can sing. I can't do that," she reminded her sister.

The joy vanished from her face and eyes. "True, but what good has singing done me?" Eve's mouth turned down at the corners. "So far, all it's ever done is get me in trouble." She continued to pout.

She took the hat from Eve. "No, you got yourself into trouble. Not your singing." Eliza returned the hat back to its box. "Besides, when Seth comes back, it may not be all that bad."

Eve flopped down on Eliza's bed. "Oh, it will be bad. He'll come back and hang me." She dramatically flung her arm up over her eyes.

Eliza frowned at her sister. "You don't believe that."

"Yes, I do!" Eve popped up into a sitting position. "He's going to find out that I killed Lucas," she groaned as she lay back down and hid her face under her arm once more.

"You are being overly dramatic." Even as the words passed her lips, Eliza wondered what Seth would find.

Eve stood and walked to the mirror. "I suppose I am." Eve's gaze connected with hers in the glass. "After all, I'm not positive I killed him. But..." Her face went pale. "There was a lot of blood, Eliza."

Eliza saw real worry reflected in Eve's eyes. She walked over and wrapped her arm around her sister's shoulder. Even though Eve had a way of rubbing her the wrong way, Eliza still loved her and wanted the best for Eve. "The marshal is a good man. Give him time to figure out exactly what happened to Lucas. If you did kill him, Seth will give you the chance to defend your actions."

Eve nodded. "I keep thinking I should leave before he comes back."

"What would that prove?" Eliza dropped her arm and moved away. She straightened up the room and spread the wrinkles out of her quilt. "Besides, if you did kill Lucas and then ran, it makes you look as if you can't be trusted. Then instead of thinking it was an accident, Seth and the jury will think you killed him on purpose." She changed out of the wedding dress and hung it on the armoire.

Eve continued to stare into the mirror and play with her curls. "Do you think if Lucas is alive, the marshal will tell him where he can find me? I don't know what I'd do if he shows up here."

Buttoning her day dress, Eliza answered, "I don't think Seth will tell him where you are, but then I don't know what will happen. I do know Seth Billings is a good man and will protect you should Lucas decide to come nosing around." Eliza slipped her feet into a pair of shoes and then repinned her hair. She looked at her wedding dress and sighed. Once again, Eve had taken the fun out of her afternoon.

She walked back into the dress shop portion of the house and sat down at her sewing machine. Eve followed close behind.

"Are you going to sew now?" she asked, scooping up her pocketbook and heading to the door.

Eliza laughed. "I can tell by your quick exit that you know I am."

"The noise of that thing gives me a headache." Eve opened the door. "Oh, don't expect me for dinner tonight. I'm going to have dinner with the Hardings. They are such nice people."

Eliza barely got out the words, "All right," and Eve shut the door. She sighed. Her sister sucked the energy right out of a room.

Thankful for a few moments of peace and quiet, Eliza walked to the kitchen. She put on a pot of tea and sat down at the table. The trees were beginning to bud and she could hear the birds singing outside the window.

So far the weather was staying warm. She prayed her wedding day would arrive bright and sunny. Even though they weren't marrying for love, Eliza wanted to remember it as a happy day.

She poured herself a cup of tea from her new teapot. Jackson had been so thoughtful to have gotten it for her. He really was a good man. Eliza sighed. But was being thoughtful and a good man enough to keep them married for years?

Jackson smiled down at Peter. “What do you think?”

Peter turned the ring around, catching the light from the open doorway. The white stone flashed rainbows all about the smithy. He looked up with a wide grin. “Ma is going to love it. She won’t even let me touch the rock you gave her.” He frowned. “Says it’s too special to be played with.”

Jackson ruffled the boy’s hair and took the ring back. “She’s right. I had a hard time getting them.” He felt a moment of happiness knowing that she valued the stone he’d gotten for her.

The boy tilted his head up and licked his bottom lip. “I sure would like a stone like that. I'm sure George would want one, too.”

“I’m sure he would.” Jackson returned the ring to the small black box he’d acquired from Mrs. Miller’s general store. “But that cavern is a dangerous place. I don’t want you boys going anywhere near it, ya hear?”

Jackson wished he hadn’t told Mr. Miller about the spot in front of Peter. It hadn’t taken the boy long to ferret out exactly where the cavern was located.

“I hear,” Peter grumbled. His shoulders slumped as he returned to his broom. Peter focused on the floor as he swept.

Had he sounded mean when he’d issued the warning? Jackson wasn’t sure. He knew the boy was curious about the cavern and wanted a stone of his own.

He'd only meant to warn the boy to stay away because it was dangerous.

"How about we take a break?" Jackson asked.

Peter looked up at him. "All right." He leaned his broom against the wall and turned to face him.

"I'll wager Mrs. Velarde over at the diner has some fresh cookies and cold milk. Why don't we head over there and see?"

Jackson took off his leather apron and walked to the door. He hung a wooden sign that read Be Back in Fifteen Minutes on the door and waited for Peter to join him.

The little boy walked with his head down, studying the toes of his boots. Jackson didn't know if he should say any more about the cavern or leave it. They continued on in silence. No, he'd leave it. If the boy wanted to say something more, he would.

The apple, apricot and peach trees around Cottonwood Springs were filled with red, pink and white blossoms. Their sweet fragrance mingled with the scent of fresh-cut wood from the sawmill.

Cottonwood Springs had turned into a nice place to live. It seemed that the gossips were happy to hear about the upcoming wedding, and he'd noticed several of the older ladies going into Eliza's sewing shop. He prayed they would give up on spreading rumors about them for a while.

"Pa, do you think I can go play with George on Sunday?" Peter asked as they walked up to the door of the diner.

The bell jingled as they entered. "I'm not sure. We'll have to ask Eliza." He placed his hand on the boy's slim shoulder.

They walked up to the counter, where Mrs. Velarde had several trays of cookies and pastries. Peter climbed up onto one of the tall stools. Jackson decided to stand beside him. He placed a large hand on the boy's back to balance him until he was firmly seated.

"Well, hello, boys. What can I get for you this afternoon?" Mrs. Velarde asked, coming to stand on the opposite side of the counter.

Jackson grinned at her. "Peter here would like a cookie and a tall glass of cold milk." He liked the fact that she turned to Peter to take the little boy's order.

"Good choice, Peter. I have pecan praline, sugar and oatmeal raisin. Which would you like?" She reached under the counter and produced a white milk jug with little pink flowers on the side. Mrs. Velarde poured milk into a glass and set it on the counter for him.

Peter leaned forward and stared at the trays of cookies. "I think I want an oatmeal raisin, please."

She winked at Peter. "Another good choice. I just put those out so they are still warm." Her amber eyes turned on Jackson. "How about you, Mr. Hart?"

"Just a coffee for me." He sat down on a stool beside Peter.

"Coming right up." She pulled two cookies from the farthest tray and set them in front of Peter on a small plate. "That second cookie is on the house." She winked at Peter again.

The bell over the door jingled once more. Mrs. Velarde sighed heavily when she saw her newest customer. Her mouth turned down. Jackson twisted on his stool to see who had caused the woman such unhappiness.

Eve Masters stood in the doorway, blinking. She looked around and then hurried to his side. "Oh, Jackson, I'm so glad you are here. I wanted to talk to you about the wedding. Do you think we can move to a table? I'd like to sit down and have a nice cup of tea." She snapped her fingers at Mrs. Velarde.

The older woman turned to her and glared. "I've asked you not to snap your fingers at me, Mrs. Masters," she reminded her in a stern voice.

Eve ignored her. "We'll be moving to that table." She pointed at the one in the window. "Please bring a pot of tea and more cookies." Eve turned away before Jackson or Mrs. Velarde could respond.

Peter scrambled from his seat. He grabbed his cookies and followed Eve.

Jackson took the coffee mug Mrs. Velarde sat down in front of him and Peter's glass of milk. He looked at the older woman and sighed. "I'm sorry about that."

"It's not your fault. She's been difficult since the day she arrived." She shook her red head and sighed again. "How can two sisters be so different?" Mrs. Velarde turned away, not expecting an answer.

He took the drinks and walked to where Eve and Peter waited. As Jackson slid into his chair, he told her, "That wasn't very nice. Mrs. Velarde isn't your servant."

Eve waved her hand in dismissal. "She's used to it, I'm sure."

Jackson didn't want Peter thinking he could treat people with such ill-mannered behavior. So took a deep breath and continued. "No she isn't. So stop snapping your fingers at her and start treating her nicer. She can ban you from the diner and then where will you eat? And don't say with Eliza because I won't put up with that behavior at our table, either." There, he'd said it.

He held his breath waiting for tears or scorn to come from Eliza's twin sister.

She surprised him by saying, "You're right. I'll apologize." Eve stood and walked to the counter, where Mrs. Velarde was pouring hot water into a teapot.

Peter looked up at him. "Ma and Aunt Eve sure are different, aren't they?"

Jackson was thankful that they were. He couldn't imagine being married to the spoiled Eve. Eliza was kind to everyone and never asked for help. Sometimes he thought she might be too kind, but after witnessing Eve's behavior, he'd take Eliza's loving nature any day. He realized Peter was waiting for an answer and nodded.

Eve returned to the table and smiled at him. "All better. Now, the wedding is in two days. Where are you going for the honeymoon?"

Jackson spewed warm coffee across the table.

Eve mopped at the front of her dress with a napkin. "Don't tell me you haven't planned the honeymoon?" she sputtered.

"Well, no," he admitted, wiping his mouth. "Sorry about that." He indicated her dress and the coffee stains that were quickly spreading.

She shook her head and finished mopping up the spill. "It was my fault. I have a way of being abrupt."

Mrs. Velarde hurried over with the teapot and a cup. She looked at Jackson and grinned. "I'll get you a fresh cup of coffee. You sure you don't want a cookie, too?"

Jackson was sure he'd choke on a cookie. The last person he wanted to talk to about a honeymoon was Eve. "No, thanks."

"I wouldn't mind a damp cloth, if you have one available," Eve said, laying the wet napkin on the table.

"Of course." Mrs. Velarde hustled off to take care of their orders.

Eve turned her gaze back to him. "Well, I have thought about the honeymoon. Kind of figured you wouldn't have thought about it and I think it would be nice if you took my sister someplace nice."

Jackson set his cup down. "Eve, I have a blacksmith shop to run."

"Yes, and I have a sister who needs a honeymoon." She leaned forward. "Plus, what would the gossips say if you didn't take her away for a couple of days?"

He hadn't thought about that. Since they were getting married on Saturday, he could shut the shop down Saturday and Sunday and reopen on Monday. Would that be long enough? It would have to be, but where would he take her? "I suppose you have an idea of where we should go."

Eve grinned. "As a matter of fact I do. Glendale is a half-day ride from here. I stopped there on my way here. You could go there, spend the evening and return Sunday evening."

Mrs. Velarde placed a new cup of coffee in front of Jackson and a plate of sugar cookies in the middle of the table. She handed Eve a damp cloth. "Can I get you anything else?" She asked, wiping her hands on her white apron.

"No, thank you," Eve answered. She scrubbed at the coffee stains and then picked up a cookie and bit into it. A soft groan issued from her throat before she finished chewing.

A smile touched Mrs. Velarde's lips. "Then I will leave you to your conversation."

"These are wonderful, Mrs. Velarde. Thank you." Eve smiled up at the older woman.

She returned her smile, nodded and then left.

Eve turned back to Jackson. "So what do you think of that idea?" she asked and then took another bite of cookie.

He looked at the tabletop. "I suppose that can be arranged."

"Do I get to go?" Peter asked, wiping a milk mustache onto his shirtsleeve.

Eve laughed. "Oh, no, dear. I've made arrangements for you to spend the night with George and his family. Julia said she has a kitten for you."

Peter bounced on the seat. "Thank you, Aunt Eve."

"Now wait a minute," Jackson protested. "We should make sure with Eliza that this is all right with her."

"Why?" Eve truly looked perplexed.

Jackson frowned. "Because she might not want a honeymoon and she might not want Peter going to the Harpers."

Eve handed Peter another sugar cookie. "Every woman wants a honeymoon, Jackson, and as for Peter spending the night with the Harpers, they are friends. I'm sure she won't mind."

Jackson felt certain that Eliza wouldn't like the idea that her sister was helping to plan their honeymoon. His head ached and he really wished he'd stayed in the smithy this afternoon. "Well, I think I'll check with her at dinner, just to be sure."

"Oh, don't ruin the surprise," Eve whined.

He looked at Peter, who was finishing up his cookie and milk. "I don't know..."

"Well, I do. Eliza and Charlie didn't have a honeymoon. She deserves one. And if you want to keep the gossips happy, you'll give her one." Eve took a drink of tea and then gently set her cup down. "Look, Jackson, this will be a good time for you and Eliza to have some quiet time alone. She'll be thrilled to get away, and Peter here is happy to play with his friend. The gossips will focus on something else and when Eliza gets home they'll be ordering dresses from her again. It's a winning situation."

Jackson studied his soon-to-be sister-in-law. He liked the notion that he could give Eliza something her deceased husband hadn't. It would be a memory that couldn't be compared to her life with Charlie. Still, planning this without Eliza's input didn't feel right. "But do we have to keep it a secret?"

Eve and Peter shared a smile. "Of course we do. She'll be so happy."

Jackson wanted that kind of happiness for Eliza, even if it were for a short time.

Chapter Eighteen

Two days later, Eliza slipped into her wedding dress. Thanks to Eve, her hair was curled and hanging around her shoulders. Rarely did Eliza wear it down, but today was special and she wanted to feel pretty. And she did.

"Jackson is sending a buckboard around to collect you in five minutes. You look beautiful." Eve smiled in the mirror at her.

"I thought I was going to walk to the church," Eliza protested. "I really don't need a buckboard to take me. It's not that far."

"Sure you do. Mr. Miller will be driving and will help you climb aboard. Besides, Jackson has a special treat planned, so we aren't going to the church."

Eliza's head began to spin. It seemed her sister knew more about her wedding than she did. Eliza studied the happy expression on Eve's face. So far, the time had been moved up two hours. She was no longer getting married at noon; now it was to be 10:00 a.m. Not in the church as she'd planned but someplace mysterious. "Is there anything else I should know?" Eliza asked, watching her sister's face.

Eve shrugged. "Not that I can say," she answered, fiddling with one of her own curls.

Eliza slipped her feet into the cream-colored slippers that Mrs. Miller had sent over. Her gaze moved to the bridal bouquet that Eve had put together. The flowers were a rich purple. Eve had wrapped green ribbon around the stems pulling it together, and the cream-colored centers matched her shoes and veil.

"Hurry—I just heard Mr. Miller pull up out front." Eve grabbed her by the arm and tugged.

Eliza pulled away. "I'm coming. No need to drag me out the front door. This isn't a shotgun wedding, you know." She walked to the table and picked up the bouquet. Her heart raced in her chest.

She followed Eve out of the house and took several deep breaths. The smell of flowers and sawdust filled her senses. The sun shone brightly and the birds chirped happily in the trees. It was a beautiful day to get married.

True to Eve's word, Mr. Miller helped her into the buckboard. "You look lovely, Mrs. Kelly."

Eliza swallowed. "Thank you."

He helped Eve into the back and then climbed up beside Eliza on the bench. "Nervous?"

She attempted a smile. "A little."

As he guided the horse out of town, Mr. Miller commented, "I don't think you have a thing to be worried about. Jackson Hart is a fine man. Granted, I haven't known him long, but I respect him just the same."

"Thank you, Mr. Miller."

He nodded and focused on directing the horse along a narrow path. A smile began to take form as Eliza realized they were heading to the clearing where she and

Jackson had shared lunch and he'd surprised her with the rainbows of light.

Eve complained as they hit a rock. Eliza couldn't make out her words but she was sure they weren't ladylike. Their mother would have slapped her arm. For a brief moment Eliza allowed herself to think about their parents. Once more, neither would be at her wedding. Tears filled her eyes and she willed them away.

Today wasn't a day for tears. It was a day of joy, and she would be happy. Jackson had planned the day to be special. She knew her husband would be a thoughtful man. He'd already proved it by planning the wedding in what she thought of as their special spot.

Jackson stood beside Reverend Griffin. He wore a dark brown suit with a white shirt and brown vest under a long-sleeve jacket. His trousers matched the jacket, and he'd chosen to wear black boots. His hair was combed down, and his blue eyes ran over her swiftly. Even white teeth flashed as he smiled at her.

Her heart beat even faster as he hurried to the buckboard and offered to help her down. His rough hands encircled her waist and he lowered her to the ground. He leaned forward and whispered, "You are so beautiful."

Eliza inhaled the rich scent of leather and warmth that she'd come to recognize as Jackson's personal scent. "Thank you." Her voice sounded breathless in her own ears.

He released her and held out his elbow for her to take. Once she'd slid her hand inside, he covered it with one of his and then led her to where Reverend Griffin still stood.

The reverend smiled at her and the small group of

people who stood around them. He cleared his throat and began the wedding ceremony.

Jackson listened to the reverend as he spoke of love and marriage. He knew that Eliza didn't love him and, to be honest, he couldn't say he was in love with her, either. But today, when she'd arrived in a cloud of lavender, his heart had done a little flip-flop.

Even now as she looked up into his face and spoke her wedding vows, his heart hammered against his chest. Could she see it through his suit? He found himself focusing on the sea of rich dark coffee that was her eyes. Eliza Kelly was an attractive woman. He knew she was just as beautiful on the inside as she was on the outside. If he could fall in love with anyone, Jackson was sure he could fall for Eliza.

The reverend drew him from those thoughts. "Will you, Jackson Hart, have Eliza Kelly to be your wife? Will you love her, comfort and keep her, and forsaking all others remain true to her as long as you both shall live?"

Hadn't he already promised to comfort and take care of Eliza? Yes, he had the day he'd agreed to bring her to Cottonwood Springs. But love? No, he'd not promised to love her. Could he do it now? He knew Eliza could be the one person he might allow himself to fall in love with. With that thought he heard himself saying, "I will."

Reverend Griffin nodded and then continued. "Jackson, please repeat after me. I, Jackson Hart, take thee, Eliza Kelly, to be my wife, and before God and these witnesses I promise to be a faithful and true husband."

Jackson had no trouble repeating those vows after

the reverend. He kept his eyes locked on Eliza's sweet face. He wanted her to know that he intended to keep his promises.

Then the reverend continued. "Jackson, do you have a ring?"

"Yes, sir. I do." Jackson pulled the ring he'd fashioned from metal and stone from his pocket. He prayed Eliza would love it.

A soft gasp escaped her as the light hit the stone and small rainbows splashed her dress. She looked up at him and mouthed, "Oh, Jackson, it's beautiful."

The reverend continued. "Good. Now, once more repeat after me. With this ring I thee wed, and all my worldly goods I thee endow. In sickness and in health, in poverty or in wealth, 'til death do us part."

Jackson looked into Eliza's face. Her brown eyes shined up into his. Trust radiated from her face. She was willing to take the chance on him that he would be a good husband. He repeated the last part of the vows with joy in his heart.

Her hand shook as he slowly slid the ring onto her finger. She smiled as the sun hit the stone, casting mini-rainbows upon them. He wondered if she thought this, too, was a promise from God.

"You may kiss your bride."

Jackson swallowed. This was their wedding day and he wanted this kiss to be special. He wanted Eliza to know that he would try to be a good husband to her. For a brief moment Jackson wondered if a woman could sense those things in a simple kiss. He prayed Eliza could.

Chapter Nineteen

Eliza's breath caught in her throat. Jackson lifted the half veil. Her eyes drifted shut as his head blocked out the sun. She felt his large hands caress the side of her neck and lower jaw as he tilted her face up to meet his. For one breathless moment their mouths met. A slight tingle entered her lips.

Just as quickly, he pulled away and smiled down at her. She missed the feel of his hand upon her face but didn't have time to focus on that. Noise erupted about them.

She felt her cheeks fill with heat as the men whistled and tossed their hats into the air. Rebecca and Julia Harper ran up to give her hugs while the men all pounded Jackson on the back and pumped his arm in strong handshakes. Congratulations filled the air.

"Lead the way back to the church, son," Reverend yelled over the noise.

Jackson grabbed her hand and pulled her toward the buckboard. He quickly scooped her up and set her on the wagon. She smiled and tossed her bouquet over her shoulder as he climbed into the other side.

When Eliza sat down and looked back at the crowd, she saw that nine-year-old Anna Harper had caught the flowers. The young girl's face paled and then a light pink blush filled her cheeks.

"Ready?" Jackson asked as he released the brake.

She nodded. The congregation was scattering to their wagons to join them at the church for cake and punch. Eliza sighed.

Jackson looked over at her. "Are you sorry you married me?" he asked, then stared straight ahead.

Eliza straightened her hat. "No." Shyness enveloped her like a warm blanket.

She glanced through her eyelashes at him. "Are you?"

He shook his head. "No, I believe we did the right thing."

Jackson pulled the team up to the church and turned to face her. He opened his mouth to speak but was interrupted by the small crowd descending upon their wagon.

Jackson set the brake and jumped down. He hurried to her side and gently lowered her to the ground. The women pressed in on them, forcing him back a few steps. Eliza missed him almost immediately. She could only imagine her frustration had she actually been a young bride in love.

Mrs. Walker grabbed her and hugged her tight. "We are so happy for you. I hope you didn't mind our meddling too much but well…we were only doing what we felt was right."

Jackson made a snorting sound behind them.

Eliza patted the woman's shoulder. "It's all right, Mrs. Walker. I'm sure we will be very happy."

Tears filled the older woman's eyes and she made a swipe at her cheeks. "I believe you will be."

Others crowded around and began moving toward the tables and chairs that had been set out on the lawn of the church. For the next two hours, Eliza felt like the belle of the ball. She was hugged and wished well more times than she could remember.

After eating cake and drinking punch, she and Jackson opened wedding gifts in front of everyone. As soon as the last package was cleared away, Jackson announced their departure. "Ladies and gentlemen, thank you for coming but if we are to make it to our destination today, Eliza and I must be leaving."

His words were met with several disappointed "awws" and a few wolf whistles from the men who weren't so gentlemanly.

Eliza stared at him, wondering what he was up to. She'd expected to spend the afternoon with family and friends. He took her hand in his large one and began walking to the buckboard.

"Peter!" he called.

The little boy came running. "I thought I was staying with George," Peter said as he slid to a halt in front of them.

Jackson ruffled the boy's hair. "You are, but don't you want to say goodbye?"

Confused, Eliza hugged Peter.

"Bye, Ma. Have fun." His words brought laughter from their friends and neighbors. He waved to Jackson. "Bye, Pa!" Then he returned to his marble game with the group of boys he'd been playing with earlier.

Jackson helped her up onto the wagon, hurried around to the driver's seat and then turned the horse toward the smithy. The crowd behind them yelled goodbye and waved.

Anger boiled to the surface. She was tired of not knowing what was really going on. Once they were out of earshot, Eliza demanded, "Jackson Hart, what are you doing?"

"Taking you back to the house, where you can pack an overnight bag. I've been told we're expected to go on a honeymoon."

She noted that his shoulders had squared at the use of his full name. "By who?" Eliza asked, searching his face as his jaw hardened and his hand gripped the reins tighter.

He pulled the wagon up in front of the house.

Eve came bounding down the stairs with Eliza's travel bag. "I packed a few things for your trip," she told Eliza, handing her the satchel.

Jackson jumped down from the wagon and stomped off to his room.

"What's wrong with Jackson?" Eve asked.

Eliza narrowed her eyes at her sister. "Did you tell him I wanted a honeymoon?"

Eve giggled. "Of course I did. He would have never thought to take you to a nice hotel if I hadn't suggested it and made the arrangement for Julia to take Peter."

She sighed as the anger drained from her body. "And did you tell him to keep it a secret from me?"

Realizing her sister wasn't happy, Eve planted her hands on her hips. "Would you have gone if we hadn't kept it a secret?"

Eliza watched Jackson walk back across the yard. He'd changed into a pair of blue pants and the blue shirt he'd been wearing the last time they'd traveled together.

"I'm not sure," she answered honestly, "but I would have liked to have known I was going on a trip."

Jackson tossed his own bag into the bed of the wagon. He pulled himself up and looked to see if she was ready to go. His blue eyes reminded her of sapphires.

"I need to change." Eliza scrambled from the wagon before he could dismount again and help her. "I'll be right back." She grabbed Eve's hand and pulled her back inside the house.

Once in her room, Eliza pulled her hat off and began removing her wedding dress. "I really wish you had let him decide if he wanted to take me somewhere. Where are we going, anyway?" she demanded, kicking off her slippers.

"Can't tell you that—it's a surprise," Eve said in a teasing voice.

Eliza handed her the wedding gown and moved to her armoire and pulled out her yellow dress with little orange flowers on it. She pulled it over her head and then hurried to the mirror and pulled her hair up into a ponytail. She tied a matching yellow ribbon around the band, holding her hair into place. "I guess I'll find out soon enough," Eliza mumbled to her reflection.

"I packed your blue dress, your pink dress with the white flowers and a silk nightgown." Eve picked up the purple slippers and carried them to the armoire.

"Thank you. So I take it we aren't going to be gone long?" She heard the question in her voice and wondered if her sister would answer.

Eve grinned at her. "Only until tomorrow evening. Relax, Eliza, have some fun. You don't get married every day."

* * *

They arrived in the town of Glendale just before sunset. Jackson studied the town with unease. It was much bigger than Cottonwood Springs, and the people hurried along the streets as if they didn't know one another. Big trees and lots of flowers decorated Main Street.

He chanced a glance over at Eliza. She'd been quiet most of the trip, offering him a nervous smile from time to time. Her big yellow hat had shaded her face most of the afternoon. It bothered him that she wasn't talkative and didn't seem natural.

"It's a pretty town, isn't it?" Eliza said in a soft voice.

Jackson grinned as he looked upon her face. "Yes, it is. Do you have any idea where you'd like to stay?" he asked, looking up and down the building fronts for a hotel or boardinghouse.

"I've never been here, so I'm not sure." She searched, as well. Her brown eyes seemed to drink in all the sights at once.

He pulled in front of a general store and set the brake. "We'll go inside and ask around. How does that sound?"

Eliza smiled and nodded. She waited until he'd hopped down and then offered him her hand. Jackson marveled at how light she felt as he helped her. Once her feet were on the ground, he released her hand and she surprised him by slipping her arm into the crook of his.

They stepped up onto the sidewalk and once more he was amazed at the way people avoided making eye contact with them. With all his senses on alert, Jackson guided her to the store.

The bell over the door announced their arrival. It took a moment for his eyes to adjust to the darker room.

A blend of smells that included spices, leather, coffee and kerosene tickled his nose.

Long wooden counters stretched along both sides of the store. The drawers and bins built into them were labeled as spices, ground sugar, coffee, tea, flour, eggs and seeds, among other things. Several glass cases sitting on the countertop displayed expensive items, such as pens, perfumes, jewelry and silverware. Behind the counter he could see shelves covered the walls from floor to ceiling. They were stocked with pots, pans, dishes, bottled medicines and countless other goods.

Eliza moved toward the ready-made clothes, boots, shoes and bolts of fabric. His gaze followed her as she ran her hands over the material. He noticed a large jar of buttons and a memory tickled his thoughts.

A man's voice interrupted his thinking. "Can I help you or the little lady? We're getting ready to close up for the evening."

Jackson started toward where the merchant stood behind the counter. He was a short man with a balding head and glasses perched on the tip of his nose. "My wife and I are looking for a place to stay tonight." It felt funny calling Eliza his wife.

His shoulders seemed to relax a little. "Mrs. Myrtle's boardinghouse is two streets over. Has a white picket fence around the front and a blue door. You can't miss it. Nice place, good eats."

Eliza returned to Jackson's side. She slipped her small hand into his and waited.

"Thank you." He nodded to the storekeeper and turned to leave.

"Before you folks leave, I should warn you. The Society of Bandits have been coming into town late at night.

Normally, I wouldn't be closing this time of day, but they are a mean bunch, and with them lurking about we're all shutting down early. If I was you I'd get the little lady inside now, while it's safe." He came from behind the counter and followed them the rest of the way out the door.

"I'll do that," Jackson said, helping Eliza back onto the wagon. He waited until after the man had locked the store door and turned around before saying, "Thanks for the warning."

The merchant tipped his hat and hurried down the sidewalk.

Jackson drove the wagon to the end of the block and then headed in the direction the storekeeper had indicated.

"Who do you suppose the Society of Bandits are?" Eliza asked him, looking around with fear in her eyes.

He didn't like seeing fear on her lovely face. Jackson scanned the street for the boardinghouse. "I was hoping you'd heard of them and could tell me."

She shook her head no.

He continued to search for Miss Myrtle's boardinghouse. Just as the man had said, a large two-story house with a white picket fence and blue door stood in the center of the block.

A sign with flowers around the base announced the name of the boardinghouse. Jackson parked and hurried Eliza to the door. He tried to open it, but the knob refused to turn. It was locked.

Jackson knocked. While they waited he turned so that he could keep his gaze on the road behind them.

The sun had lowered and was almost down. Jackson didn't like this. He didn't like it one bit at all.

The door behind him opened, and he heard Eliza's fear-filled gasp.

Chapter Twenty

Eliza took a step back. The man who opened the door was almost as big as Jackson. He wore an old brown coat with what looked like tobacco stains all over it. His shirt was unbuttoned several buttons. Dark hair hung about his face. Hollowed-out black eyes stared at Eliza. His appearance was frightening but not nearly as scary as the gun he held in his hand.

Before she could register that the gun was pointed at the floor, Jackson shoved Eliza behind him. She held on to his waist as she eased her head around him and peaked at the rough-looking man. Jackson slowly backed away, pushing Eliza back and farther away from the door.

In a low voice Jackson said, "We don't want any trouble."

A small round woman peaked out from behind the gunman. She saw Eliza and pushed the man to the side. "Move, Sam, and let them inside."

Jackson stood perfectly still.

Eliza watched as the woman slapped Sam's hand. She had short grey hair and steely grey eyes. Not much taller than herself, the older woman was thin, but she carried a sense of authority about her.

"And put that gun away," she barked at the unkempt man.

Sam set the gun on a table beside the door.

She turned around and gave them a huge toothy smile. "Are you here to rent a room?"

Jackson continued to eye the man. "We were but…"

She waved the rest of his words away. "Oh, don't mind Sam. He's been as jumpy as a bullfrog every since the Society of Bandits arrived. 'Course, who can blame him. The Bandits are one of the meanest bunch of men I've ever had the displeasure of meeting."

Eliza came from around Jackson and stood beside him once more. She watched Sam disappear down a side hallway. "I'm Eliza Ke…Hart. This is my husband, Jackson," she introduced, extending her hand out to the woman.

"My name's Myrtle Harvey, and I am the owner of this fine establishment." Myrtle shook Eliza's hand firmly. Her palms were callused and scratched as she squeezed Eliza's. She pulled Eliza farther inside the room.

"I only have two rooms left. One's done up in blues and the other in greens. Which would you like?"

"That depends on the cost," Jackson said as he followed them into the sitting room.

Myrtle hurried around a small desk and produced a slender, bound book. She pushed it across the wood for them to sign. Her gray eyes met Jackson's and she grinned. "I like you, so I'll only charge you a shiny fifty-cent piece."

Eliza tried to hide her smile behind her hand. Fifty

cents a night was the going rate. A big sign outside the front door had shown the prices for a week, five days and nightly. She assumed in his rush to get her inside, Jackson had overlooked it. Then she heard him grumble, "Me and every other fella that comes up the sidewalk." He signed Mr. and Mrs. Jackson Hart to the ledger.

Myrtle winked at Eliza and laughed. "Got that right."

The sound of Jackson's rich laugher joining the other woman's warmed Eliza's heart. She tried to remember if she'd ever heard him laugh like that. Her gaze met his and held. Something in his look seemed to steal her breath away.

Myrtle cleared her throat. "If you would tell me which color room you'd like, I'll get you up to it."

Warmth filled Eliza's cheeks and she turned her attention back to Myrtle. "I think I'd like to see the blue room." If Myrtle liked blue as much as Eliza thought she did, the room was probably very nice.

Jackson handed the innkeeper a fifty-cent piece.

Myrtle dropped the money into a drawer and then pulled a key off a rack behind the small desk. "That's a good choice." She stopped and relocked the door before leading them up the stairs.

Eliza hurried after the older woman.

As she stomped up the staircase, Myrtle laid down the law. "Breakfast is at six, dinner at noon, supper's at seven. I'll have no cigars, pipes or liquor anywhere within the house, and I don't abide cussing." She stopped in front of a door with the number one painted on it. "It's pretty, but I don't think it's anywhere near as nice as your man's eyes."

This time Jackson's neck and checks turned a light

red. Eliza simply couldn't hide her grin. She focused on the door, trying not to laugh at Jackson.

As the door opened, Eliza could see that it was a nice-size bedroom. A blue-and-white nine-patch quilt covered the full-size bed. Her gaze hurried from the bed to the small dresser and lamp beside it. She walked inside and ran her hand over the writing table that sat just inside the door. A wooden chair had been placed in front of the desk. Just as she thought—the room was lovely.

Her gaze continued around the room. A tall armoire rested in the far corner, and a blue sheet hung from ceiling to floor beside it. Eliza wondered what the purpose of the sheet was but decided not to ask.

Blue-and-white dollies covered the surfaces of the tables. The kerosene lamp was blue. Dark and light blue rag rugs, mixed with browns, littered the floor. Sheer light blue curtains covered the only window. Now she knew why Myrtle called it the blue room. "It's beautiful," Eliza said at last.

Jackson moved farther into the room. He walked to the curtain and looked behind it. "What's this for?"

Myrtle winked at Eliza. "If your wife is shy, she can change behind it."

"Oh." Once more color traveled up Jackson's neck and face. "I see."

The old woman laughed again. "Well, if there aren't any more questions, I'll be leaving you two alone." She walked to the door.

Jackson's voice stopped her. "Before you go, I'd like to know if Sam is one of your boarders?"

Myrtle ran a hand through her gray hair. "No, Sam is my son. He's big, like you, and with the Bandits hanging around town, he likes to open the door for me after three in the afternoon."

Eliza asked. "Who are these Bandits?"

"You two get settled and then come down for supper. We can yarn some more then." Myrtle shut the door behind her as she left.

Silence hung between them. They hadn't discussed their sleeping arrangements, and Eliza felt a knot form in her belly. Would Jackson expect a true wedding night between them? And if so, would she be able to resist him?

Jackson ran his hands through his hair. Now what? His gaze moved to the bed and then jerked away. A soft pink filled Eliza's cheeks and she averted her eyes, as well. "I'll go get our bags and take care of the horse and wagon."

"That sounds good," Eliza answered as she walked over to the window.

He thought about telling her there was a washbasin behind the blue curtain but decided to let her find it on her own. "Lock the door behind me, and don't let anyone in but me. I've got a bad feeling about this group of men they keep calling the Society of Bandits."

She nodded. He opened the door and put one booted foot over the threshold. Her voice called out to him. "Jackson?"

He turned.

"Be careful out there," she said.

A smile pulled at his lips. She cared about him. "I will. Be right back." Jackson shut the door. He listened until he heard the lock turn and then hurried downstairs to find out where he could house the wagon and horse.

Mrs. Harvey sat at the desk in the sitting room. Sam Harvey sat in a chair off to the side. She looked up at him and a dimple flashed in her cheek. "I figured you'd be right down."

"I need to take care of the horse and buggy."

She nodded. "Sam, take Mr. Hart out back and show him where the lean-to is."

Sam stood and slapped a big hat on his head. The man had pulled his hair back from his face with what looked like a string of rawhide.

"And, son, tell him about the Bandits." She looked at Jackson. "We'll sugarcoat it at supper for the missus."

"Okay, Ma." Sam led the way to the door.

An hour later, Jackson came back inside, feeling jumpy. The Bandits were a mean lot who enjoyed terrorizing the good citizens of Glendale. According to Sam, they burned homes and tortured and hung men at random. Their favorite sport seemed to be running off the local ranchers' livestock. At night they came into town and drank at the Ole Drinking Hole Saloon until the wee hours of the morning. Jackson was glad he and Eliza were only staying for a day.

He tapped on the door. "Eliza, it's me," Jackson called through the door.

The lock clicked and her white face peeked around the door frame before she pulled the door open slightly. "What took you so long? I was getting worried." Eliza let him in.

He walked past her and dropped both of their bags on the bed. "I'm sorry. Sam decided to show me the lean-to, we got to talking and I lost track of time. I'm sorry." Jackson turned around and pulled her into his arms. He was happy that she didn't pull away.

Her small hands came up and rested against his back as she hugged him back. "I know it's silly, but I thought maybe that Society of Bandits had gotten you. I wish we knew more about them."

Jackson rested his head on her soft hair and inhaled the sweet scent of vanilla. "I'm fine. Thank you for worrying."

His heart melted at the thought that she'd been worried about him. Would he ever get used to her caring for him?

Eliza pulled away. "There is a basin of water and a clean cloth behind the changing curtain if you'd like to wash up before supper." She folded her hands in front of her dress and watched him.

Wanting to make her happy, Jackson walked to the curtain. He stepped behind it and found the basin full of fresh water. "I was thinking we might head back early tomorrow."

"Why?"

Jackson splashed water on his face. He didn't want to tell her of the dangers they might face if they were to wait too late in the day to travel. "I just thought you'd like to get back to Peter."

Eliza's soft laugh flowed to him like dust particles on a light breeze. "He's fine with Julia. I'd like to look at the fabric at the general store and then I thought we might stroll around the town and see what all they have here, unless you are concerned about those Bandits."

Fresh worry had entered her voice. How could he refuse her? Jackson vowed to stay close to her and not allow anything or anyone to hurt her. "Of course we can do that." He wiped his face dry with the clean towel.

"Do you think it will be safe?" Worry filled her voice.

"Probably as long as it's daylight. Sam said that the Bandits usually leave town when the sun comes up."

"What else did he say about them? Did he say they were killers? Or are they just a bunch of kids making mischief? I wish we knew more about them. Why do you suppose Myrtle wanted us to wait until supper to tell us about them? Do you think they will come to Cottonwood Springs?"

Jackson was grateful that his bride had found her voice again. The quiet Eliza wasn't nearly as fun as the talkative one, plus, with her asking so many questions at once he could pick and choose which ones he wanted to answer.

He splashed a little water on his hair and finger-combed it down before coming around the curtain and answering her. "I'm not sure why she wanted to wait, but if we hurry, we can go downstairs and you can ask her."

Eliza turned around and smiled at him. "I'm ready."

His eyes drank in her appearance. She'd changed into a pink dress with little white flowers. Her hair was pulled up but instead of her normal tight bun, Eliza had allowed wisps of hair to hang about her face. Her earlier curls hung down her back, gathered once more with a little pink ribbon. "So am I." He opened the door and held out his arm for her to take.

A tingle spread where her fingers touched his bare skin. His heart decided now was the time to pick up the beat. He glanced back into the room and the bright blue quilt on the bed. How long would he be able to keep his agreement that theirs was a marriage of convenience only?

Chapter Twenty-One

Eliza sighed as he opened the door to their room. Dinner had been unique, to say the least. Myrtle kept up a constant conversation about the Bandits and their latest escapades. From what the older woman had said, they didn't seem that dangerous to Eliza.

The Bandits' main interest seemed to be in cutting the ranchers' fences and running off livestock. Still, she hoped the local sheriff would be able to catch them soon. "Do you think Seth is aware of those men?" she asked Jackson as she sunk into the chair in front of the writing desk.

"I'm not sure, but he should be." He closed the door and walked to the bed. Jackson sat down, lit the kerosene lamp and sighed.

"Maybe so, I'd hate for those men to come to Cottonwood Springs." She lifted her hands to her hair and began releasing the pins that held it up.

"Eliza, I think you should know that those men are more dangerous than Myrtle and Sam let on down there." He reached down and pulled off his boots.

Eliza watched as he wiggled his toes. "How so? They seemed mild enough to me."

"Yes, but they didn't tell you the whole story. Those men do more than harrass ranchers and steal cattle. They also burn down homes, barns and fields. They have already killed two men and have no qualms about killing again." He ran his fingers through his hair.

"How do you know this?" she asked, wishing she didn't know it now.

Jackson pulled his shirt out of his waistband. "Sam told me while we stowed away the wagon."

Eliza sighed. "Why didn't they just tell me?"

"Myrtle thought it would be better not to scare you. I don't want to scare you, either, but I felt you should know the truth." He looked at the bed and began unbuttoning his shirt.

"What are you doing?" Eliza asked, averting her eyes from his chest.

"Getting ready for bed. I'm tired." Jackson's shirt hit the floor a few feet away from her.

A few seconds later she heard his pants join the shirt. Still keeping her eyes on the floor, Eliza protested, "But we haven't talked about sleeping arrangements."

The hem of the quilt began sliding down the bed. She listened as Jackson pulled back the sheets. He didn't say a word. She heard the mattress squeak as his weight descended upon it.

"All right, you can have the bed." Her voice cracked. Keeping her eyes averted from him, Eliza hurried to stand behind the changing curtain.

Now what? There was no place to sleep. A cabinet with a washbasin was all that was behind the curtain. The sound of the covers rustling filled the too-quiet room. She looked about the small changing space and realized she hadn't grabbed her satchel.

A soft chuckle met her ears before Jackson asked, "Did you forget something?"

"You know, a gentleman would have offered me the bed," she called back to him, half mad.

The sound of him yawning reached her ears. "I suppose you are right."

Hadn't they agreed to keep the marriage pure? Well, maybe *pure* wasn't the right word. Had she not made herself clear? Eliza felt sure she had.

A soft snore greeted her ears. Was he asleep already? She eased her head from behind the sheet and sighed. He was.

Advancing quietly toward the bed, Eliza looked down on him. Jackson had made a pallet out of the quilt. He lay on the floor with one arm thrown over his head and the other resting on his chest. His relaxed features presented the most handsome man she'd ever seen. Gone were the worry lines. His forehead was smooth, his jaw unclenched.

Eliza realized he'd only been teasing her about sharing the bed and was grateful. She picked up her bag and carried it behind the screen.

As she changed, Jackson's snores got a little louder. The white cotton gown came to her knees. The lacy top with short sleeves felt cool against her overly warm body. Eliza looked in her satchel for the cover-up that went with the gown. Eve hadn't packed it.

His snores continued to fill the silent room. Eliza blew out the lamp and then slipped to the opposite side of the bed. She pulled back the sheet and eased onto the bed.

Once under the covers, Eliza closed her eyes and tried to ignore the big man snoring softly on the floor. The mattress felt soft against her back and she sighed. It was hard to believe that she and Jackson were now man and wife. She continued to listen to his soft snores and soon found herself drifting toward sleep.

Jackson awoke the next morning with a knot in his back from sleeping on the floor. Eliza's steady breathing told him she was still fast asleep. For a few moments he allowed himself to dream of what his life would be like if he and Eliza turned this into a real marriage. They had already made it through some tough times and had worked through them. They hadn't disagreed on the main decisions; instead, they gained a mutual respect for one another.

He sat up, forcing away the thoughts of true marriage. Cool morning air shivered over his warm flesh. Careful not to wake her, Jackson moved to his valise and pulled out fresh clothes.

He carried them behind the changing curtain and bathed the best he could with cold water from the washbasin. Jackson dressed and then picked up his soiled clothes and boots. After stuffing the dirty clothes into his bag, he sat down in the wooden chair and pulled on his boots.

Eliza continued to sleep. Her hair splayed across the white pillow; her long eyelashes created shadows on her cheeks. Her generously curved lips were slightly parted, and as she drew in each breath they moved as if she were getting ready to speak. Jackson couldn't help the grin that pulled at the corners of his mouth. The woman even talked in her sleep.

He walked over to the window and looked outside. Sam and a few other men stood in front of the house. Jackson made the decision to go join them.

Drawn to the bed for one more look at Eliza's sleeping face one thought crossed his mind then swelled up somewhere near his heart and lodged. This woman belonged to him. They may not have been intimate, but in all the ways that mattered they were bound together. He'd made a promise to keep and protect her, and Jackson Hart never backed out of a promise. With that thought in mind he slipped out the door.

The house was quiet as he made his way down the stairs. The smell of a fresh new day greeted him as he stepped outside.

Glendale was ten miles closer to the Colorado boarder than Cottonwood Springs. The change in temperature could be felt on the morning breeze.

Sam waved him over. "Morning, Jackson. This here's John Freeman, Asa Johnson and his son, Cord."

Jackson shook hands with each man. His gaze moved over the horse behind John Freeman. It looked to him as if the horse had been ridden hard. She kept lifting her back leg, and he couldn't help but think she might have a rock lodged in her shoe.

"Mind if I take a look at your horse's shoe?" he asked John.

"Go ahead." John held the animal's head while Jackson approached it.

Sam continued speaking while Jackson lifted the horse's back hoof off the ground. "John was just telling us that the Carter place was burned to the ground last night. Phillip and his wife, Caroline, just barely made it out."

"If you ask me, someone should send for the marshal. It's his job to uphold law and order." Asa spat on the ground.

"What about the sheriff?" Jackson asked, taking out his pocket knife and digging a stone out from under the horse's shoe.

John shook his head. "He up and left. Not sure what they said to scare him off, but one morning his office was cleared out and he was gone."

Jackson moved to the other side of the horse and examined its other back shoe. "So you have no law?"

"None at the moment." Sam rocked back on his heels. "You want to apply for the job?"

Jackson stood and patted the horse's rump. "I'm not a lawman, I'm a blacksmith."

"And a darn good one, I'd wager," John said, rubbing his horse's nose.

He wondered if he should feel flattered but decided not to. "Anyone can dig a rock out from under a horse's shoe." Jackson shrugged.

"True, but not everyone would volunteer or even notice that the animal was uncomfortable. Thank you." John held out his hand. After shaking Jackson's hand, he remounted. "I am heading over to Wheel's Road to tell the folks up there about the Carters and warn them to be on their guard."

Sam nodded. "We'll spread the word here. Thanks for stopping by, John."

John nodded and then spun his horse around.

"We best be getting to the Glendale newsroom," Asa told his son, Cord.

As they walked down the sidewalk Sam explained, "Asa owns the only newspaper in town. He'll have the news about the Carters' place circulating by noon. Come on, let's go get us some breakfast before Ma throws it out to the hogs."

Jackson followed Sam inside. The smell of bacon and coffee filled the sitting room. He heard a noise at the top of the stairs and turned just in time to see Eliza floating down toward them in a dress of blue.

When she reached the bottom step her brown eyes met his and a soft pink filled her glowing cheeks. "Good morning."

Jackson bent down and kissed her cheek. It felt soft against his lips, reminding him of their wedding kiss. She'd been soft and sweet then, too, and it had taken all he had to release her. He slowly lifted his head, wanting to kiss her lips but knowing now wasn't the time. Instead, he offered her his arm.

Sam continued walking toward the smell of breakfast. "If you lovebirds will follow me, we'll have breakfast."

Eliza ducked her head but slipped her small hand into the crook of his elbow. He patted her hand and followed Sam.

The dining area was a narrow, long room with a sideboard that held platters of bacon, scrambled eggs, fresh bread, jams and a crock of butter. A coffeepot sat on a hot brick at one end of the makeshift bar. Plates, silverware and cups sat on the other end.

Sam walked to the plates and began working his way down the buffet. Eliza followed his example and Jackson picked up a coffee cup and headed to the pot at the other end of the table.

Myrtle hastened into the room from a side door. She held a plate of flapjacks in one hand and a jar of syrup in another. Jackson moved out of her way and went to sit down at the table.

"I hope you both slept good." Myrtle set the flapjacks and syrup on the buffet table.

Eliza smiled. "We did. Thank you."

Jackson watched her fill the plate in her hands. She piled it high with eggs, bacon and two biscuits. Her face scrunched up and then she added two pancakes and poured a generous amount of syrup over the top of them. For such a little woman she seemed to be prepared to put away a mountain of food, he thought.

He was surprised when she set the steaming plate in front of him and then walked back to the buffet, where she began filling another plate. This time she placed less than half of what she'd taken for him onto her plate.

"This smells wonderful, Myrtle," Eliza offered.

Myrtle gave her a toothy smile. "Thank you. I hope you enjoy it."

Sam sat beside Jackson and began shoveling food in his mouth like it was his last meal. He slurped his coffee and clanked his silverware against his plate.

"I'm sure we will," Eliza said as she returned to sit beside him.

He took the fork and knife she offered him and smiled his thanks.

Her hair was up in its normal knot and once again she'd allowed curls to escape about her face. Jackson liked the softer look. He leaned over and, for her ears only, said, "Thanks for getting my plate, but you didn't have to do that."

"You're welcome. Will you say the prayer, please?"

Sam stopped eating and lowered his head. Myrtle sat down, as well, and Jackson tried to hide his grin as he, too, lowered his head and then asked the blessing on their food, throwing in a quick request for protection on their ride home.

As soon as he finished, Myrtle asked, "What are your plans today?" She looked at them expectantly.

Jackson answered, "Eliza wants to see the town and maybe stop in the general store for a few supplies." He picked up his fork and took a big bite of the hotcakes. Sugar coated his tongue and he sighed with satisfaction.

Myrtle grinned across at him. "I'll be sure and give your wife my secret recipe before you head out."

"Thanks, Myrtle. He's never sighed like that over my cooking."

Jackson turned his head to look at his pretty new wife. Was she offended that he hadn't shown the appropriate pleasure at her cooking?

"I'm teasing you, Jackson," she assured him.

Myrtle laughed. "New husbands take things so seriously."

Jackson looked at her. "How did you know we just got married?"

Sam scoffed but continued to eat as if he'd not made a sound.

"It's in both of your eyes." She rested her elbows on the table and looked dreamily out the window. "I remember when I first fell in love. Everything seems rosier. Don't you agree, Eliza?"

Eliza choked and sputtered.

Jackson felt as shocked as Eliza sounded. Did they appear to be in love? Surely Myrtle was mistaken, Eliza couldn't possibly love him as a wife loves a husband.

Chapter Twenty-Two

"Are you sure you're all right?"

Eliza nodded. She continued to walk beside him but didn't meet his gaze.

"You sure? I thought you might just choke to death in there," he teased.

She gritted her teeth. "I just needed some fresh air."

"Uh-huh. It's a good thing I don't eat a large breakfast. You got us out of the house so fast Myrtle thought your skirts were on fire."

Eliza watched the corners of his mouth twitch. She playfully swatted him on the arm. "Oh, she did not."

His laughter caused several people to look in their direction. Jackson didn't seem to notice. He opened the general store door and the bell rang out over their heads.

Eliza inhaled the many fragrances and looked toward the front counter and the drawer labeled Tea. She walked up and waited for the merchant to turn around. The sound of Jackson's boots on the wooden floor told her he'd followed her to the counter.

Mr. Roberts, the owner, turned to face them. "Oh,

good. I'm glad you came back. What can I get you today?"

"I'd like a pound of tea, please," Eliza answered.

"All right. Is there anything else?"

"I'd like to shop around a bit," Eliza answered. She looked to see where Jackson had gone and found him standing against the wall watching them. His arms were crossed over his chest.

She'd thought he would do a little shopping, too, but he didn't seem to be interested in anything but her. Eliza felt the hair on the back of her neck begin to prickle. She walked over to Jackson while Mr. Roberts measured out her order. "Aren't you going to look around?" she asked, trying to ignore the butterflies that had decided to take flight when she looked into his blue eyes.

A couple of older gentlemen entered the store. The merchant looked up at them and called, "Morning, Jeb, Ike."

They waved and moved to a small table off to the side where a checkerboard sat.

Jackson answered her, "No, I don't need anything from here. You go ahead and look."

"Is there someplace else you'd like to go?" she asked, watching as the older men began setting up the game board.

Jackson tilted his head. "Trying to get rid of me?" He dropped his hands to his side.

"Only if you're thinking about dragging me to the smithy. I'd rather stay here and shop while you go do that," she confessed, knowing he probably couldn't resist going to see what the local blacksmith shop looked like.

"I don't know, Eliza. We probably should stick together." His gaze moved to the street outside.

"Really, Jackson. I'll be safe in here, and I promise not to leave the store." She placed her hand on his arm. "I'd feel better knowing you were enjoying yourself while I shop."

He reached up and touched one of the curls that framed her face. His knuckles brushed the side of her cheek. "All right, but only if you promise not to leave here without me."

It was all Eliza could do not to lean into his hand. "I promise."

Jackson dropped his hand back to his side. "I'll be back in half an hour." He spun on his booted heels and left her staring after him.

Eliza walked to the bolts of fabric and began picking out several patterns that she knew wouldn't be in Cottonwood Springs. Her thoughts went to the dresses, shirts and hats she could use each print for. She also thought about what notations she'd need to go with each fabric.

Twenty minutes later she paid Mr. Roberts for the fabric, notations, tea and a windup toy and lemon drops for Peter.

As she placed the change in her reticule a man and woman entered the store. The woman hurried to the counter and handed Mr. Roberts a long list. Her husband walked to where the two older gentlemen were still playing checkers and lit up a foul smelling cigar.

She tried to ignore the stench, but soon her eyes were watering and she felt as if she couldn't breathe. He offered cigars to the other two men. One accepted; the other declined. Soon both men were filling the room with the foul odor.

Eliza decided to step out on the porch for a breath

of fresh air. The thought that she'd promised Jackson she'd stay in the store gave her pause.

The woman's husband blew another cloud of stench into the air. Eliza felt light-headed. Her throat clogged up and she began to cough. She looked longingly out the door.

A bench that rested under the window looked inviting. Eliza called to Mr. Roberts, "I'm going to sit on the bench outside. When Jackson returns, he'll pick up my packages."

He nodded that he heard her as he continued to tally up the woman's order.

Eliza pulled the door open and hurried out to the sidewalk. She sucked in great gulps of fresh air. How in the world could anyone stand to smoke those disgusting things? And his wife, how did the man's wife live with that? Eliza thanked the stars above that Jackson wasn't a smoker.

As her lungs cleared she looked around. Lots of people now filled the town. Wagons rolled down the dirt street. Several little boys were playing some type of game with a ball and sticks. Their dog raced about barking. She sat down on the bench to wait for Jackson.

Her gaze moved down the rows of shops and Eliza sat up. Was that a dress store? How had she missed it earlier? She stood and walked to the edge of the sidewalk to get a better look. It was a dress shop. Excitement raced through her as she thought of all the different pattern ideas she might get there.

Eliza hurried back inside the store. She tried to hold her breath as she marched up to the counter. "Mr. Roberts?"

He looked in her direction. "Yes, Mrs. Hart?"

"Would you be so kind as to tell my husband when he returns that I ran across the street to the dress shop?" she asked while trying not to breathe too deep.

"Yes, ma'am. I'll do that."

Eliza offered him a big smile. "Thank you." Then she rushed from the store.

She'd just crossed the street and was almost to the door of the dress shop when a tall, thin man grabbed her elbow. Eliza tried to jerk away from him, but he held fast.

His rich calm voice stopped her from screaming. "So this is where you've been hiding." He pulled her toward the alley.

"Let go of me." Eliza jerked hard away from him. "Or I'll scream," she threatened.

He stopped. "Why would you scream? I'll just explain that you are my wife and we've had a little spat." Confusion laced the words. "I just want to talk to you. Say I'm sorry, honey." His dark eyes and smooth voice worked toward calming her down.

Instead, they placed fear in her heart. The man was demented! "I am not your wife."

"No, she's my wife. Unhand her now."

Eliza felt as if she might melt into the ground. Jackson stood a few feet away, looking angrier than a bear whose cub had been threatened. His legs were spread and his fists clenched.

Whoever the man was, he dropped her arm and stared from her to Jackson. "But…"

Eliza ran to Jackson.

His words came out cold and hard. "Go into the dress shop, now."

Fury radiated from his very being. Eliza didn't know

if the rage was directed at her or the man who'd dared to try and force her into the alley. She stared into his ice-blue eyes.

"For once, do as I say." Jackson ground the words out through clenched teeth.

She turned and ran to the dress store. The bell announced her arrival, but Eliza paid no heed to it. She turned and watched Jackson through the glass window.

He marched right up to the man and growled something. She couldn't make out his words and was tempted to go out onto the porch so she could hear better.

The man spread his hands out in front of him and began talking hastily. Again, she couldn't make out their words. Whoever the stranger was, he was explaining fast and backing up.

He had straight black hair and a black mustache. Dark black eyes the color of polished jewels stared at Jackson as he moved away from him.

"May I help you?"

Eliza ignored the woman and continued to watch her husband put the fear of God into the other man. She heard the woman clear her throat and decided she'd better answer. "No, thank you."

The store owner came to stand beside her. "My, that is one big man," she gasped.

Eliza watched the stranger turn on his heels and hurry away. Jackson turned to the window. Anger laced his features and she remembered her promise. Day two of her marriage and she'd lied to her husband and disobeyed him. A sick feeling entered her stomach.

The other woman noted, "And he's madder than a cross-eyed bull." Her hand trembled as she reached for her throat.

"It's all right. He's not angry at you," Eliza tried to assure the woman. She turned to the door as Jackson's boots pounded up the sidewalk.

He opened the door and growled, "Let's go."

For a brief moment, Eliza pondered refusing but then she saw the look in his eyes and came to her senses. Jackson had every right to be angry with her and she was grateful he'd shown up when he had. She walked toward him, and the owner of the dress shop stepped in front of her.

"You don't have to go with him, you know." Her blond hair shimmered in the sunlight that flowed from the big window. Fear filled her soft green eyes.

Eliza offered her a timid smile. "Thank you, but he's my husband. So I do have to go."

A flash of defiance entered the other woman's eyes. "I'll help you."

Without being told, Eliza had the inclination that the woman before her had been hurt by a man. "Thank you for caring. But I can assure you even though he's angry with me right now, Jackson won't harm me." She gave her a hug and then pulled away.

"Are you sure? He looks mad enough to hit someone." The woman looked from Jackson to Eliza.

Eliza glanced over her shoulder at her new husband. He did look mad enough to hit someone. She didn't know him very well, but Eliza knew deep in her heart that Jackson Hart would never hit a woman, especially her. She turned back to the dressmaker. "You're right, he does look pretty angry. But I can assure you, he has never hit me and he never will."

She nodded. A deep sighed exited her lungs. Her hands grabbed Eliza's and squeezed. "All right, but if you should ever need a place to run to, my door will always be open to you."

Eliza smiled. "Thank you." She returned the squeeze to the other woman's hands and then released them.

Jackson cleared his throat and asked, "Ready?"

His voice was much softer now and he seemed to have relaxed. Eliza walked toward him. "Yes, I'd like to go home."

Jackson reached out and pulled her close to him. He held her against his chest and let her listen to the rapid beat of his heart. When he'd seen her being pulled toward the alley, his heart had jumped with fear. Why hadn't she stayed at the general store like she'd promised?

If he hadn't seen her cross the street, he might not have been there to stop the demented stranger. Jackson still didn't understand how the man could have mistaken Eliza for his wife. The only thing that had saved the man from a good beating was that deep in his eyes, Jackson could read that the man believed he'd found his long-lost wife.

What caused a man to go crazy and mistake one woman for another? He buried his face in Eliza's neck and held her tight for a few minutes longer. Jackson knew the other woman was watching him but he didn't care. All he cared about now was making sure Eliza was safe and unharmed.

He leaned back and looked into her face. "Are you all right? Did he hurt you?"

"No. He didn't hurt me. I think he was just delusional. He thought I was his wife. It was frightening.

I'm so glad you came along." She looked up at him with clear brown eyes.

Jackson pulled her back against his chest. "I know. I'm sorry I wasn't there to protect you."

Eliza shook her head. "No, I'm the one who is sorry I didn't keep my word. I should never have left the general store." Her hands moved up his back and Jackson felt her squeeze him close.

What was he going to do? He knew he was falling in love with Eliza. His heart had lurched in his chest when he'd thought she was in danger. Jackson determined in his heart to fight feelings of love.

Chapter Twenty-Three

Eliza climbed down from the buckboard before Jackson could help her down. He'd been even more silent on the way home from Glendale then he'd ever been before. Deep down Eliza felt she'd lost his respect.

He handed her her bag. In a cool voice he said, "I'll put the horses and wagon away." Jackson sat back down and clicked his tongue. The horses headed to the barn.

Tears burned the back of her eyes. She'd lost something very special today. The sun was going down, and Eliza just wanted to crawl into her bed and cover up her head. She opened the door and lit a kerosene lantern for added light.

The house seemed quiet without Peter. She'd missed the little boy during the short time they'd been gone. Like a sleepwalking person, Eliza made her way to her bedroom.

She wondered if Jackson would move into the house tonight or stay in his room. With no one to impress she expected him to stay in his room.

Tomorrow she'd deal with where he'd sleep once he moved into the house. Weariness swept over her. Eliza pulled her covers down on the bed and crawled in between her cool sheets.

She blew out the lantern and then allowed her silent tears to flow. Eliza cried for what she'd lost with Jackson, she cried for herself and she cried because she'd lied to Jackson and broken a promise.

When all her tears were dry, she cried out to the Lord. She asked for direction. And she asked Him to help Jackson forgive her.

The knowledge that she needed to apologize entered her tired mind. She'd do it first thing in the morning. Once the decision was made, peace enveloped her. The sun sank and Eliza fell into an exhausted sleep.

The next morning, she awoke to sunlight and rainbows flooding her room. Eliza yawned and stretched. She turned over. Jackson sat in a chair beside the bed, asleep.

When had he come in? She felt bad that he'd slept in the chair. Eliza pushed back the covers and tiptoed to her bag. She pulled out the yellow dress and slipped it on over her nightgown. Then she walked to the kitchen.

Her packages from the day before were on the table. Eliza carried the fabric and notations to the sewing room. She collected the things she'd gotten for Peter and placed them on his bed, except for the candy. She decided to keep that in the kitchen as a special treat.

After starting the coffee, Eliza made a batch of pancakes, fried sausage and eggs. The coffee's rich aroma filled the house. As she worked, she tried to figure out how she and Jackson were going to coexist when he didn't trust or believe in her anymore.

Eliza set the table and waited for him to come to the kitchen. She sipped on a cup of tea and looked out at the garden spot in the backyard. Every year she planted a plot. She wondered if she should this year, too.

Her gaze moved to the hallway that led to the bedrooms. To keep from thinking about Jackson, she forced her mind to focus on the garden. She told herself that working in the soil was something she'd always enjoyed. Since the Tuckers weren't returning until next spring she decided to go ahead and plant vegetables and herbs.

The sound of Jackson moving about drew her attention. Again she tried not to think about facing him and the apology she knew would need to be said.

Eliza turned her thoughts back to the subject of gardening. She'd need to go to Mrs. Miller's store and buy seeds. And since her own place still had a garden spot, maybe she'd plant two gardens. She could can most of it and share the extras with her neighbors and friends.

Jackson walked into the kitchen with one hand clutching his lower back. He didn't say anything, just headed straight for the coffeepot.

Even rumpled from a rough night he was still the handsomest man in all of Cottonwood Springs. "Good morning." Eliza stood and got a plate. She filled it full of food and then set it in his spot at the table.

"I said you don't have to do that. I'm capable of getting my own breakfast," Jackson growled at her.

Eliza frowned. "I'm sorry. I always get Charlie's meals and just assumed I'd do the same for you." She watched him sit down slowly at the table.

"I'm not Charlie." He took a sip of his coffee.

She tried to hold back the tears. "No, you're not."

Jackson's head came up. "What's that suppose to mean?"

Eliza sighed. "It means you can get your own breakfast from now on."

They sat in silence. He sipped his coffee and she rotated her teacup in her hands as she watched him. Charlie would not have snapped at her like that. She realized as soon as she had the thought it was a lie. Charlie had snapped at her often.

Eliza knew their marriage hadn't been perfect, but since his passing she'd made him out to be more than he was. Charlie was a good man who'd loved her and she had loved him, but he wasn't perfect. At some point along the way, she'd colored him in her mind as an ideal husband.

"You loved Charlie, didn't you?" Jackson asked as he set his cup down.

"Yes, I did."

"Did you ever lie to him? Break a promise to him?" he asked. His gaze had moved out the window.

Eliza sighed and set her cup down, too. "You mean like I did to you yesterday?"

Blue eyes swung around to study her. "Yes."

"No, I didn't. For the past five years I've done what I wanted to, when I wanted to. I didn't answer to anyone. I'm used to the way it has been since Charlie died. I'm not saying what I did was right. I shouldn't have left the general store. I did so to get away from that foul cigar smoke. Then I saw the dress shop, so I told Mr. Roberts where I was going and then went. I acted impulsively." She stopped talking and picked up her teacup again. "I really am sorry, Jackson."

"Your impulsiveness could have gotten you killed." He took a sip of his coffee and continued to study her over the top of the cup.

Eliza didn't know what else to say. He was right. She could have been killed. "I know, and I've already said I was sorry. What more do you want me to say?"

"That you won't lie to me again or break your promises."

He leaned forward on his arms and waited.

The words burned her throat as she spit them out. "And if I say that, will you believe me?"

His Adam's apple bobbed as he swallowed. "I'll try."

She nodded. "Then so will I."

Confusion crossed his features. "What? Try to keep your word? Or believe that I'll keep mine?"

"Both."

Jackson sighed. "Fair enough." He rubbed the muscles in his lower back.

Eliza offered him a weak smile. "Would you like for me to make you a cup of willow bark tea? It will help your back feel better."

He pulled his plate to him. "Thank you for offering but I need to get to work. I'll eat and then head on over to the smithy."

Eliza stood. Her mind worked as he ate. He couldn't continue to sleep in a chair, and she wasn't going to share her bed.

Jackson's chair scraped against the hardwood floor as he stood. His plate was empty. She watched as he drained the last of his coffee. "Was that our first argument?" he asked.

She nodded. "I believe it was."

He walked to her and laid both hands on her shoulders. "Don't husbands and wives kiss and make up when they argue?"

Surely he wasn't planning to kiss her.

* * *

Jackson wanted her to know he was no longer angry. He cupped her face in his hands and gently touched his lips to hers. One hand slid into her hair and the other snaked around her back. He pulled her to him and deepened the kiss, pulling her even closer. Holding her in his arms like this felt amazing, felt right.

When he pulled back, she looked as dazed as he felt.

She moved her hand to cover her heart and sighed. "That wasn't supposed to happen."

"Time for me to get to work." He hurried out the door, leaving her looking mystified.

Within a few minutes he opened the smithy to the group of men who stood outside its doors. "Morning, gentlemen."

The men echoed, "Mornin'."

He walked to the forge, his mind on Eliza and the kiss they'd just shared. She'd seemed to enjoy it as much as he had. Jackson stoked the coals and blew on them to start the fire. Eliza's lips had tasted like sweet honey and she smelled of vanilla. He could get used to kissing her.

Bart Hamilton pulled him from his musings. "How was Glendale?" He blew his nose on a white handkerchief.

"It's a nice town but has some problems."

Hank Browning, the livery owner, stepped up beside him. "What kind of problems?"

Jackson looked pointedly at Hank's ten-year-old son, Carl. "The kind that I should be telling the sheriff instead of you guys." He smiled to take the sting out of his words. Truth was he didn't want rumors running wild before he could speak to Bob James, the sheriff.

"Carl, run over to the sheriff's office and ask him if he'll come on over here."

"All right, Pa." He took off running down the road.

Carl turned to Jackson. "While we're waiting for the sheriff, would you mind looking at May Bell's shoes?"

Jackson followed him out into the sunshine. He noticed the other men had settled on barrels and wagon beds around the front of the smithy. They were talking and laughing as if they didn't have a care in the world. He wondered why they weren't at work.

Hank held his mare, May Bell, steady while Jackson examined each shoe in turn. "She needs four new shoes," he finally said, dropping the last hoof.

"I was afraid you were going to agree with me," Hank replied, looking uncomfortable.

"What's the problem?"

"May Bell belongs to the Widow Simmons. She boards her with me, but I know she doesn't have the money to pay for new shoes and shoeing. But she also won't take charity." He stroked the mare's starred forehead.

Jackson nodded. "Leave her here and I'll get her fixed up this afternoon."

Hank studied him. "What about payment?"

"I'll take care of it."

"Mrs. Simmons isn't going to take charity."

Jackson rubbed the horse's back. "Does she know May Bell needs shoes?"

"I haven't mentioned it," Hank admitted.

He grinned. "Then don't. If she asks, you can tell her you brought her over here to be shod, but if she doesn't ask, then don't tell."

Hank nodded. "I knew you were a good man."

Jackson ignored the comment. "If she asks, tell her to come see me. In the meantime, I'll think of some way to let her pay for the shoes. I'm sure Eliza will have some thoughts on the matter. I'll ask her tonight."

"Sounds good," Hank agreed.

Carl ran back to them. He panted. "The sheriff's on his way."

Hank placed a hand on Carl's shoulder. "Good, son."

Jackson walked back inside the smithy. Should he tell the sheriff about Glendale's bandit problem in front of the other men? Or keep it between them? He wasn't sure.

The thought that the Society of Bandits might come to Cottonwood Springs bothered him. He didn't want those men anywhere near his family. And he felt sure the other men would feel the same way about their families.

Chapter Twenty-Four

"Are you sure you have to go tonight?" Eliza paced the sitting room. She didn't like that Jackson had joined up with the posse that was headed back to Glendale.

Jackson nodded. "Sheriff James seems to think we should take care of the problem there so that it doesn't come here."

Eliza licked her lips. Her gaze moved to where Peter sat on the floor playing with a calico kitten. He seemed engrossed in his new pet, but she lowered her voice, anyway. She didn't want to worry the little boy. "Can't you wait until Seth comes back? I'm scared for you."

"No, we don't know when the marshal will return, and we don't know when the Bandits might get tired of Glendale and come here instead." He walked up to her and pulled her against his chest. "There's nothing to be afraid of."

His heart beat against her ear. Its steady rhythm should have given her some comfort, but it didn't. All day she'd tried to push the memory of his kiss away. Now all she wanted for him to do was kiss her again. She didn't want him going and getting himself killed.

Jackson moved her away a tiny bit and looked into her eyes. "Sheriff James needs all the men he can get to back him up. We'll be home in a couple of days and the Bandits will be behind bars, where they belong."

"I understand." Really, she didn't, but Eliza knew that was what he wanted to hear.

He leaned down and kissed her forehead. His lips felt hot against her cool skin. "Don't worry for us. Pray for us, Eliza. Pray everyone gets out alive."

She nodded, not trusting herself to speak.

Jackson placed his hand under her chin and tilted her head back. His lips found hers. This time the kiss was urgent and full of emotion. Her hands crept up the front of his shirt and around his neck. It was as if he was trying to say how he felt in that one moment.

When he pulled away, she felt weak-kneed. Eliza tried to convince herself it was because of worry. She released him and twisted her hands in her apron. When had she started feeling these deep emotions for him?

"I've got to go." Jackson picked up his change of clothes and turned away.

Peter jumped to his feet and came running toward them. He stopped in front of Jackson. "You be careful, Pa."

Jackson stooped down and hugged the boy. When he released Peter, he ruffled his hair. "I'll be careful. And you take care of your ma while I'm gone."

Peter stood a little taller. "I will, Pa."

Jackson hugged him once more and then stood. He hugged Eliza again and breathed into her ear, "I'll be back as soon as I can."

She nodded and then released him. Peter and Eliza followed him onto the porch. Ten or more men were waiting for him by the smithy. She recognized the women and children that were saying goodbye to them. Did they think they might not make it home? She bowed her head to say a quick prayer over each of them.

Father, please keep and protect each man who is leaving today. I know they are going so that they can protect this town and their loved ones who live here, but I still fear for them. Lord, I'm asking You to bring them home safe to their families. Watch out for Jackson. I love him.

She held her breath, wondering where that confession had come from. Did she love him like a wife is supposed to love her husband? Eliza knew she did, but she also knew she could never tell Jackson. She continued on with her prayer.

Thank you, Lord. Amen.

The sound of their horses thundering through town drew her head up. She watched Jackson ride away beside the sheriff. Her throat felt dry and scratchy.

Eve walked up the steps. "I'm sorry he had to leave so soon after you two just arrived home," she stated.

Peter turned and ran back into the house. Eliza assumed he was going to get his kitten.

She cleared her throat. "Thank you, Eve." The other ladies walked away. Some talked to each other but most kept their heads down and hurried home.

"How about I make you a fresh pot of tea?" her sister offered, taking her arm and turning her back to the house.

Eliza nodded. "That would be nice."

They went back inside. Eve led the way to the kitchen. "Was that group, the Bandits, as bad as the other ladies are saying?"

Eliza looked about the kitchen for Peter. He was nowhere in sight. "I'm afraid so." Eliza sunk into a kitchen chair. She called out to Peter.

He came from his bedroom, holding the kitten against his chest. Was it her imagination or were his eyes red from crying? She had planned to tell him to take the kitten to the barn, but after seeing his face decided one more night in the house wouldn't hurt anything. "I don't want that kitten sleeping in your bed. You need to get an empty box from the barn to put her in."

A big smile filled his face, revealing a gap where he'd lost a baby tooth. "I'll get a big one so she can't get out. Thanks, Ma." He hurried out the back door.

"I went to the bank this morning and deposited all my money," Eve stated as she continued to make tea. "Mr. Bickel, the banker, said he expects to see you in a few days. What did he mean by that?" She sat down across from Eliza.

"He knows that now that I'm married, I'll be coming back in so that I can take out a loan and start rebuilding my house and business." Eliza looked out the window. Shadows were beginning to cover the ground as the sun sank in the sky. Would the Bandits make her a widow again before she got the loan? Eliza pushed the thought away.

Eve's soft voice drew her attention. "Why don't you borrow the money from me?"

"We've been through this, Eve." She sighed.

"I have lots of money, and I'm willing to share it with you."

Eliza offered her sister a wobbly smile. "I know and I thank you, but I have to do this my way. Besides, you are going to need your money. Don't you want a house? A horse and buggy? And other things?"

"Well, sure I do, but I can help you, too." Eve reached out and took Eliza's hand. She gave it a little squeeze. "I know I haven't been the best sister, but I love you and I really want to make it up to you."

Eliza opened her mouth to protest. At the same time someone knocked on the back door. She sighed again.

Eve jumped to her feet. "Don't worry, I'll get it. It's probably Peter trying to get an oversize box inside." She hurried to the door and opened it.

A gasp filled the air.

Eliza looked up in time to see Eve try to slam the door shut. "No!"

A man's voice drifted through the door. "I just want to talk to you. Please let me in."

"Run, Eliza!" Eve screamed. She released the door and took off running to the front of the house.

She couldn't have run, even if her life did depend on it. Her feet felt as if they were frozen to the floor. He was a tall, thin man with dark eyes and straight black hair. He'd shaved his mustache off, but Eliza recognized him as the man who'd tried to force her into the alley the day before in Glendale. "It's you."

He advanced farther into the room. "My name is Lucas Masters. I've been looking for my wife, Eve, for several months now. I'm sorry I scared you yesterday, but I thought you were her."

"Lucas, you get away from my sister." Eve had returned to the kitchen and she held a fireplace poker in her hands.

Lucas looked at his wife. "I'm not going to hurt her or you."

"After the way I left you? I don't believe you aren't out for revenge. How much have you had to drink, Lucas?" Eve's eyes shone with unshed tears and something else.

Eliza realized her sister loved the man standing between them.

He held his hands out in front of him. "I haven't had a drink since the day you left, Eve. When I woke up and realized what had happened, I decided to change my life."

"Sure you did." Eve continued to hold the poker out in front of her. "Eliza, come stand by me," she ordered.

When had her sister become so brave? Eliza looked from Eve to Lucas. He stared at Eve like a starving man looked at a steak. "Let's all calm down."

They both looked at her, Lucas with relief and Eve with disbelief. Eliza would have laughed if the circumstances had been different. Especially at the look on her sister's face.

"Mr. Masters, please sit down." Eliza indicated the chair that sat the farthest away from her and Eve.

He did as she asked. "I only want to talk to you, Eve."

"Eve, lower the poker. I don't think he means to harm either of us."

"I don't," he said, looking only at Eve.

Eve continued to hold on to the poker but she pointed it at the ground as Eliza asked her to do. "I don't trust him."

"I don't blame you, sweetheart, but I've changed," Lucas said.

Eve shook her head no. Tears spilled down her face. "I asked God to change you, but He never did."

Lucas disagreed. "He did change me, Eve. After you

left, I had no money and no place to go. So I ended up at the church. The preacher there, Reverend Don Pope, helped me. He taught me about Jesus and what He did for me. Reverend Pope led me to the Lord, Eve." Tears now spilled down his cheeks, as well.

"How can I believe you?" Eve asked.

Eliza searched Lucas's stricken face. Had he expected Eve to simply take him at his word?

Lucas sighed. "All I can do is tell you and allow you to watch me and see if I've changed."

"How did you get money to follow me?" Eve asked suspiciously.

"I worked."

A very unladylike laugh tore from Eve's throat. "A gypsy work?"

"You married a gypsy?" Eliza heard the shock in her voice and then felt her cheeks go pink. She'd known Lucas had worked in a traveling show, but she'd had no idea that meant it was a gypsy show.

Eve nodded. "Kind of explains why Father and Mother weren't happy about my marriage, doesn't it?"

"I'll say," Eliza agreed. She could just imagine the looks on her parents' faces when they found out their daughter had eloped with a gypsy.

Peter entered the kitchen with a big wood box on his head. "Ma, help," he called.

Eliza hurried to the little boy and pulled the heavy box off.

He smiled up at her, while the kitten tried to claw its way up and over his shoulder. "Do you think this one is big enough?" Peter asked. His gaze moved to Lucas. "Who's that?"

"I'll introduce you later. Let's go take care of the kitten." She led Peter to the bedroom. As they went she prayed Eve and Lucas could work out their differences.

Her thoughts turned to Jackson. She wanted to be a real wife to him, too, but even as the thought entered her mind, Eliza shoved it back into the dark. It was wishful thinking, and she no longer allowed herself to wish for what she knew could never be.

After a week of rounding up the group of outlaws that called themselves the Society of Bandits, the Cottonwood Springs men were headed home. Jackson was bone-tired. His gaze moved over the ragtag group of men.

Seven of the Bandits were riding with their hands tied behind their backs. The Cottonwood Springs men were riding on all sides of them as guards. Sheriff James rode in the lead, and Jackson brought up the rear guard.

Hank fell back and rode beside him. "I imagine you are ready to get home to your lovely bride, aren't you?"

Jackson grinned across at him. "I'd say I'm looking forward to seeing Eliza about as much as you are Lilly."

"I don't know. Lilly wasn't happy with me when I left."

None of the ladies had been happy to see their husbands leaving. Jackson knew they were worried and he couldn't blame them. He'd been worried, too. "I'm sure she's forgiven you by now."

"True. Lilly doesn't hold a grudge long. But just to make her happy, I'm planning a trip tomorrow afternoon to Denver. She always enjoys going there." Hank grinned back at him.

Jackson didn't think Eliza held grudges, either. She'd only shown him kindness. The few times he'd angered her, she hadn't stayed angry. He thought about the kiss they'd shared after their first spat. She'd been sugar and spice.

And the kiss before he'd left had taken his breath away. As silly as that sounded, Jackson knew it was true. He'd thought about that kiss every night he'd been gone.

"From the look on your face, I'd say Eliza doesn't, either." Hank chuckled.

Jackson grinned. "No, she doesn't. I'm looking forward to getting home to her and Peter." Jackson liked the sound of home and of finding Eliza there to welcome him back.

"I better get back in formation since we're almost there." Hank touched his heels to his horse and moved back into his position beside the last prisoner.

Jackson hadn't enjoyed leaving Eliza and Peter, but thanks to the need to round up the outlaws, he'd made friends with the men of Cottonwood Springs.

A little while later, Jackson climbed out of the saddle. He brought up the rear as each prisoner was escorted into the small jailhouse. "They're going to be crowded in there, aren't they, Sheriff?"

"Can't be helped," Bob answered.

Since it was a two-cell jail, the sheriff put three in the first cell and four in the second one. "It's only for a few days, boys, and then we'll be sending them on up to Durango."

Jackson felt sure that knowledge was little comfort to the prisoners. He waited until the last cell was closed and locked and then walked out onto the sidewalk.

They all said their goodbyes. He watched the other

men leave and then turned to Bob, who stood in the doorway. "Isn't your wife waiting for you, too?"

"She is but I'm the only law here right now. Until the marshal comes back, I'll be staying put." He hung his hat on a nail beside the door.

Jackson wanted to go home, but something in the sheriff's eyes stopped him. "Why don't you go on home and tell her you're back? I can stay here with the prisoners for a few hours," Jackson offered.

Bob studied him for several long minutes. "Don't you have a new wife waiting at home for you?"

Jackson nodded. "I do."

"Then you should head on home. My wife is used to me being gone for days. In the morning when she hears we're back, she'll come to me." He turned around and walked back into the jailhouse. His spurs jiggled.

Jackson followed him. "You need a deputy."

The sheriff laughed. "You volunteering for the job, son?"

"Nope. Just thinking out loud." Jackson didn't want to leave the lawman alone. Over the past week, he'd gotten close to several of the men, but Jackson had discovered that he respected and liked Bob the most. He was fair to both the prisoners and the men who'd followed him to Glendale.

The sound of boots hitting the sidewalk outside alerted the two men that someone had arrived. They both turned toward the door. The sheriff had one hand on his gun.

"Afternoon, gentlemen." The Reverend Griffin stepped inside. "I'm here to relieve you."

Jackson offered, "Evening." And then waited to see

what the sheriff had to say about the reverend offering to watch the prisoners.

"Much obliged, Reverend. I'll be back by six. How's that sound?" Bob walked to the door and pulled his hat off the nail. "Coming, Jackson?"

Jackson looked at the smiling preacher. He knew without being told that if Bob trusted him to take over that the good reverend was up for the job, even if he did look too small to handle the men behind bars. "Yes, sir." He hurried after Bob.

When they were out of earshot of the jail, Jackson asked, "Do you think he can handle those men?"

Bob laughed. "With one hand behind his back. Our reverend is as tough as nails." He turned toward his street. "I'll see you tomorrow."

Jackson stood for a few moments watching him walk away. He was about to head in the direction of the smithy when the reverend called to him from the porch of the jailhouse.

"Tell your mother I said hello."

He looked over his shoulder to see who the preacher was talking to. Not seeing anyone, he turned back around and walked the short distance back to where the preacher stood. "My mother isn't here, reverend."

The preacher laughed. "Sure she is. I had a nice visit with her this afternoon."

Jackson's stomach dropped. His palms broke out in a sweat and his head began to ache.

Please, Lord, don't let her be here. She will ruin everything.

Chapter Twenty-Five

So this was what people meant when they talked about having a bad mother-in-law. Charlie's mother had been like a second mother to her, nothing like the woman who now stood before her. Eliza held her hands to her head and counted to twenty as the woman continued to rant.

"Why do you coddle that boy so much? Don't you know you are just ruining him?" Ida Hart pursed her lips as if she'd just eaten green persimmons.

Eliza didn't answer. After three days of constant complaining and criticism, she knew nothing she said would soften the older woman.

She picked up her sewing and studied Ida Hart, her mother-in-law. Blond hair with streaks of gray topped her head. Hard blue eyes that were a pale robin's egg color were magnified behind black spectacles. A long nose held them up. Thin lips were permanently pursed and full of venom.

Ida looked nothing like her son. To be honest, Eliza couldn't wait for Jackson to come home. Maybe it was all a mistake and Ida had the wrong Jackson Hart. It was ridiculous to think that such a thing was possible, but Eliza prayed it was so.

"Well?" Ida demanded.

Eliza took a deep breath. "Mrs. Hart, I don't see the point in answering your questions."

Ida dropped her own sewing into her lap. She glared at Eliza over her spectacles. "I can't imagine what my son sees in you."

That was it. The last straw of the evening. Eliza stood. She calmly laid her sewing back in the basket and turned to Ida. "I do believe I will be going to bed now. Excuse me."

As she left the room, Eliza heard Ida mutter, "It's simply rude to leave one's guest sitting up."

Eliza walked to the kitchen and poured herself a cold cup of tea. She carried it to her room and closed the door. Again she asked herself how Jackson could be that bitter woman's son. During the short time she'd known him, he'd not been rude or mean-spirited.

In the short time she'd been there, Ida had run off everyone who'd come to visit. Even Eve had quit coming around. Eliza walked to the window and looked out at the night sky. Eve and Lucas seemed to be trying to make their marriage work. It had taken Lucas almost three full nights and days of talking to convince Eve that he'd changed. He'd confessed he'd never been married before, that he'd been drunk and stupid. He'd been afraid Eve was beginning to hate him because of the drinking and made up the excuse of having another wife to give her a real reason to leave him.

Then Ida Hart had shown up on her doorstep. Her first complaint was that no one had arrived to pick her up in Durango when she'd stepped off the train. The second complaint was that she'd had to learn from a total stranger, Mrs. Hattie, that her son had moved to Cottonwood Springs, New Mexico. The third big complaint came when she'd learned upon arrival that he was married and planning to adopt a six-year-old boy. After that, she lost count of all her mother-in-law's complaints.

Even Peter avoided the older woman. He either stayed in his room or the barn playing with his kitten, Mrs. Whiskers. She smiled as she thought about the little spitfire. It had drawn blood with its sharp claws on more than one occasion. She looked down at her newly acquired scratch.

"Eliza! I need another blanket," Ida called from her room.

From where she stood, Eliza called back, "Look in the chest at the foot of your bed."

Eliza stared out into the night and prayed for patience.

"You could have come and got it for me," the woman complained. The sound of the trunk lid slamming down filled the silent house.

The tea tasted bitter and Eliza sat the cup on her side table. Next she pulled her dress off and slipped into a soft cotton nightgown. The fabric felt cool on her skin and she sighed.

Her head still ached. Eliza decided that if she let her hair down, her head would feel better. She worked the pins out and ran her fingers through the silky strands. Then she moved back to the window.

A man's shadow slid across the yard and under a tree. Eliza watched as the dark form inched toward the house. Her heart began to pound and unwanted thoughts of last year when Maxwell Evans had broken into her house through one of the bedroom windows, grasped her by the throat and cut off her air.

Just when she thought she'd scream, Jackson's whispering voice called out to her, "Eliza."

"Jackson?" she whispered back.

"Yes, let me in." He stepped from the shadows and into the lantern's light.

With trembling hands, Eliza unlocked the window and stood back as he crawled inside. His body had to double over as he worked his way through the opening. Once inside he pulled her close and gave her a hug. "I'm sorry if I scared you," he whispered over her head.

Eliza enjoyed the feel of his arms about her. She'd missed him more than she cared to confess. Easing back, she looked up into his handsome face. "What are you doing?"

"Sneaking in. Shhhh, I don't want her to hear us." Jackson's blue eyes darted to the door.

So he knew his mother was in the house. She didn't know whether to feel relieved or annoyed.

"Eliza! What are you doing in there?" Ida demanded from the other side of the door. "Did I hear you talking to someone?"

She jumped at the sound of Ida's sharp voice. Eliza stepped away from Jackson and started walking toward it.

Just as her hand touched the knob she heard Jackson whisper, "Don't let her in."

Eliza glanced over her shoulder and saw that he stood statue-still. His blue eyes resembled saucers. Was he afraid of his own mother?

Eliza's voice sounded shaky as she answered, "I'm

getting ready for bed, Mrs. Hart." She held her breath, praying Ida would go to her own room and leave them alone.

Ida made a rude noise before informing her, "You sound sick."

Eliza opened the door a crack. She peeked around the wood. "I'm fine. Please keep your voice down. I don't want to wake Peter."

Ida huffed and crossed her arms over her chest. "You scared me half to death and all you can think about is the boy?"

She'd not argue with the woman. "Yes. Good night, Mrs. Hart." Eliza shut the door and then leaned on it for support.

Jackson stood with wide eyes. His breathing seemed very rapid. Was he having a heart attack? Did he fear his mother that much? She locked her bedroom door and hurried to his side.

Jackson sat down on the windowsill and ran a shaky hand through his hair. He'd almost allowed himself to forget about his mother. It seemed no matter where he went she eventually hunted him down. His gaze moved to Eliza.

She stood beside him, studying his face. What did she see? The fear of a child? Or a cowardly man? He took her hand in his and proceeded to throw one leg over the windowsill.

"Where are we going?" she whispered.

Jackson continued and soon stood outside in the night air. He inhaled as much of it into his lungs as he could before answering. "We need to talk, away from here." Holding out his hand, he waited for her to join him.

Eliza looked out the window at him. Her eyes searched his. “Wait just a second.” She pulled back into the room.

He heard fabric shifting and within a couple of minutes she was back at the window, looking out at him. She’d changed into a simple day dress and a pair of slippers. Her hair hung about her shoulders. Coffee-colored eyes met his, and she smiled.

Jackson helped her over the windowsill and thanked the Lord that it was low to the ground. As soon as she stood beside him, he took her hand in his and hurried away from the house. He didn’t know where they were going but knew they had to get far enough away that they could talk freely. Away from his mother’s sharp ears and even sharper tongue.

Her hand felt soft, warm and small inside his. “Where are we going?” she asked again.

Jackson stopped and looked around. They were a good distance from the house now and standing under a large cottonwood tree. “I guess we can stop here,” he answered, still keeping his voice low.

She continued to hold on to his hand. Eliza looked up at him; questions filled her dark brown eyes. He’d missed her so much over the past few days and now that he was home, his mother would complicate things even further.

He broke the silence. “When did my mother arrive?”

“Three days ago.”

Jackson heard the tired sigh in her words. “I’m sorry. I know she can be a little overbearing.” That was the understatement of the year.

Eliza nodded. “Yes, and she is a little put out with you.”

It was his turn to sigh. "I'm sure she is."

They stood listening to the night sounds for several minutes. Crickets chirped and insects buzzed about them. A half-moon hung in the sky, giving them just enough light to see each other clearly.

"How is Peter?"

She smiled. "Good. He has been going to the diner every day and helping Mrs. Velarde. I'm not sure how helpful he's been, but she's paying him in cookies, which seems to give him added energy every night. Oh, and before I forget, he's named the kitten Mrs. Whiskers."

"I'm sure my mother loves that," Jackson groaned.

He was surprised to hear Eliza giggle. "I'm not sure your mother loves anything." As soon as the words were out of her mouth Eliza gasped and covered her mouth. Speaking through her fingers she added, "I'm sorry, Jackson, that was a most unChristian thing to say about your mother."

Jackson grinned. "Maybe so, but it's the truth." The woman didn't even love him. He led Eliza to the base of the tree and then sat down. She followed him down, still holding fast to his hand.

Once he was seated with his back to the trunk of the tree, Eliza leaned into his side and laid her head on his shoulder. "I still shouldn't have said it," she said.

He enjoyed her closeness. The scent of vanilla drifted up to him. "What are we going to do?" He rested his head on the top of her soft hair.

"I don't know. I'd cleaned up the spare room for you to use when you got home but then Mrs. Hart arrived and now she's staying in there."

So she'd given him the spare room? He'd hoped that

after that kiss they'd be sharing her room. But he should have known better. After all, theirs was a marriage of convenience. Jackson sighed again. "We'll think of something. I might have to sleep on the floor for a while in your room."

Eliza nodded. She looked up at him. "I also talked to Mr. Bickel at the bank. He's going to give us a loan. You need to go in tomorrow and sign some papers. Oh, and Mr. Woosey, Peter's teacher, says he is doing really well in school." Eliza's chatter told him she felt uncomfortable.

"Mr. Woosey? I thought we were going to wait until the fall to start Peter in school." He breathed in her soft vanilla scent, enjoying the feel of her pressed against his side.

Eliza nodded. She first rested her hand on his chest and then her head. "We did, but Mrs. Hart thought he should be in school now. I confess, most of the time I give her her own way. It's easier."

Jackson had to agree it was easier, but maybe now was the time to stand up to his mother. He was a grown man with a wife and son. Tomorrow morning he was going to move his mother's things into the room off of the smithy. That would give Eliza back the house, he could have the spare room and his mother would be out of the way.

Most of the time.

He could only imagine what kind of fit she was going to throw.

"What happened in Glendale?" Eliza asked, tilting her head and looking up at him.

Her soft lips were close enough to kiss. She moistened them with the tip of her tongue. Memories of other kisses flooded his mind and for just a moment he thought about claiming them once more.

But then he felt her shiver and she ducked her head again. Jackson moved his arm to encircle her shoulders and share his warmth. Disappointment filled him at the missed kiss. "We rounded them all up and no one was hurt. The sheriff knows his business. He had us working like a well-oiled machine, and those bandits didn't know what hit them."

"I'm glad." She snuggled closer still. "I feel bad for Mr. Hamilton."

Jackson shook his head. Would he ever get used to the way she changed subjects in midthought like a person changes shoes? "Why?"

"While you were gone Millie ran away. She left a note saying not to follow her. It said she is a married woman now and would write again once she was settled."

"How did she get married without them knowing it?" Jackson asked, confused at the way women seemed to approach marriage nowadays.

Eliza yawned. "Proxy. At least that's what she wrote. Mrs. Hamilton has been a bundle of nerves all week."

Jackson didn't know what to say about that, so he held his tongue. He'd add the Hamiltons to his morning prayer list.

He moved his back to sit more comfortably with her cradled against his side. A warm breeze drifted through the new leaves in the tree above their heads, creating a sort of lullaby. An owl hooted in the distance.

Jackson allowed himself to enjoy the peace of the evening. His gaze moved to the house. The light from Eliza's room shone through the window. He noticed another window's light flickered out and realized his mother must have blown out her lantern.

Eliza nuzzled her face into his chest. Sleep had claimed her. She whispered something in her sleep.

He stroked her hair and wondered if his mother would destroy the bond that was beginning to form between them. Jackson couldn't deny that he was falling in love with Eliza and hoped that maybe she was with him, too.

But one word from his mother and their newfound love would shatter like a mirror hitting a hardwood floor.

Chapter Twenty-Six

Eliza woke the next morning in her own bed. She stretched and yawned like she did every morning upon waking, but something was different. The scent of leather and earth teased her nostrils. Then she remembered Jackson was home.

She lifted her head and looked into Jackson's dark blue eyes.

Heat filled her cheeks as she recalled how he'd carried her back to the house and laid her gently on the bed. She'd thought she was dreaming and begged him to stay.

"Good morning," he whispered. He sat in the chair beside her bed. He, too, stretched and yawned.

Eliza heard the huskiness in her voice as she whispered back, "Good morning."

Jackson sat up straighter and ran his hands through his rumpled hair. Keeping his voice low he asked, "Eliza, who is Maxwell?"

She sat up and scooted against the headboard. Her hands went into her lap. Eliza realized she must have been talking in her sleep. "A bad memory."

He nodded. "From childhood?"

She tried to iron out the wrinkles in her dress with her hand. Eliza couldn't meet his gaze. What had she said that would prompt his interest? "No. Last year he was after Rebecca. While we were visiting at my house, Maxwell broke in."

Jackson stood and sat down on the edge of the bed. He took her hand in his larger, stronger one. "Did he hurt you?"

"It's not important." Eliza tried to pull her hand away. She wasn't sure she wanted to share the horrible memories.

He nodded. "I see. Too painful to share." Jackson released her hand. A hurt expression filled his eyes and she felt immediately bad.

Eliza sighed. "He slapped me around a bit."

Jackson nodded. "I can see why you still fear him."

She shook her head. "I don't fear Maxwell, Jackson."

He cocked his head to the side and studied her. "Then why do you dream about that night?"

"I don't know. He paid for his crimes by hanging. Maxwell can't hurt me or anyone else ever again." Her hand trembled. Why did she still dream of him? Eliza had no answer.

Jackson captured her hand in his once more. He rubbed his thumb in a circle in her palm. Tingling sensations traveled up her arm and into her hair. "You fear someone breaking in, and each time you dream it is Maxwell's face that comes through the window."

Eliza watched his thumb. She tried to focus on what he said and realized he was right. She'd thought those fears were gone but if she was talking in her sleep, they must still be there tormenting her. "How do you know that?"

"Because I've been hurt before, too, and fear is one of the reasons that until now I've stayed on the move."

Anger boiled at the thought of someone hurting Jackson. "Who are you running from?" she asked, turning her hand over in his.

"Myself, my mother, everyone."

"Eliza! Who's in there with you?" Ida demanded from the other side of the room. "If my son knew what kind of woman he married, you'd be out on the streets before I could utter—"

Jackson crossed the room and jerked open the door cutting off her words. "Mother," he growled.

She planted her hands on her hips and looked at him with reproach. "When did you sneak in?"

"We'll be out in a few moments, Mother." He shut the door in her face.

They heard her stomp her foot. "I'm getting dressed and when I come back you better be ready to answer some questions, young man."

Eliza wondered if Ida woke up each morning and took hateful pills. She scooted off the bed and moved to her armoire, opened it up and pulled out a peach-colored dress. What had he meant by "everyone"? She felt as if Ida had ruined the moment.

"I better go change and get back here as quick as possible." Jackson walked over to her and lifted her face to meet his. "Please, if she says something about me that you don't understand, let me be the one to explain it to you."

She nodded. "I will."

It didn't take a genius to know that Jackson and his mother had deep problems. What she couldn't understand was what made Ida so bitter and Jackson so fearful.

Jackson leaned down and brushed his lips across hers. He looked deeply into her eyes. Then he rested his forehead against hers and sighed. "I'd better go." He slipped out the window and ran across to his room.

Eliza touched her lips with trembling fingers. They tingled where his had been moments before. She glanced at the side of the bed and saw where he'd made a pallet. Eliza picked up his bedding and pillow. Without thinking, she pressed her face into his pillow and inhaled his scent.

Her emotions were high. It seemed over the past few weeks things had spiraled and she'd been caught in the downward spin. She wasn't sure what was going to happen from here but the one thing she was sure of was that Jackson had melted a part of her heart that she'd thought would be frozen forever.

If only she could give him the children she knew he'd want with time. But Eliza knew that dream would never come to pass. She felt moisture dampen her face as a lone tear eased past her troubled heart and onto her cheek.

Jackson took a deep breath and reentered the house. He felt as if his legs were weighted down with wrought iron. Before he left the smithy, he'd hung a sign on the blacksmith shop saying he was closed. But if an emergency came up he could be reached at the house.

He found his family in the kitchen. Eliza stood at the stove stirring fried potatoes, his mother sat at the table nurturing a hot cup of either tea or coffee and Peter played on the floor with the toy Eliza had gotten him in Glendale. A perfect picture to an outsider but to him it contained all the ingredients for disaster.

Peter saw him first and jumped up. The little boy wrapped his arms around Jackson's legs. "I missed you, Pa."

Jackson swung him in the air and said, "I missed you, too. I hear you've been working for Mrs. Velarde after school." He set a giggling Peter back onto the floor.

He puffed his little chest out. "Yep, she pays me in cookies."

Ida scoffed at the table. "Like that is any type of payment," she muttered just loud enough for them all to hear.

Peter looked up at him with big eyes. Jackson knelt down in front of him and said, "I'm proud of you, son."

Ida slapped the tabletop hard enough to jiggle her cup and saucer. Malice dripped from her tongue as she yelped, "Proud? What is there to be proud of?"

Peter's chin began to quiver. Jackson hugged him and whispered in his ear, "Everything."

"Now see here." Eliza turned from the stove and pointed a wooden spoon at Ida. "I'll not have you speak to my son like that."

Ida stood and faced Eliza with a snarl on her lips.

Jackson set Peter back down and took a deep breath. It was time to stand up to his mother, time to stand up for his new family. "Mother, that's enough." He heard the anger in his voice and for the first time allowed her to hear it, too. "This is my home, and you will respect my wife and son or you can leave."

She clutched her fists on her hips and glared at him. Her words were filled with contempt. "Really? You really think you can throw me out?"

Jackson looked at Eliza. Her face said it all. She was struggling with anger, disbelief and something more that he couldn't quiet decipher. "Eliza, would you take Peter to the diner and have breakfast? I need to talk to my mother."

Eliza took the skillet off the stove and laid the spoon down. Her brown gaze turned to their son and she offered the boy a sweet smile. She held out her hand to Peter. "Come on, Peter. Mrs. Velarde makes the best banana nut pancakes."

Peter ran to her and grabbed her hand. His frightened eyes looked between Jackson and Ida. "All right."

Eliza stopped in front of Jackson. She gave him a hug and when he bent down to return the embrace she whispered in his ear, "Be kind but be firm. Don't lower yourself to her level of behavior."

He pulled back and was surprised to see a sweet smile on her lips for him. This woman understood him without knowing what drove him and his mother to such behavior. Something he didn't fully understand himself. All Jackson could manage was a nod.

"Oh, please. I've been in this town long enough to know you two are not in love, so you can stop the act." Ida sat down in a chair and crossed her arms and legs.

Did it look as if they were in love? Jackson released Eliza and watched her lead Peter from the room. He took a deep breath and faced his mother.

When he heard the front door close, Jackson walked over to the table and sat down. "Mother, why are you here?"

She huffed. "I'm your mother. Do I need a reason to be here?" Ida picked up her cup and swirled the liquid around inside, much like she did his emotions.

He ran his hand through his hair. "Yes. All my life you have had a reason for everything you've done. I won't pretend to understand your reasoning, but I know you have one. So, what is it now?"

Ida raised her head and looked proudly down her nose at him. "I followed you because I care about you."

Jackson hardened his heart. He wanted to believe his mother loved him but past experiences told him it wasn't true. "Try again."

Her eyes regained their hardened glint. Ida's thin lips smiled, but no warmth entered her face. "All right, I came to tell you I am getting married."

Who would marry her? She was a bitter woman who treated everyone as if they were something that needed to be scraped from her shoes. Jackson didn't believe her.

She stood to her feet. "I know you don't believe me. I'll prove it." Ida set her cup down and stomped to her room.

Jackson stared out the window while he waited for her to return. Even if what she said was true, that really didn't explain why she'd taken the time to find him. His mother was up to something, but what?

Ida stalked back into the kitchen. She held a thick envelope in one hand and the other was closed into a fist. "Here." She thrust the envelope into his hands

Jackson frowned down at the envelope. "What is this?"

She dropped back into her chair. "Your inheritance."

Jackson felt a laugh build in his throat. They'd always been poor. Whatever was in the envelope couldn't be much of anything. He allowed the mocking laugh to burst from his throat.

"Open it," Ida ordered. She looked over the rim of

her cup and watched as he slid his finger under the flap and looked inside.

The mocking smile slipped from his face. Money filled it to the rim. Not small notes but large ones. "Where did this come from?" Jackson gasped.

"Your father left it." She snarled the word *father* as if it left a bad taste in her mouth.

Jackson studied her face. "But you told me Pa ran off and left us penniless."

"I know what I said, Jackson. I lied." She stared at him.

None of it made sense to Jackson. Why would she lie? What really happened? Had she lied to him all his life? He asked one question, the one that burned his tongue and summed it all up. "Why?"

"Because I hated you. I hated that your father loved you enough to leave money to take care of you. Did you know you look just like him? I wanted you to suffer like I suffered. Making you suffer almost felt like I was making him suffer, even if he didn't know it." Her eyes took on a crazed look. She continued to watch his every expression.

Was his mother truly crazy? He felt betrayed and confused. "You said he left because of me." His voice sounded as small as he felt.

"Oh, come on, you didn't really believe that." She searched his face and laughed harshly. "You did!" She shook her head. "I'm a better actress than I thought. He left because of me. The night he ran out on us he gave me that—" she pointed at the envelope "—and said, 'Make sure my boy is raised right.'"

Jackson looked down at the envelope. So his father had cared about him. "Why didn't you use this money when I was a kid? It would have made both our lives easier."

Ida sat down. Another harsh, bitter laugh tore from her throat. "He left money for our everyday lives, too, and even sent more from time to time." She pointed at the envelope he held. "But that money had your name on it."

She wasn't making any sense. Why would the woman not want to use the money to make her life easier, his, too? Confusion must have revealed itself upon his face because she continued. "Don't you understand? If I had used the money to make your life easier, he would have won."

Jackson decided his mother really was a little crazy. What she said, was saying, made no sense. How would making his life harder affect his father? The man never looked back. He had no idea what their lives were like.

Her voice rose to a near scream. "I wasn't going to touch the money. It's been sitting in the bank all these years."

He looked down at the money. "Why give it to me now?" he asked cautiously.

"I wasn't going to but—" she looked at her clenched hands, lying in her lap "—he said I should." She opened her hand and looked at the ring inside it.

Jackson watched as she slipped a small gold band with tiny diamonds imbedded in the gold on her finger. Her eyes took on a dreamy look for just a moment before she shielded them once more.

He tore his gaze away from her and focused on the apple orchard outside the window. Not really seeing it but trying to get his thoughts together. She'd said his father had sent money to them through the years. Each letter or wire would have had his location on it. She'd known all these years where his father was and hadn't told him. Even when she knew he'd left to find the man who'd sired him, she'd kept his true location a secret.

Jackson felt anger well up again. "Do you know where Pa is now?" he asked around a lump in his throat.

"Buried in California. I got the letter a few weeks ago."

There was no end to the cruelty of the woman before him. Did she realize what she had done and was still doing to him? Did she even care? He'd never know his father. Never really know if the man cared about him.

Joy filled her voice as she announced, "His death was the best news I've ever gotten."

Jackson's mind reeled. "How so?"

"I'm free to marry again." She continued to stare down at the ring on her finger. "All these years Jasper and I had to hide our love, and now we are free to announce it to the world." A smile tugged at her lips, and her eyes softened as she thought of the blacksmith from home.

Just to make sure, Jackson asked, "Jasper? The man who trained me?"

Ida nodded. "He was willing to train you so that you'd move on and be out of our lives forever. Why do you think he sent you off as a journeyman as quickly as he did? Whispered lies to you that your father was in this state and that state and then last summer hinted he was in Colorado. I'll tell you why. With you out of the house we were able to be together all these years."

A thought came to Jackson. He didn't want to believe it, but if his mother was confessing he needed to hear it all. "Mother, did Pa know about Jasper?"

Sorrow filled her eyes. "Yes, he shouldn't have come home early that day, but he did."

Jackson understood. His pa had caught his mother with the other man. "And that's when he left."

Silence hung between them. All these years he'd thought it was his fault his father had left. He'd been told by his mother that his size had caused her not to be able to bear any more children. She'd told him that birthing him had torn her up inside and because his father wanted more children he'd left. Now Jackson realized they'd all been lies told to a ten-year-old boy. None of the lies made sense; if his father had wanted more children he would have taken Jackson with him when he left. At least, that was the hope Jackson clung to now.

Ida stood. "Now that you know, I'm heading home. Jasper is waiting for me and we're getting married. It's been a long time since I've been truly happy."

Jackson studied her face. He didn't see a happy woman. The choices she'd made in life had shaped her and him. The wrinkles in her forehead and around her mouth were permanent markers of the frowns she'd worn over the years. He pulled his shoulders back and raised his head. From this day forward, he'd not allow her spiteful words to hurt him. For the first time in his life, he realized that her mistakes were not his fault.

She turned to leave the room. Jackson wouldn't let her go like this. He reached out and gently grabbed her arm.

Jackson pulled his mother to him and hugged her. "I hope you and Jasper have a long and happy life."

Tiredness seeped into his bones. The thought of putting up with her verbal abuse all the way to the train station left him feeling drained. Then he remembered

Hank had said he and his wife would be going to Durango.

"I'll go ask Mr. Browning and his wife if they will escort you back to Durango." He continued to hold her arm but reached for the money on the table. Jackson pulled out a large bill and tucked it into her hand. "Stay with Mrs. Hattie until your train arrives to take you home."

Ida tried to give him the money back. "I won't take that money—it's his."

He pressed it deeper into her palm. "No, it's mine. It was always mine, and I want to make sure my mother is safe until she gets home."

Ida looked up at him. Her eyes hardened. "You do realize I never want to see your face again, don't you?"

Her words cut like shattered pieces of glass into his chest. "Yes, but I love you. More importantly I love the Lord, and the Bible says to honor your mother and father. So, maybe after you are married and happy, you'll change your mind about seeing me." Jackson gave her another quick squeeze and then hurried to make arrangements for her to leave.

He just prayed Hank would forgive him for asking this favor. Ida Hart liked to make everyone miserable. Jackson prayed his friends would understand.

Jackson sighed. To be fair, he'd lay it all on the line with Hank and if he refused to take her to Durango, Jackson knew he'd drive her and see that she was on the next train home.

Regardless of what she'd said and done she was still his mother. He loved her and would continue to try to forgive her for the lies she'd told him that had shaped his life.

Chapter Twenty-Seven

Eliza smiled when she saw Jackson enter the diner. He looked deep in thought, and she wondered how it had gone with his mother. When his gaze connected with hers, he offered a small grin.

"Hi, Pa!" Peter looked around Jackson. "Where's Mrs. Hart?"

Jackson pulled out the chair beside Peter and across from her and ruffled the boy's hair. "She's on her way home."

She saw Peter's grin before he stuffed a large forkful of pancake into his mouth. Eliza felt the same way but wondered how Jackson felt about the situation. She found his piercing blue eyes searching her. "Are you all right?"

"Yes. For the first time in my life, I believe I am. My mother and I discussed a few things and she's a happy woman now." He reached across and captured her hand in his.

Eliza nodded. She wanted to know more but felt as if this wasn't the place to discuss what had happened between him and his mother. Also, she was having a hard time concentrating as he turned her hand over and traced the lines in her palm with his rough finger.

"I was thinking maybe we could go down to the fishing hole and spend the rest of the day by the river. What do you say to that?" he asked, raising his eyes and looking into hers.

"Really? I want to go!" Peter squirmed in his chair like a new puppy.

Jackson laughed. "Yes, really." He released Eliza's hand and hugged the boy around the shoulders. "I've missed my family and think we should have fun today."

"Can Mrs. Whiskers go, too?" Peter asked, excitedly.

"She sure can." Jackson answered before looking back to Eliza.

Eliza hated to spoil his good mood, but she did have a sewing shop to run and he had the smithy. "What about our businesses? I can't just close my shop."

Unhappiness laced Peter's face. Eliza hated disappointing the boy but she had a fitting with Charlotte Walker around ten that she couldn't miss. Now that she was a married woman again, Mrs. Walker had come in and ordered several dresses for both of them. Eliza was counting on that money to help with the rebuilding of her home.

"I'll put a note on the blacksmith saying I'm at the river with my family and if it's an emergency to come find me." Jackson grinned across at her as if that were the answer to all their problems.

Eliza grinned back at him. "Well, I have a fitting with Charlotte Walker this morning that I can't miss. So you and Peter go on without me."

Peter's face lit up. "All right!" He started to climb down from the table.

Jackson grabbed him by the back of the shirt and set him back in his chair. "Hold on, little man. Finish your milk while I talk to your ma."

"What about this afternoon? Can you sneak away for a little while?" Jackson's eyes pleaded with her to say yes. At least that's what Eliza told herself as she looked into their depths.

She grinned. "I suppose I could take a lunch break and come down for a little while. That way, I can pack you men a lunch and then get back to work later. I shouldn't miss too much business in that hour."

He nodded and picked up her hand again. "I would have liked to have had you with us all day but we'll take what we can get. Isn't that right, Peter?" He began rubbing small circles on the back of her hand.

Peter was busy trying to drink the whole glass of milk in one guzzle. He nodded his head and continued drinking.

"I'd better get back to the house. I'll be down there around noon. Are you going to your normal spot?" she asked, gently removing her hand from his and standing. Eliza could still feel the warmth of his finger in her hand.

"Yes. We'll be in close to the bend in the river by the largest cottonwood trees." A mischievous gleam was in his eyes, and Eliza wondered if he knew the effect his drawing on her hand had had.

Peter finished his milk and smiled up at her with a white mustache. "Bye, Ma. Can we go now, Pa?" The little boy had dismissed her as sure as any adult would have.

Eliza waved to them as she left the diner. The bell jingled as she stepped out onto the sidewalk. A quick glance at Charlie's watch told her it was closer to ten than she'd figured. Thankfully it didn't take long to return to the shop.

Charlotte stood on the porch. Her foot tapped as she waited with arms crossed. When Eliza got within speaking distance the young woman said, "I was about to leave."

"I'm sorry, Charlotte. Let's go inside. Would you like a cup of tea?" She tossed her pocketbook onto a nearby table and turned to face her young ward.

Charlotte laid her small bag down. "No, thanks. Ma wants me to hurry. She says Mr. Dillon from Durango is due today with supplies."

"Then let me grab the dress and we'll get started." Eliza hurried to her sewing machine and scooped up the finished garment. It was a golden color with little flecks of black throughout. The rich black would bring out the blues in Charlotte's eyes.

"Thank you." Charlotte took the dress and moved behind the new changing curtain that Eliza had put up shortly after returning from Glendale.

Eliza gathered her pins and pin cushion and pulled out a stool for Charlotte to stand on. "This is to be your dress for your birthday party, isn't it?"

Charlotte stepped out and the fabric flowed around her. "Yes, my birthday was a couple of weeks ago but since Ma wasn't giving you her business then, I had to wait on the dress."

If Charlotte realized how rude her statement had sounded, it didn't show on her face as she stepped up onto the stool. "I'm sorry about that," Eliza said as she pulled the fabric into place and prepared to pin up the hem. "Please stand a little taller, Charlotte, so I can get this edging just right."

Charlotte did as she was asked. "Me, too. I would have liked for Millie to have seen it before she left town."

Eliza stopped working. Something in the girl's voice alerted her that she had a double meaning behind her words or was about to tell her something she felt was important. "I was sad to hear Millie left like that. Why do you suppose she left?"

Charlotte sighed. "Just as I thought." She tsked and shook her head.

"What did you think?" Eliza asked, going back to her pinning. Maybe if she didn't act interested, Charlotte would stop beating around the bush.

Charlotte sighed dramatically. "That she didn't come and tell you that she burned your house down."

The moment he saw her Jackson knew Eliza had been crying. He laid down his cane fishing pole and walked up the slight incline to meet her. He took the basket she held tightly in her hands. "What's wrong?"

"Hi, Ma!" Peter called from the riverbank. He waved at her and then held up a string of fish.

She smiled and waved back. But Jackson could see her eyes weren't smiling. Something had upset her and he wanted to know what.

As if she sensed his growing frustration, Eliza answered him. "Let's get Peter's lunch and then I'll tell you."

Jackson nodded and walked with her to the base of the big cottonwood tree. He watched as she prepared their meal on a checkered quilt. She didn't meet his gaze and wasn't talking; both actions worried him.

"Peter, pull the lines out and come have some lunch," she called to the little boy.

"Aw, can't I eat and fish at the same time?" He looked from the river to her and back again.

Jackson cleared his throat. "Let the boy fish and we can talk. I've got something I want to tell you."

Eliza nodded and fixed a plate for Peter. He watched as she made a sandwich out of thick ham and cheese. She added dried apple slices to the side. "Do you mind taking it to him?"

"Be happy to." He took the plate from her and turned to take it to Peter.

"Thank you. Oh, and Jackson?" When he turned back to look at her, Eliza added, "Tell him if he eats all those apples, I'll give him a slice of cherry pie, too."

Jackson nodded. Fear and concern nipped at his heels as he hurried to give the boy his plate and then returned to her. She handed him a plate that matched Peter's, only she'd added potato salad and a pickle to his. "Thank you."

She waited until he was seated and then pulled a mason jar from the basket. Eliza handed it to him with a watery grin. He brushed her fingers with his as he took it. She leaned against the tree and closed her eyes.

"Aren't you going to eat?" he asked, setting his own plate to the side.

Eliza looked at him. "No, I'm not hungry. You go ahead."

"All right, and while I do that you tell me what has you out of sorts." He unscrewed the jar and took a sip. Rich black coffee coated his tongue.

"Do you remember me telling you that Millie Hamilton left town while you were gone?" She caught her bottom lip between her teeth and her eyes filled with tears.

He wanted to gather her in his arms and comfort her but had the feeling that wasn't what Eliza wanted at the moment. "Yes." He dreaded to hear that the girl was dead or worse.

Eliza filled her lungs with air and then blurted, "She left because of me."

His heart constricted in his chest at the sight of the tear that trickled down her cheek. It was all Jackson could do to make himself sit still and listen. "What makes you think that?"

"Charlotte told me this morning that Millie was the one who set my house on fire. Millie had been practicing smoking and her mother had almost caught her. She'd tossed the cigar away and it caught the house on fire. That girl was always trying to please her friends. She was so guilt ridden about it that she ran away from home. Charlotte says Millie's ma would have died from embarrassment if anyone knew about it so before she was found out, Millie left. Oh, Jackson! I'm the reason that girl up and married a stranger."

He couldn't take it any longer when she buried her face in her hands and her shoulders shook from her sobs. Jackson pushed up and hurried to her side. He sank down beside her and gathered Eliza onto his lap. "Shhhhh, it's not your fault. None of it is."

"I shouldn't have left her to take care of the house and shop," she wailed against his chest.

Jackson rubbed her back and said a silent prayer that the Lord would give him the right words to help her see she wasn't to blame for Millie's actions. She cried until his shirt was wet and then she cried some more. He was beginning to worry that Millie's leaving had been the last straw for Eliza. So much had happened in such a short time. Would she be able to pull out of this?

His gaze moved to Peter, who sat by the river playing with the kitten and eating his sandwich. Thankfully the little boy was absorbed in his lunch and the fishing poles. "Eliza?"

She sat up and wiped her red-rimmed eyes. "I'm sorry, Jackson." Eliza moved to scoot away from him, but he held her fast.

"You have nothing to be sorry for, Eliza. Please stay. I want to tell you something, too." He let her go enough to move from his lap. She sat next to him and looked out to where Peter fished.

"I'm sorry. I forgot. Please tell me." She offered another watery smile.

Jackson took a deep breath and then exhaled. "I've decided not to go to Silverton."

She pulled a handkerchief from her sleeve and blew her nose. "Why not?"

Was that hope he saw in her eyes? Jackson didn't allow himself to think about that. He pressed on. "My mother and her fiancé led me to believe my father was there. For years I've been chasing after my pa."

Eliza tilted her head sideways. "And she told you he's not there?"

Jackson nodded.

"So where is he and why were you chasing after him?" She frowned. "I'm confused. Maybe you should start at the beginning." Eliza picked up a dry apple slice and nibbled on the edges. She moved so that she faced him.

Never had he told anyone his story. Would she turn from him when she learned how much his mother hated him? How his father deserted him? He didn't know, but he knew it was time to reveal who he was to her.

"All my life my mother told me that my father left us because when I was born I was too big for her body and the doctor told her she'd never have any more children. She told me he wanted lots of children and that because of me she couldn't have any more." Alarm leaped in her eyes and she covered her mouth.

It looked as if she were going to speak but he stopped her with a raised hand. "When I was ten, Ma sent me to our local blacksmith, Jasper Morgan. He agreed to apprentice me. She was a bitter woman and never showed me the kind of love a mother should, so when Jasper showed kindness and taught me a trade, I felt blessed. Then one day, Jasper said I'd learned all there was to learn and that it was time I go journey myself out for a while. I told him I'd do that and search for my pa at the same time."

He looked up into the trees. The breeze had picked up and the leaves shook above him. Jackson looked to Eliza. It was as if she sensed he needed to continue. "Jasper told me he'd heard my pa was down Texas way. So I went there. No one had heard of him. So after about five years, I headed home. Once again Jasper told me someone had spotted my pa in Nebraska, and so it went. I'd go where he would say and at each place there had been no sign of him. Well, as you can guess the last time I was home, he said my pa was in Silverton, Colorado."

Eliza nodded. "So where did your mother say he was this time?"

"Buried in California. It seems she's known all along

where he was but never told me. And now she's marrying Jasper."

"Oh, Jackson, I am so sorry." Eliza reached forward and hugged him.

He allowed her to hold him and returned the hug. "I should have known that they were lying. I should have known Ma was having Jasper send me all over the country so they could be alone."

Eliza leaned back on her heels. "How could you have known? Your mother made her choices—you had nothing to do with that."

"No, and I have come to realize that she lied to me about a lot of things. My pa didn't leave because of me. He found out about Jasper and couldn't stand to be in the same town as them." He shook his head and wondered if Eliza would realize that she couldn't control what Millie did, either.

"So he didn't leave because she couldn't have any more children?" She began making him another sandwich.

"No, I think she made that up, too." Jackson wasn't sure why but he had the feeling that she had a second reason for asking.

Eliza looked at him. Disbelief filled her face. "But why would she do that?"

"She isn't quite right in the head, Eliza. I think my pa leaving like that and offering to take care of me was too much for her. Instead of taking the blame for what she'd done, she blamed me." Jackson realized that by talking it out with Eliza he was beginning to understand his mother a little better.

"That is so sad." Eliza shook her head. "You would

think she'd be thrilled that your father offered to take care of you."

Jackson nodded and took a bite of sandwich. He'd said more in the past half hour than he'd probably ever said at one time with her.

She chewed and stared down at the riverbank where Peter played. From the look in her eyes, her thoughts were miles away.

He turned his focus on Peter, too. The little boy had given up on fishing and was now skipping rocks across the water. Someday he'd have to explain that doing that so close to the poles scared the fish away, but for now he'd let the boy play and Eliza think.

After several long minutes, she sighed. "Thank you, Jackson. Like your mother, I guess Millie made her decisions, too. She didn't have to leave. She could have come and talked to me. I wouldn't have said anything to her mother or anyone else." Eliza looked into his eyes. "I'm sorry about your mother," she offered.

"Don't be. I'm glad she came and I learned the truth. Now I can move on with my life and so can she." He dusted the crumbs from his hands and stood. "I think I'll go check on Peter."

As he walked away, Jackson couldn't help but think that Eliza was holding something from him. Something important that could affect their future. But what?

Chapter Twenty-Eight

A few days later, Peter ran into the kitchen. Eliza smiled. "Ma, are you about ready?" he asked. His cheeks were red and his green eyes bright.

Eliza walked over to him and felt his face. It was cool to the touch. "Are you feeling all right?"

The little boy laughed. "Yeah. I've just been running bunches." He grabbed her hand and tugged. "Pa says I can help hold nails and stuff for the men while they work."

Satisfied the color was probably from the excitement of going to his first barn raising, Eliza allowed Peter to pull her toward the kitchen. The smells of cinnamon and spices filled the air. She'd been baking since before sunrise. He dropped her hand and took off for the back door.

"Peter, come here and help me carry the pies out to the wagon."

He stopped and looked over his shoulder at her. "But, Ma. I want to go get Mrs. Whiskers. She'll like going to the barn raising, too."

"No, sir, that cat is staying in our barn. You don't

want her to get lost today do you?" She held out a warm peach pie for him to take.

"No, I guess not." He took the pie and sighed. Eliza picked up the picnic basket, which held a platter of fried chicken, a bowl of mashed potatoes and two jars of green beans.

"I've never been to a barn raising. Have you?" Peter asked, holding the pie and inhaling its fragrance.

"Yes, I have. They are a lot of fun, but you will be working, so be mindful of what is going on around you. I don't want my favorite little boy to get hurt."

Peter smiled. "I will. I'm going to be a good helper to Pa."

Jackson entered from the hallway. "You two about ready?"

"I think we have everything," Eliza answered while Peter nodded.

"Good. Lead the way, Peter." Jackson motioned for Eliza to follow Peter ahead of him.

The boy held the door while balancing the pie. He stared out the front of the house with a quizzical look on his face. "Where's the wagon?" he asked.

Eliza wondered the same thing as she joined him on the porch.

Jackson closed the door behind them. "I figure we can walk." He took the pie from Peter and grabbed Eliza's free hand with the other.

They started walking down the sidewalk toward town with Peter following behind. The sun peeked over the mountain and the crisp morning air filled her lungs as she walked.

Why were they walking? She looked at him with a frown. His eyes sparkled as if he were up to something.

They rounded the corner and she was shocked to see so many wagons along Main Street. Granted, town was normally busy on Saturdays but this Saturday was designated for the Vaughans' barn raising. Everyone should have been on their way out to the farm, not still in town.

Jackson stopped and turned to face her. His beautiful blue eyes smiled down at her.

"What's going on?" Eliza asked, searching Jackson's face.

He grinned at her. "Well, plans changed. I talked to a few of the men and we've decided to have a house raising in town today."

Peter groaned and kicked at a stone. "I wanted to raise a barn, not an old house."

Jackson laughed. "What if I told you it's our house we're raising?"

"I guess that's all right," Peter answered grudgingly. He saw his friend George and asked, "Can I go play?"

Jackson nodded and then turned his attention back to Eliza. She realized he'd planned this as a surprise for her. Would the man never cease to amaze her? Eliza's breath caught in her throat. "Our house?"

"Yep, complete with a sewing shop in the front and a home in the back." Jackson leaned his forehead against hers. "Surprise." He grinned.

The scent of leather, coffee and earth filled her nostrils. Is this why he'd been so quiet? How long had he been planning it? She had so many questions but didn't know where to start with them. Befuddled, Eliza admitted, "I don't know what to say."

"How about, I would like to see the plans," he teased.

With him this close, Eliza longed for a kiss more than she wanted to see the plans. She tilted her head back and brushed his lips with her own. When he didn't pull away she felt heat enter her cheeks at her bold behavior. "Thank you for thinking of this." Her voice came out a whisper.

A smile tugged his lips upward. "You're welcome." He gave her a quick hug and then stepped away.

Eliza took a deep breath. "I'm ready to see the plans now."

Jackson touched her cheek and led her to the group of men and women who waited for them. He listened as she thanked them all for coming. His lips still tingled where she'd brushed them with hers. Had gratitude been the only reason she'd kissed him or did she really care for him?

His thoughts had been on their relationship day and night since his mother's departure. Jackson knew Eliza to be a strong Christian woman and he knew deep in his heart and mind that she'd never betray him like his mother had betrayed his father.

He'd spent the past week reading his Bible and praying. There were so many things he didn't understand. How could a mother not love her son? Why would you lie to a child and scar him with your words? He'd asked God these questions and still didn't have the answers. But what he did have was the assurance that his marriage to Eliza hadn't been an accident. He hadn't been an accident.

During those times in the Word, God's love had covered the hurt and scars. Jackson felt like a new man. A man who could conquer the world with Eliza by his side.

"Oh, Jackson, you did a wonderful job on the plans.

I love that the shop is separate from the house." Eliza smiled up at him. Her coffee-colored eyes sparkled.

"I'm glad. Now go help the women and let us menfolk get to the building," he teased.

The men chuckled.

Jackson squeezed her free hand before releasing it and then handed her the peach pie. He watched her walk away, then turned to the work at hand, even though he would have enjoyed nothing more than spending the day with her.

At noon, they stopped and everyone filled their plates with all the goodies the women had cooked up. Jackson looked for Eliza and Peter. He found them both sitting on a blanket in the shade of the drugstore.

As he sat down beside them, Eliza said, "It's going up nicely. I can't believe how much you men have done already."

Jackson smiled and allowed his gaze to move over the building. The outside walls were up and the windows and doors were being built and would soon be in place. "It sure is. It helps that we have over sixty men working on it."

Peter grabbed a chicken leg and said around a mouthful, "I helped, huh, Pa?"

Jackson reached over and mussed the boy's hair. "You sure did."

"Now that the walls are up, is it all right if I play with George this afternoon?" Peter asked, tossing the chicken bone on his plate.

"I don't see why not. You worked hard this morning," Eliza said, handing him a napkin.

Jackson smiled at his family. He couldn't wait until the house was finished and they could move in. His stomach growled, reminding him to eat. "Just be sure to stay away from the work site since you aren't helping," he warned Peter.

The little boy grinned mischievously as Eliza pushed a slice of pie in his direction. "Oh, we will. George and I have plans this afternoon. We won't be bothering you all."

He noticed Eliza looking at the boy with a frown. "What kind of plans?" Suspicion dripped from her voice.

"We're going to play treasure hunt," Peter whispered.

Jackson wondered how one played treasure hunt but didn't give it another thought as people began to cheer. He stood up to see what all the noise was about and was glad to see Seth Billings riding his horse into town.

Rebecca jumped up to greet her husband. She picked up her skirts and ran to where he'd pulled his horse to a stop and jumped down. Seth grabbed his wife and swung her around. He kissed her soundly to more cheers from the townspeople.

Jackson turned to see Eliza's reaction. A big smile graced her face and her brown eyes looked up at him longingly. Did she want that kind of relationship, too, or was it just wishful thinking on his part?

He finished his lunch and hurried back to work. It was better not to dwell on those things just yet. He'd known for a while that he loved Eliza and up until now had only hoped she returned those feelings.

His job this afternoon was to nail the boards together and hand them off to Hank, who made sure they went to the next person. He heard a soft laugh and looked to where Eliza sat sewing with a small group of women.

Red-hot pain sliced through his thumb as he hit it with the hammer. He yelped and stuck the digit in his mouth.

Deeper laughter came from beside him. Hank slapped him on the back. "You might want to focus more on your work and less on the ladies, if you get my drift."

Jackson scowled at him. It was none of his business if he wanted to stare at Eliza. Hank looked in the direction of the ladies; Jackson followed his gaze and found Eliza looking at him. Concern filled her eyes.

He held up his throbbing thumb for her to see. Seemingly satisfied he wasn't seriously injured she went back to her sewing and her visiting.

Another howl of pain filled the air and Jackson looked to see young Benjamin Cooper sucking his thumb and grinning at Selena Martinez. "It appears you aren't the only one that isn't focused today." Hank chuckled before walking away to get more boards.

Jackson spent the rest of the afternoon hammering and building inner walls. He smiled his approval each time he passed a working man. His jaws were starting to ache from holding the grin in place.

As dusk began to settle over the small town of Cottonwood Springs, Jackson called a halt to the work. He thanked each man for coming out to help and the women for cooking up such fine dishes. Many of the men promised to come back the following Saturday and finish up the house.

He watched as families got into their wagons and headed home. His gaze moved about as he searched for Eliza and Peter. The women had cleaned up the many makeshift tables and stored away all the food.

Jackson spotted Eliza's basket sitting next to the side of the house.

Where was she? His heart hammered in his chest as he saw Julia and Richard Harper looking around also. Anna stood off to the side, wringing her young hands, and baby Holly clung to her mama's neck.

Richard advanced on him like a wild boar. "Have you seen our boys?"

Jackson took pleasure at the way Richard had acknowledged Peter as his son. The pleasure quickly drained away as he saw the worry in Julia's eyes. "No. Last I saw of Peter he'd mentioned the boys were going on a treasure hunt."

Richard frowned. "Treasure hunt? What kind of treasure hunt?"

Anna stepped forward. "Pa?"

"Not now, Anna."

Fear laced Anna's young voice as she tried again. "But, Pa. I might know where the boys are."

Richard spun around to look at his daughter. "Well, why didn't you say so sooner? Are you hiding something?" he demanded.

Julia placed a hand on her husband's arm. "That's not important now, dear." She bent down and smiled at Anna. "Honey, where do you think they went?"

"I wasn't hiding anything from you, Pa. I told Mrs. Hart about an hour ago when she asked me where they were playing." Anna's lips trembled.

Jackson's heart sunk. They'd been gone over an hour? "Where are they playing, Anna?"

Anna shrugged. "I'm not really sure. I overheard Peter telling George that he knew where some pretty rocks were and that they should go find them." She quickly added, "Mrs. Hart seemed to know where they were because she said, 'Oh, no' and took off running when I told her."

Jackson's pulse began ragging. Sweat broke out on his back and face. *Oh, Lord, please don't let them be where I think they are.*

Chapter Twenty-Nine

Eliza's side hurt. She'd run most of the way to the hill where she and Jackson had gotten married. Jackson's horse was tied to a tree not far from where they'd said their vows. Her heart pounded in her head.

She knew without being told that Peter had ridden it there. As soon as Anna had told her the boys were looking for pretty stones she'd known where Peter was going.

Why hadn't she warned him not to come here? Jackson had said it was dangerous inside the cave. Peter had asked her several times for the white rock that hung in her bedroom window. She should have realized he might come looking for one of his own.

Catching her breath, Eliza began to climb the side of the small hill. She pulled her skirts up so that she wouldn't trip on them. When she got to the top, her breathing felt shallow and painful.

Her gaze scanned the grass-covered wall for the opening. It was almost concealed by a large shrub bush. Eliza hurried to the gap in the rocks and yelled inside, "Peter! George!"

Neither answered.

The thought that she should go find Jackson and George's father nicked at her brain but she chose to ignore it. One or both of the boys could be hurt and time might be running out.

Eliza squeezed through the opening. Her dress caught on a sharp rock and she jerked it free. The sound of tearing material reached her ears but she ignored it. Sunshine shone through the cracks in the walls of the hillside, providing just enough light for her to inch down the narrow pathway. "Peter!" she called again.

A whisper of sound met her call. She thought the words she heard were "down here." It sounded as if the words had come from her left.

Pressing her back against the wall, Eliza continued on into the ever-growing darkness. It seemed to open into a cave of sorts. She saw another opening and slid inside. "Peter!"

"Ma! Down here."

This time his voice was louder and closer. Eliza pressed on in the dusky light. "I'm coming!" She had no idea where the path was leading her but the incline said down, and Peter had yelled he was "down here."

His voice came even louder now. "Hurry, George is hurt!"

Fear crept into Eliza's hairline. She did as Peter said and quickened her pace. Just as darkness seemed to suddenly enclose her she felt her shoes slipping in something wet. Her feet flew out from under her and she began to slide. A scream tore from her throat.

Eliza grabbed for the wall as she continued to slide down. Sharp rocks cut into her fingers and palm. Then she felt her body go airborne.

Oh, Lord!

The air whooshed from her body as she landed. Tears stung her eyes as pain shot up her back and down her right leg. Light filled the cavern she'd landed in. Eliza pulled herself up into a sitting position and called, "Peter!"

"I'm here, Ma." His small arms wrapped around her and held on tight.

Eliza hugged him back even as white-hot pain shot through her body. "Where's George?"

"Over here. I pulled him to the side so he wouldn't be in the way if you fell, too." Peter pointed to the right side of the cavern.

Eliza tried to stand but her ankle twisted and she fell back to the ground. A gasp of pain ripped from her throat. Blackness threatened to cloud in behind her eyes. Eliza fought to stay conscious.

Peter let out a cry and clung to her. "I'm sorry. Pa told me not to come here. I should have listened."

She patted his arm. "It's all right, Peter. I think my ankle is just sprained. Let me go so I can check on George."

He released her and said, "He bumped his head when we fell down here. I can't get him to wake up."

Eliza pulled her body over to the little boy's limp form. Each movement sent a new wave of pain and nausea. She pressed her back against the wall and then ran her hands though George's fine hair. A lump the size of a goose egg met her touch.

"Peter, did George just fall asleep or was he already asleep when you landed?" Panic filled her. She put her hand on George's chest and felt the gentle rise and fall of his steady breathing.

Peter crouched down beside his friend. "He landed and went right to sleep. I don't think he even knows he's hurt."

Eliza thanked the Lord she hadn't hit her head, as well. She needed to be able to think straight, to figure out a way to get all three of them out safely.

Her gaze moved upward and she gasped. Large rocks that looked like icicles hung above her head. Their sharp tips pointed at the ground, at them. On the floor and walls were clumps of smaller white rocks.

"Try not to touch the rocks on the wall. Some of them are real sharp," Peter said, holding up a hand that had several small cuts.

She remembered her own fingers and palm being cut as she'd fallen. Eliza looked down at her right hand and saw that she was bleeding from several deep cuts. "Peter, tear the hem of my skirt so I can wrap it around my hand and stop the bleeding."

Peter picked up a stone and used its sharp edge as a knife. He sliced into her skirt and then ripped off a big piece. "Is this big enough?" he asked.

"Yes, thank you."

She held out her hand and the little boy lovingly wrapped the fabric around her palm. He tucked it in and leaned back. "I'm sorry, Ma."

"I know you are. Don't worry. Jackson will come for us." Eliza closed her eyes against the pain and worry.

Lord, please let Jackson know where to find us and, Father, I ask that You keep him safe when he gets here.

Jackson tried not to panic. He looked at Anna. "Can you go to my house and get the horse back for me?"

The girl looked to her father, who nodded his consent and then turned to Jackson and demanded, "What are you thinking?"

"That they've gone to the cavern I found a few weeks ago."

Julia gasped. "The boys have been talking about that place for weeks." She covered her mouth. Terror filled her eyes as she looked at them.

Richard grunted. "I'm going with you." He turned to Julia. "You take the girls and go home."

Jackson interrupted, "Maybe she and the girls could go to our house and wait for us. You're going to need one of your horses."

"In that case, I'll take the team over to your place and leave the wagon there." Richard nodded.

Anna came running to them. "Your horse isn't there, Mr. Hart."

He realized that either Eliza or Peter must have taken it. "Mind if I use one of yours?" he asked Richard.

"No, but I think we should hurry." Richard climbed aboard the wagon and took off for the house.

Julia began to follow him on foot. Jackson stopped her. "I'm going to run over to the Millers' and get a rope and a couple of lanterns. You and the girls make yourself at home."

Julia said as she clutched little Holly to her side, "Bring our boys home safe."

His gaze grabbed and held hers. "I'll do my best."

She nodded and then hurried after her husband.

An hour later, Jackson and Richard arrived at the hillside. Jackson's horse neighed in greeting. "That's my horse. They're here." He jumped from his borrowed horse. Jackson hung the coil of rope across his shoulders and balanced the lantern he carried as he ran up the hillside.

Lord, please let them be safe.

The prayer became his mantra as they raced against time to get up the hill. “The opening is up here,” he called down to Richard, who had tied up their horses and now hurried after him.

When Richard stood beside him, Jackson explained where they were going. “I’m praying they took the right tunnel and not the left but I’ll be honest, I’m pretty sure they took the left, and if so, we’re going to have to be very careful.” He tied a rope around his waist and then handed the other end to Richard. “Tie that around your waist. There are wet spots along the path, if one of us slips and starts to fall, maybe the other can stop him.”

A grim-faced Richard did as asked, then nodded. “You lead the way.”

They lit the lanterns and then started into the caves. Just inside, he saw a scrap of blue material with little white dots. Eliza’s dress. Jackson prayed for safety as they went. He chose the left tunnel first, praying his instincts were wrong. “There’s water here, so watch your step.”

“What’s that?” Richard asked, shining his light on the right side of the wall. Blood smears coated the sharp rocks.

“Blood, try not to touch the sides of the walls. Some of these rocks are razor sharp.”

“We should have worn gloves,” Richard stated.

Jackson acknowledged the comment and pressed on. He came to the edge of a drop off and called out, “Eliza, Peter, George!”

Eliza's frantic voice called back, "Jackson be careful! There's a drop-off!"

A relieved smile tugged at his lips. "I know. I'm standing on the edge of it. Is everyone all right?"

"My ankle is sprained and George has a knot on his head," she answered.

"Is George hurt bad?" Richard called down.

Eliza answered, "I don't know. He's unconscious. We need to get him to the doctor."

Jackson turned to Richard. Richard's face was pale and his hands shook. He prayed Richard would get a hold of himself. "You are smaller than me. Take the rope and tie one end around your waist."

While Richard did as he was told, Jackson called back over the ledge, "Peter, are you hurt?"

The boy answered in a scared voice, "No, sir."

Jackson silently thanked the Lord. He turned back to Richard. "I'm going to lower you down first. Tie Peter to the rope and I'll haul him up. Then Eliza and lastly George."

"Why does my family come last?" Richard demanded, new fire lighting his eyes.

Jackson understood the fear the other man was feeling, so he ignored the anger. "George is unconscious. Peter is too small to hold him while I pull them up. Eliza is hurt and can't hold him, so it is up to you to carry your son out of that cave."

"You're right. I'm sorry." Richard bowed his head.

Jackson clasped a large hand on his shoulder. "No need to be sorry. I understand how you feel. We're going to get him to the doctor."

Soon Jackson had his family back, and together they

had hauled up Richard and George. "Peter, you take the lantern and lead us out of here."

The boy had been unusually quiet but nodded his head and took the lantern. "Richard, you and George next. I'll help Eliza and we'll bring up the rear." If any of them should slip and fall he'd be there to catch them. For the first time in his life, Jackson was thankful for his large build.

Eliza held on to his waist with her left hand and hobbled along beside him. Her pale face and clenched teeth spoke of the intense pain she felt in her ankle. But not one word of protest came from her lips.

Once out of the caves, Jackson placed a hand on Peter's small shoulder. "Go to Doc's place and ask him to meet us at our house. Tell him he has two patients. One with a head injury and the other with a sprained or broken ankle. Can you do that, son?"

Peter rubbed his toe in the dirt. "Yes, sir."

"Good. Hurry."

Peter took off like a shot. He climbed aboard Jackson's horse and was out of sight before the others could mount up. Jackson stood Eliza next to a tree and then held on to George while Richard got on his horse. He handed the limp little boy up to his father, then Jackson went to his borrowed mare. His gaze moved to Eliza. What would be the best method for getting her on the horse?

As if she read his mind, Eliza offered him a weak smile. "Just set me in the saddle. I'll hang on. I promise."

She felt lighter than his anvil as he picked her up and placed her on the horse's back. He heard her intake of breath and knew the move had been painful for her.

Jackson looked into her pale face. His heart ached for the pain she felt.

He swung up behind her and tried to avoid touching the injured ankle. Turning the horse toward town, he saw Richard still waiting for them. George slumped in front of his father.

"Get him to town, Richard. We'll be right along."

Richard didn't have to be told twice. He whipped his horse into action. Within a couple of minutes they were out of sight.

Eliza leaned against Jackson. He tugged her close and whispered into her ear, "Eliza, I love you more than words can say."

She heard his rapid heartbeat in her ears as he whispered words of love and encouragement to her. Tears filled her eyes. She loved him, too, but couldn't saddle him with a barren woman. Someday he would want children. Once he learned she couldn't give him the children he desired, would she love him enough that, should he ask, she'd release him from their marriage of convenience?

In a louder voice Jackson repeated, "Eliza, do you understand that I love you? I've known for a long time, but today when I thought I'd lost you, I realized I never want to be without you."

She didn't know what to say. Eliza held her breath and closed her eyes. To say she didn't love him, too, would be a lie, and she'd vowed never to lie to him.

"Don't you love me, too?"

She heard the hurt in his voice. "I do," she replied.

"Then why can't you tell me so?" he asked, hugging her closer still.

It was time to tell him the truth. Her heart ached almost as painfully as her ankle. Tears streamed down her face. Thankfully she saw the lights of town and knew she'd gained a reprieve from telling him the whole story, even it only for a few hours. She answered him truthfully, "Because, I know what you will want besides my love and I can't give that to you." A sob tore from her throat and she buried her face in his chest and wept for the love she felt sure she'd soon lose.

Chapter Thirty

The next morning, Eliza awoke in her bed feeling miserable. A lot had happened during the past few hours. The doctor had wrapped her ankle and given her medication for the pain. He'd said George had a concussion and would need to be monitored for several days. Jackson had offered the Harper family their house until George was able to return home. Julia had agreed, saying she could help Eliza with Peter and the chores. It all seemed like a dream.

She noticed that Jackson's shirt hung on the back of a chair and a pair of his boots set beside the bed. Since the pain medication had put her to sleep, Eliza could only assume Jackson had moved his things back into her bedroom the previous night.

Her bedroom door cracked open and Peter looked inside. "Are you awake, Ma?"

Eliza smiled. "Yes, I'm awake."

He walked into the room and shut the door behind him. "Does your ankle hurt much?"

She patted the mattress beside her. "Not too bad. Come sit beside me."

Peter did as she asked. His eyes shimmered in unshed tears. "I'm real sorry you got hurt."

"I know you are. It's all right, Peter, I'm going to be fine." She picked up his small hand and held it tight.

"Pa said that, too."

"He did?"

Peter nodded, looking down at their hands.

"What else did he say?"

"Just that he loves me and that I'm never to go out to the stone caves again." His bottom lip began to tremble.

Concern filled Eliza. The little boy was very upset. "Did he punish you?"

"No. My other pa would have whomped me good. Then he would have told me that the whompin' hurt him more than me because he loved me so much." Peter looked into Eliza's face. "Why didn't Jackson whomp me good?"

She offered him a soft smile. "I don't know, but don't worry. I'm sure he loves you and is trying to think of a good punishment."

Peter's face brightened. "You really think so?"

Eliza nodded. "I'm sure of it."

He sat quietly for a few moments. "Do you think he'll make me get rid of Mrs. Whiskers?" The tears returned to his eyes. "My other pa made me get rid of our puppy because he caught me playing in the henhouse."

Her heart went out to her son. "No, I don't think that will be your punishment." She lowered her voice and whispered as if her next words were a big secret. "I think Jackson likes your kitten as much as you do."

Peter giggled.

They sat in comfortable silence. Peter began to look worried again and Eliza felt sure he was thinking about and beginning to dread whatever punishment Jackson thought up. She'd have to remember to mention it to Jackson.

Her stomach growled and Peter smiled. "Are you hungry, Ma?"

"I am and a little thirsty, too."

Peter jumped from the bed. "I'll go tell Mrs. Harper." He ran from the room.

A few minutes later, Jackson arrived carrying a tray. "Peter says you're awake and want to eat." He smiled at her as he set the tray on the bedside table.

Eliza pushed herself up until her head rested against the headboard. "I thought Julia would bring me breakfast, or is it lunchtime?" Her words came out harsher than she'd intended.

He frowned. "It's still breakfast. She's feeding George so you got me instead."

She offered him a smile. He handed her a bowl of warm oatmeal. "Can you handle that?"

"I believe so." She took the bowl and spoon and began to eat. The oatmeal had maple syrup in it, and she savored each bite.

Jackson closed the bedroom door and pulled the chair up beside the bed. "I've been doing some thinking about what you said yesterday. I'd like to discuss it with you, if you don't mind."

She'd known he'd want answers. Eliza had just hoped he'd wait until she felt better. But truthfully, she wasn't sure she'd ever feel better about this. So she nodded her consent.

He sat down. "Explain to me what you meant yesterday. What will I want that you can't give me?" He placed his elbows on his knees and leaned forward.

Eliza swirled her spoon in the gooey cereal. "Charlie and I were married for three years. After two, we began to wonder why we didn't have children so, I went to the doctor. He deemed me healthy but said that I probably couldn't have children. I know someday you are going to want more children, Jackson. And I can't have them."

"I see." He folded his hands between his knees. A frown drew his brows together. Confusion filled his deep stormy eyes.

"No, you don't. I've seen the way you look at Peter. You want children. I can't give them to you. So if we keep our marriage—" she paused searching for the right words "—a marriage of convenience, then when you are tired of me and want a real wife who can give you children, we won't have bonded in that special, intimate way. And you will be free to go." She'd spoken so fast, Eliza felt as if she'd run two miles. She sucked air into her lungs and waited to see what his reaction would be.

Jackson stood and walked to the window. He played with the white stone and watched the miniature rainbows dance about the room. Did he want children that badly? Bad enough to never have a true marriage with Eliza? To never hold her? Truth be told, he'd never thought about having children of his own.

He walked back to where she lay. Her face was pale. Dark brown hair rested on her shoulders and her beautiful eyes were filled with sorrow.

Instead of sitting on the chair, Jackson sat on the edge of her bed. He was careful not to move her leg. "Yesterday, when I thought I would lose you, I didn't want to live any longer myself. You have become my everything. Up until I met you, my life was lonely and boring."

She started to speak and he stopped her by holding up a hand. "Let me finish." At her nod he continued. "Then you came along and it hasn't been boring since. I'm no longer lonely. Because of you, I am now a part of a real family."

"But, Jackson, I can't have children. Someday you are going to want them and then what?"

He took the bowl from her hands and set it on the table. "We have Peter and if we want more children there are orphanages full of them."

A tear slipped down her cheek. "But they won't be blood of your blood or flesh of your flesh."

"No, but I will still love them. Peter wasn't born to us, either, but I love him just the same. My heart ached at the thought that I might have lost him yesterday." He reached forward and wiped the tears from her face.

She shook her head. "No. Charlie said it didn't bother him, either, but I saw the longing in his eyes."

Jackson gently took her face in his hands. "I'm not Charlie. I love you, Eliza. If God sees fit to grant us children, so be it. But if He doesn't, I am content to be a husband to you and a father to Peter."

"Do you mean that?" Her eyes searched his face. She reached up and touched the cleft in his chin. Her palm cupped his jaw as her eyes looked deeply into his.

He could tell she wanted to believe him. Jackson leaned forward and kissed her. As he pressed his lips against hers, he silently prayed that God would let her feel the love he felt for her. That God would convince her that he was speaking from the heart. Jackson felt her arms snake around his neck. Her fingers curled into the hair at the nape of his neck.

When they pulled apart, he leaned his forehead against hers and said, "I love you, Eliza Kelly Hart. With or without children, you are my life. Please say we can be a real family."

Eliza moved her head back and looked deeply into his eyes once more. He prayed she could see his unwavering love there. She pulled his face to hers and gently kissed his lips again. When she broke the kiss, Eliza sighed. "Yes, I'm ready to be a real wife and make this a real family. I love you, Jackson Hart. I think I always have."

Epilogue

"Are you sure? I mean, I never thought, well at one time I thought. But not now. Are you sure?" Eliza looked at Dr. Clark. "I've been sick with this stomach flu for a couple of weeks. Are you sure it's not the stomach flu?"

He shook his head as he walked to the washbasin. "Most women don't question me, Mrs. Hart. I've been a doctor for over thirty years and I've never been wrong in this case."

"Never? But the other doctor, he said…" Eliza felt the words close in her throat. Why was she arguing with him? This was an answered prayer.

After washing and drying his hands off, Dr. Clark walked back to her. "Never. Whatever that other doctor told you might have been true at the time. But I'm positive you will be having a baby in six short months. All the signs are there."

She just couldn't believe that she was going to have a baby. Eliza found herself protesting again. "But the other doctor, he told me that since I'd not gotten in the family way after two years of trying that I probably never would."

Doctor Clark sat down on a stool in front of her. He took her cold hands between his much warmer ones. "That was with your first husband, right?"

Eliza nodded. Could it be true? Did she dare believe that she and Jackson were going to have a baby? Fear of being that happy crushed any hopes she might have.

He gave her hands a gentle squeeze. "And he laid the blame at your feet, didn't he?"

Again Eliza nodded as tears filled her eyes. She remembered the day like it was yesterday. The coldness in the other doctor's voice, the disappointed look in Charlie's eyes. The words echoed in her memories. *"You will never have children, Mrs. Kelly."*

The doctor rubbed her hands in his, pulling her back to the present. "Eliza, some doctors won't consider that it could be the husband with the problem and not the wife." A smile touched his lips and he continued. "But I am of the mind-set that you are a healthy young woman who is three months pregnant. Now, go on home and tell that husband of yours to get ready. He's about to become a new papa. And put that other doctor's words right out of your pretty little head."

Eliza couldn't contain her joy any longer and squealed. She grabbed Doctor Clark and hugged his neck. "A mother! I'm finally going to be a mother!" She released him and grabbed her handbag and hat. "Thank you, Dr. Clark."

He laughed, stood and walked with her to the door. "Thank your husband. He's the one that made it happen."

She felt heat fill her cheeks. Eliza ducked her head and grinned. “I will.”

Eliza hurried from the doctor’s office and headed to the smithy. She couldn’t wait to give Jackson the good news.

The past six months had been filled with one wonderful happening after another. First, Jackson finished the house while her ankle healed and then promptly moved her and Peter in. She loved her new home and business.

Then, Eve and Lucas had renewed their vows in front of the whole church and bought a house in Cottonwood Springs. Lucas now worked at the sawmill and her sister was much easier to get along with and seemed extremely happy. To everyone’s joy, the spoiled woman of a few months ago was gone.

Eve had written to their parents to tell them they were both living in Cottonwood Springs and were happy. She’d invited them to come spend the holidays and they had answered that they would be arriving in Durango in the fall.

She couldn’t wait to tell her parents about the baby. Eliza’s thoughts turned to the new dresses she’d be making as her body grew and changed. Filled with those happy thoughts she walked into the smithy. Thankfully Jackson was alone.

He stood beside the forge, pounding a long metal pole. When Jackson saw her he set his tools aside. “Did the doctor give you something for your upset tummy?” he asked as he walked to her.

Eliza smiled. “No, he said it would cure itself in six months.” It was all she could do to hold her tongue and see if he would guess that they were going to have a baby.

He frowned and concern filled his cobalt eyes. "That's a long time to be sick. Maybe we should drive up to Durango." He pulled her against his chest and gave her a hug.

She enjoyed the feel of his arms around her for a few minutes and then leaned back to look into his face. She shook her head, trying unsuccessfully not to smile. "No, the doctor there will say the same thing."

Jackson searched her face. He saw the joy in her eyes and the way her lips twitched. "Woman, are you toying with me?"

"A little." She couldn't contain the smile any longer. "If I am going to be sick for six more months, can you guess what might be wrong with me? It's something that makes me very happy. I hope it makes you happy, too. I mean, I know we talked about it and the fact that I didn't think it was possible. But I was wrong." Eliza frowned. What if he really didn't want more children?

Jackson tried to work through the words that spilled from his wife's lips. As understanding dawned, he grinned. "Eliza Hart, are you trying to tell me we are going to have a baby?"

She captured her bottom lip between her teeth and nodded. "Oh, Jackson, say you are happy. I couldn't stand it if you weren't. I've wanted a baby for so long."

He tossed his head back and laughed. His sweet little wife's emotions were running amock. Just like any pregnant mama's should. Why hadn't he read the signs? They were going to have a baby.

Jackson picked her up and spun around. Her laughter joined his as she pleaded, "Stop, you are making me dizzy."

"Woman, you have made me dizzy from the moment you told me you were my mail-order bride!" Jackson stopped and slowly slid her down his body until she touched the ground.

Eliza looked up into his face. "So you are happy?"

"Honey, I have been happy ever since you said you'd marry me." Jackson cupped her face in his hands and kissed her lips.

He thanked the Lord above for bringing this chatty woman into his life and he hoped she'd feel his happiness and love through the many kisses they shared.

God willing, they were going to have many children, and he'd work hard to make sure Eliza was as happy as she made him.

When they parted she rested her head on his chest and listened to his steady heartbeat. She loved the sound and the man more than words could express.

He squeezed her close. "I love you, Eliza Kelly Hart."

Eliza reached up and ran her finger through the cleft in his chin. Though she knew every feature of his face by heart, she drank in his eyes, lips and hair. Being in his arms, knowing they were going to have a baby and that she was loved and could express her love for him was better than she'd ever dreamed. She grinned. "I love you, too, and I'm glad Hannah answered a mail-order bride ad for me."

Jackson nuzzled his face into her neck. "Me, too."

To Eliza's way of thinking, she and Jackson would enjoy the life that Hannah had set in motion by answering a mail-order bride advertisement. Delight caressed her like butterfly wings. Eliza thanked the Lord above for the love she'd found with Jackson. Never again would they walk alone, their love would last forever.

* * * * *

Dear Reader,

Eliza Kelly is a woman after my own heart. She speaks her mind and often too quickly. God has dealt with me about such things and so it was fun to share Eliza's story and let her be the talkative one for a change. Unlike Eliza, I can't sew dresses and clothes. I do enjoy quilting and have made several quilts. If I had been born in the 1800s I'm sure I would have learned to sew more. Yes, I admit, I enjoy going to the store and buying my clothes.

Feel free to visit me on my website and blog www.rhondagibson.net. My email address is rhondagibson65@hotmail.com. I'd love to hear your thoughts on Eliza and Jackson's story.

Warmly,
Rhonda Gibson

Questions for Discussion

1. When Eliza learns of Hannah's arrangement for her mail-order groom, she decides to stay and wait for the man to arrive. Would you have stayed if you were her? Why? Or why not?

2. How do you think Jackson's life would have been different if Eliza hadn't pulled him from the train?

3. When Eliza discovered her home and business had been destroyed, she felt lost. Have you ever had a time in your life when you felt like that? How did God help you through that time?

4. Jackson and Eliza both fell in love with Peter and wanted to take care of him. If Peter hadn't come into their lives, do you think they would have still fallen in love? Why or why not?

5. Jackson grew up feeling rejected. Have you ever been rejected, and did that rejection change your life?

6. Eliza was afraid of loving Jackson; she thought he would be disappointed in her because she couldn't have children. Is there something in your life that you feel would disappoint someone else and cause them not to love you? If so, have you taken it to the Lord and asked Him to help you?

7. Jackson felt awkward and as if he didn't fit in. How have you overcome the barriers of not fitting in?

8. Eliza liked the fact that Jackson was a gentle giant. But Jackson was convinced he was too large. Has there been a person in your life who challenged your perceptions about yourself? Share about that person and how they helped you.

9. Name people in your life who feel like family but aren't. What is it about them that makes you want to be a part of their family?

10. Which character in this book did you most connect with? And why?

COMING NEXT MONTH
from Love Inspired® Historical
AVAILABLE MARCH 5, 2013

THE COWBOY'S UNEXPECTED FAMILY
Cowboys of Eden Valley
Linda Ford
With her own business in a fledgling frontier town, Cassie Godfrey will be self-sufficient at last. But her solitary plans are interrupted by four young orphans—and one persistent cowboy.

THE HEIRESS'S HOMECOMING
The Everard Legacy
Regina Scott
Samantha, Lady Everard, will lose her fortune if she isn't married by her twenty-fifth birthday. William Wentworth, Earl of Kendrick, seems the perfect solution, but he thinks the scandalous Everard family is nothing but trouble.

A TEXAS-MADE MATCH
Noelle Marchand
Ellie O'Brien has always prided herself on making matches, but when her childhood friend Lawson Williams comes back to town, the citizens of Peppin, Texas, decide to return the favor.

BOUND TO THE WARRIOR
Barbara Phinney
After the death of her husband, Ediva Dunmow is determined to keep her villagers safe. When the Norman knight she's ordered to marry proves to be gentle and faithful, can Ediva begin to trust God once more?

Look for these and other Love Inspired books wherever books are sold, including most bookstores, supermarkets, discount stores and drugstores.

LIHCNM0213

REQUEST YOUR FREE BOOKS!

2 FREE INSPIRATIONAL NOVELS PLUS 2 FREE MYSTERY GIFTS

Love Inspired HISTORICAL

INSPIRATIONAL HISTORICAL ROMANCE

YES! Please send me 2 FREE Love Inspired® Historical novels and my 2 FREE mystery gifts (gifts are worth about $10). After receiving them, if I don't wish to receive any more books, I can return the shipping statement marked "cancel." If I don't cancel, I will receive 4 brand-new novels every month and be billed just $4.49 per book in the U.S. or $4.99 per book in Canada. That's a saving of at least 22% off the cover price. It's quite a bargain! Shipping and handling is just 50¢ per book in the U.S. and 75¢ per book in Canada.* I understand that accepting the 2 free books and gifts places me under no obligation to buy anything. I can always return a shipment and cancel at any time. Even if I never buy another book, the two free books and gifts are mine to keep forever.

102/302 IDN FVXK

Name (PLEASE PRINT)

Address Apt. #

City State/Prov. Zip/Postal Code

Signature (if under 18, a parent or guardian must sign)

Mail to the **Harlequin® Reader Service:**

IN U.S.A.: P.O. Box 1867, Buffalo, NY 14240-1867

IN CANADA: P.O. Box 609, Fort Erie, Ontario L2A 5X3

Want to try two free books from another series?
Call 1-800-873-8635 or visit www.ReaderService.com.

* Terms and prices subject to change without notice. Prices do not include applicable taxes. Sales tax applicable in N.Y. Canadian residents will be charged applicable taxes. Offer not valid in Quebec. This offer is limited to one order per household. Not valid for current subscribers to Love Inspired Historical books. All orders subject to credit approval. Credit or debit balances in a customer's account(s) may be offset by any other outstanding balance owed by or to the customer. Please allow 4 to 6 weeks for delivery. Offer available while quantities last.

Your Privacy—The Harlequin® Reader Service is committed to protecting your privacy. Our Privacy Policy is available online at www.ReaderService.com or upon request from the Harlequin Reader Service.

We make a portion of our mailing list available to reputable third parties that offer products we believe may interest you. If you prefer that we not exchange your name with third parties, or if you wish to clarify or modify your communication preferences, please visit us at www.ReaderService.com/consumerschoice or write to us at Harlequin Reader Service Preference Service, P.O. Box 9062, Buffalo, NY 14269. Include your complete name and address.

LIH13

Love Inspired HISTORICAL

Matchmaker—Matched!

For Ellie O'Brien, finding the perfect partner is easy—as long as it's for the other people in the town of Peppin, Texas. When her handsome childhood friend Lawson Williams jokingly proposes, the town returns the favor and decides a romance is in order for them. But when secrets in both their pasts threaten their future, can the efforts of an entire town be enough to help them claim a love as big and bold as Texas itself?

A TEXAS-MADE MATCH

by **Noelle Marchand**

Available in March wherever books are sold.

www.LoveInspiredBooks.com
LIH82957

Love Inspired™®

To Trust or Not to Trust a Cowboy?

Former Dallas detective Jackson Stroud was set on moving to a new town for his dream job, until he makes a pit stop and discovers on the doorstep of a café an abandoned newborn and Shelby Grace, a waitress looking for a fresh start. He decides to help Shelby find the baby's mother, and through their quest he believes he's finally found a place to belong, while Shelby's convinced he will move on eventually. What will it take to convince Shelby that this is one cowboy she can count on?

Bundle of Joy

by

Annie Jones

Available March 2013!

™

www.LoveInspiredBooks.com

LI87801